THE ALCHEMY OF

LOVE

PlaneTree

For David + Jean
You may be able to bear
to read this again
Love
Rosa

THE ALCHEMY OF LOVE

By

ROSA WAKE

Hereward
Green Lane
Kessingland
Lowestoft
Suffolk, NR33 7RH

Published 2002
ISBN 1-84294-069-4

Published by PlaneTree

Old Station Offices,
Llanidloes,
Powys SY18 6EB
United Kingdom

Manufactured in the United Kingdom

The Alchemy of Love

Synopsis

Plain Jane overhears a plot by her cousin Lisette and fortune hunter Adrian to kill her in order to inherit her money.

Without revealing her knowledge of the plot she gets away to Brighton, changes her name and opens a Modiste's. There she sees and falls in love at first sight with Dominic; he doesn't notice her.

As they become acquainted he suspects her social climbing - she suspects him of spying for Napoleon.

After many adventures, some of them nearly fatal, the truth is revealed, can the lovers be united now the Alchemy of Love has been at work?

Dedication:

My thanks to Ellie, John and Denise who, between them,
solve all my difficulties

CHAPTER 1

The sound of her own name stopped the girl in her tracks and she stayed to listen.

"Jane – plain Jane? Of course, I shall marry her, but it is you, my sweet, I love. My marriage need make no difference to our affair".

"But why, then, marry her?"

"Do not you realise, Lisette – I am marrying her money! Oh, I'll be kind to her, never fear … once I have her fortune!"

"Once you have her fortune you will not need her", replied the feminine voice reflectively. "She does not look strong – marriage may be too much for her".

"Good God!" amazement amounting to horror informed his voice. "Do I hear what I think you mean?"

"Why not? Then you would have the best of both worlds – a handsome fortune and, after a suitable, brief interval, a beautiful wife! All it needs is resolution. An accident, after all, is easy to contrive."

The eavesdropper, sick with shock, did not wait to hear the man's reply, but fled from the back of the pavilion over the soundless turf until she reached the shelter of the wood that bordered the formal garden. Breathless, she sank on to a fallen tree-trunk. As her breathing and pulses steadied and she ceased to tremble the cruel words rang again in her ears.

All her life Jane Gascoigne had known that she was hopelessly plain. Her mother, a light, frivolous woman, whose only child she had turned out to be, had made no bones about her dissatisfaction with so plain an offspring.

"Mousy, straight hair, pale face, no features to speak of and no more spirit than a cretin – she'd best be kept out of sight in the nursery!"

This to Becky, Jane's nurse, who was outraged and did her best to make up to the child for her mother's rejection: she was so successful that, not until she was five, did Jane realise what she was missing in motherly devotion. Then, with the arrival of her cousin, Lisette, aged seven, who had come as a refugee from France with her widowed mother, sister to Jane's father, the

1

inevitable comparison soon made clear to Jane what she was being denied.

Lisette was everything Mrs Gascoigne desired in a daughter: she had corn-gold hair, heart-shaped face with rose-leaf complexion and deep blue eyes shadowed by curling lashes several shades darker than her hair. She had the engaging ways of a kitten and was soon a firm favourite with both Jane's parents – and this was the girl who had just suggested her murder!

Jane's first impulse was to confront the pair, then she thought of the situation that would follow and found she could not face it. Instead she left the wood and went quietly to the house, avoiding the pavilion.

Safe in her room she sat down to think and, with hindsight, could see how Lisette's envy and resentment had grown since first she realised that, in spite of her beauty and the favour of her aunt, her position was that of a pensioner in Jane's family.

By the time the girls were in their late teens Mrs Gascoigne seemed almost to have substituted Lisette for Jane as her daughter. She looked forward to presenting her niece at Court and thus, herself, enjoying a glittering London Season – a step she had never contemplated taking with Jane. Looking back, Jane believed that she had not envied her cousin, although her father had provided, without stint, a lavish wardrobe and increased pin-money for Lisette's come-out. Unhappily, her cousin's hopes had been dashed. Within months of the great event Mrs Gascoigne fell ill and died, after a brief illness, of smallpox.

Cook said it was a mercy, her mistress would never have wanted to live so badly scarred. The housekeeper agreed, "And it was her own fault, too! All the rest of us had that Mr Edward Jenner's vaccination, even the children, but she wouldn't , not she, scared she'd get the smallpox that way. Ah, well, you could say it's a judgement!" and the two ladies nodded wisely.

Jane saw then evidence of her cousin's lack of feeling for anyone but herself. Lisette's aunt had treated her as a loved daughter, lavishing on her everything a girl could wish for, yet, when Mrs Gascoigne died, Lisette had been inconsolable, not because of her aunt's death, but because it meant the postponement of her début.

At this point in her reverie Jane shook herself impatiently and rang for her maid. She did not want to remember her own lack of grief at her mother's death. She had been far more upset over the death of Lisette's mother some years earlier. Madame Duclos had found some consolation for her heartache over the death of her husband, a casualty of Napoleon's Italian campaign, in the companionship of her quiet, reserved niece. To her Jane owed her fluency in French, spoken and written, and her expertise in embroidery and dressmaking. Indeed the dress her maid now fastened for her was one she and her aunt had created between them.

At dinner Jane answered her cousin's perfunctory enquiries as to how she had enjoyed her afternoon walk with no hint of the cataclysmic discovery which had interrupted it.

Lisette continued with an arch look, "Lucian came and was desolated to find you from home".

Sickened by her cousin's hypocrisy Jane replied calmly, "I am sure you entertained him quite adequately in my absence".

"I did my best!" Lisette's smile was that of a kitten remembering a saucer of cream.

During the rest of the meal, while they exchanged polite nothings, Jane studied her cousin unobtrusively, thinking back over the time since her mother's death.

They were in black gloves for a year and Lisette spent it alternately sulking and getting round her uncle to persuade his distant cousin, Lady Amelia Hapgood, to sponsor his niece's presentation and, what was more, again to spend lavishly on clothes and pin-money for her début.

She succeeded, but her hopes of achieving a brilliant marriage came to nothing. Looking at her with new eyes Jane realised some of the reasons for Lisette's failure. From early, ecstatic letters she had learned that her cousin had taken the town by storm. Men of the first stare had paid court to her, attracted by her beauty and practised, charming ways. However, one by one they fell away and Lisette, furious, had attributed their defection to her lack of fortune.

Continuing her critical appraisal Jane was not so sure that that was the only reason. Some of Lisette's swains could have noticed that her stocky body, stubby fingers and broad feet did not accord with her flower-like face. It was true that, once Lisette had become aware of these blemishes, she had taken immense trouble to disguise them. However, the more intrinsic deficiencies of a shallow mind and malicious wit were beyond her ability to conceal because, with her greed and her vanity, they became more obvious on longer acquaintance.

Whatever the reason, Lisette returned to Cleave Grange furiously resentful at the unkind fate which had decreed that she, the beautiful Lisette, was the poor relation, while mousy Jane stood to inherit her father's considerable wealth.

By the end of dinner Jane found the effort to conceal her painful thoughts beneath an exchange of commonplaces more than she could manage so, pleading headache, she retired to her room. There she was free to let her mind roam unchecked, without disguise. She thought back to when, as she now realised, Lisette had set her mind first to achieve a second Season and then to persuade Jane's father to leave her a substantial legacy, the promise of which she could use to encourage an advantageous offer of marriage.

Jane remembered now, unheeded at the time, hearing Lisette saying to her uncle who had remarked on her downcast looks, "I was worrying, uncle, now that my aunt is gone, who will care for me and secure my future."

He had replied bracingly, "I care for you, puss, you will always have a home with me".

"But ... but...", she hesitated artfully, "If you should die ..."

He laughed, "Now you are being morbid, I have no intention of dying for many, many years, so let me see a smile on your pretty face!"

Brave words, for within the year he was brought home from the hunt having come to grief on a Cotswold stone wall and broken his back.

4

Despite Lisette's ingratiating ways, he had done nothing to secure her future. This was revealed when Mr. Gascoigne's will was read leaving everything to his daughter. Was it only three months ago, thought Jane? She shuddered to remember the scene. Lisette had fallen into strong hysterics and for once Jane had asserted herself. She had slapped her cousin sharply on both cheeks and given her into the care of her maid, recommending a strong dose of hartshorn.

When she returned to the study her father's lawyer, a friend from childhood, viewed her with respect.

"You are going to have trouble with that one", he said. "Your father loved her but he once said to me, "Lisette is a heedless spendthrift with a pretty face, it's Jane who has the head on her shoulders – even if she hasn't the looks ..." he stopped in embarrassment. In recollecting his friend's words he had forgotten the tailpiece!

Jane smiled ruefully to herself, half a compliment was better than none she supposed. But enough of this excursion into the past! It was time to think of the future.

She had already come to one conclusion – she could not live with Lisette nor could she continue to meet Lucian on the old footing of brotherly friendliness which had continued from their childhood. She must get away, at least for a time, until she could decide on permanent plans for her future. The problem of how to achieve the departure from home without having to satisfy questions from Lisette remained unsolved when, worn out by the strains of the day, she fell asleep.

CHAPTER 2

For the next few days, while she was still trying to plan her course of action, Jane unobtrusively avoided Lucian and met Lisette only at meals. Then, some days later one of her difficulties was resolved when Lisette, reading a letter from Lady Amelia, laughed with pleasure.

"Listen, Jane. She has invited me to visit her in Bath! Of course, it's not London but it is quite fashionable these days".

Jane was careful not to show how welcome was the news. "Remember, you are still in black gloves", she reminded her cousin, "But I am sure Lady Amelia will countenance no impropriety and the change will do you good".

Lisette ignored the warning and said petulantly, "Of course, I have nothing fit to wear, even in Bath. I shall need some new clothes, it is a pity some must be black but it becomes me, does it not?" She was right. Her fair skin and golden hair were enhanced by contrast with the filmy black of her gown.

With no doubt as to the answer, Jane asked, "I expect you will need an advance on your allowance? It might be best to buy what you need in Bath rather than in Cheltenham, shops there are more fashionable.

"Oh, dear! And some of my gowns could be silver-grey or lavender, don't you think? After all, Mr. Gascoigne was only my uncle – not my father and, Jane, you are right, I <u>have</u> used up all this month's allowance. Perhaps it would be best if I had <u>several</u> month's in advance", she said in a coaxing tone, "Bath shops are expensive and I shall need some pin-money." She took it for granted that her demands would be met, however much she resented having to ask Jane for what she felt should have been her's by right.

"I'll arrange with Mr Whitney for a banker's draft", said Jane, "It had best be sent to Bath, do not you agree, it will save time". She was anxious that there should be nothing to delay her cousin's departure.

"You are right, as always, dear Jane" The hint of malice was there and Lisette went on hurriedly, she had no intention of antagonising her cousin, the keeper of the purse strings! "Then I will write immediately to Lady Amelia and accept her invitation. When should I tell her to expect me, do you think?"

Jane replied, "Let us see, today is Thursday. Next Monday would give you time to get ready. If you start early you should arrive before dark – it is not much above forty miles and the new post-chaise is well-strung."

Lisette was delighted. She had expected some opposition from Jane, but gave no thought as to a possible reason for her cousin's ready acquiescence to the visit.

Jane wrote at once to her former governess who was keeping house for her widower brother in Hampstead to ask if she could now take up the long-standing invitation to visit Miss Duke. She asked for an early reply and, receiving by return an enthusiastic assent, wrote to her man of business in London to arrange for the draft for Lisette and for a meeting with him at Hampstead on Friday of the following week.

These first steps taken, Jane battled with the feeling of desolation which beset her in the early morning hours when, sleepless, she longed for someone to help her through this calamitous time. She reminded herself, forlornly, that she had had to rely only on herself for most of her lonely life and in the morning threw off her malaise and set about completing her preparations to escape from the intolerable position in which she found herself.

To this end she wrote to her dear Becky, now living with her sister in Hove helping her to run a genteel boarding house, asking for a bedroom and parlour to be reserved for her in a fortnight's time. Becky was to write to her at Hampstead in the unlikely event that, out of the season, she could not accommodate her. Then she waited until Lisette was safely on her way to Bath to summon her housekeeper and the agent for the estate.

She announced to the surprised pair, "I shall be leaving the Grange on Wednesday when Marsden and the horses have had a rest after their journey to Bath. I am going first to London, then I shall be touring". She ignored the look of astonishment on the faces of her audience and went on, "As I am not sure where my travels will take me and how long I shall stay in any one place I shall ask Mr Whitney to deal with any matters arising here. He will pay all bills and see that you have sufficient funds for wages and so on. You can consult him in any difficulty, but I am sure you are both more than competent to keep things running smoothly in my absence". She got through her prepared speech without interruption then, recovering a little from the shock of her mistress's announcement, Mrs Reynolds said, "But, Miss Gascoigne, are you sure you will be safe? Are you taking Miss Lisette with you?"

Jane replied soothingly, "I shall be quite safe, Mrs Reynolds. I shall not trouble Miss Lisette, she will be enjoying her visit to Bath and it would be a shame to interrupt it".

She looked reassuringly at the troubled pair. "Do not worry about me, I rely on you both. Indeed, I could not go away with my mind at rest had I not such reliable people to leave in charge." And, smiling, she dismissed them.

She had no doubt that the servant's hall was in a turmoil of conjecture and that gossip was rife over all the estate but she ignored it and busied herself with her maid, Elsie, in packing a modest wardrobe. To her great relief Lucian was away (in Bath, perhaps?), so she was not required to furnish him with an explanation of her sudden departure.

By this time she had begun to consider making a completely new life for herself as the only tolerable solution to her present dilemma and had no wish to discuss her decision with him or Lisette.

As she was driven out of the gates of the Grange she wondered when she would see Cleave again. The beauty of the Cotswold Hills, green and patched with gold-grey stone, tugged at her heart. She saw in her mind's eye the wonderful panorama from Birdlip and other points of vantage and by the time they reached Cheltenham she was almost ready to abandon her bid to escape and return to the safety of her home. The thought brought her up short – it was no longer safe! With an enemy as ruthless as Lisette within her gates she would never feel secure. Thus reminded, she dismissed her coachman and entered the Posting Inn to wait with an excited Elsie for the specially hired travelling carriage which was to take them the journey of over a hundred miles to London. The coachman and groom, hired with the carriage, were trustworthy men employed by the Postmaster and could be relied upon to see their charges safely to their destination.

She had never before travelled further than Evesham, where she had visited her aunt whose house nestled in the Vale surrounded by acres of plum and cherry trees which were a heavenly sight at blossom time, and she was apprehensive over the long journey facing her, but nothing in her composed manner betrayed this unease.

They were still in Cotswold country when they stopped at Burford for a change of horses. Jane and her maid took coffee at the Bull and walked for a little way down the High Street, glad to be free for a short while from the lurching of the coach. As she climbed back into the carriage Jane sternly subdued her impulse to order the coachman to turn round and retrace his route back to Cheltenham.

It was the last time she had need to strengthen her resolve to leave her home and its problems behind her. The waters of the Windrush leading them to lower-lying Witney rippled soothingly among its meadows, gilded with buttercups and starred with daisies, and along its banks a scarf of lady smocks and celandines lay as if carelessly dropped by the goddess of Spring. Helped by the tranquillity of the scene Jane at last began to look forwards instead of back and to put behind her the misery of her last days at Cleave.

When they reached Oxford where they were to stay at the Randolph Hotel for the night she and Elsie were more than glad to leave the discomfort of the swaying carriage.

They woke refreshed the next morning ready to make an early start on their journey to Hampstead and arrived to a warm welcome from Miss Duke and her brother.

CHAPTER 3

The interview with Mr Whitney was as difficulty as Jane had anticipated. She had hoped, when thinking about it, to avoid giving the real reason for her flight from home, but realised that the lawyer was too shrewd a man to accept a spurious explanation.

She began by saying, "Mr Whitney, will you assure me that what I have to tell you will remain strictly confidential?"

He replied rather stiffly, "Miss Gascoigne, any matter between a lawyer and his client is confidential – you should know that!"

She looked apologetic, "Of course, I know, but I'm so worried – you usually call me Jane", she added inconsequentially. "I will tell you all about it and you can advise me", and she related briefly the events which had driven her from Cleave and ended with an account of the arrangements she had made with the staff there. "You will look after things for me?" she asked pleadingly.

The expression of incredulity on the lawyer's face had given way to outrage.

"We must first deal with those two villains!" he ejaculated.

"How?" Asked Jane. She had had a long time to think over the situation. "We have no proof – they have done nothing as yet, Lucian has not married me, let alone contrived an 'accident'! There is only an account of an overheard conversation which they would deny and to raise the matter would put them on their guard".

Mr Whitney became thoughtful and said, "To think, Jane, that you, a slip of a girl, should have to point out the weakness of the case to me – a man of the law! You are right, of course, until we have more evidence we can do nothing!"

"That is why I had to get away," said Jane. "I need time to think and I have a plan. At first I thought I would just go away for a while, but now I have decided to make a clean break and begin a new life for myself". She looked challengingly at the lawyer. "I could never feel that, plain as I am, any suitor would not be more interested in my money than me".

Mr Whitney attempted to protest.

"No, it is true – in any case that is what I feel – so I thought I would stay with Becky, my nurse, you remember, and use another name".

"Jane!" the lawyer exclaimed, "You cannot give up your whole life!"

"That is where you come in, Mr Whitney. I don't know how long it will be before I can feel ready to become Jane Gascoigne again and what is to be done in the meantime – about Lisette for instance? But while I am away someone responsible must know where I am and look after the Gascoigne interests and that is what I am asking you to do for me – will you?"

The lawyer looked at Jane, old beyond her years, and saw how tautly she held herself and how her hands were gripped together in her lap so tightly that the nails were white. He was filled with compassion and replied, "I will do all in my power as long as you keep in touch with me". He was privately of the opinion that, once Jane had recovered from the immediate shock, matters could be arranged more satisfactorily, meanwhile she would be safe with Becky.

Jane was so much relieved that she almost burst into tears but managed to keep her composure and the rest of the lawyer's visit was spent in arranging details. She proposed to use two of her names – Jane Darcy – and promised to write to Mr Whitney each month.

In turn, he undertook to supervise matters at Cleave Grange and manage her business affairs – including paying Lisette's allowance! He would keep Jane's alias and whereabouts a closely guarded secret.

When all this was settled she said, "I have a small problem. I brought Elsie, my maid, with me so that my removal from Cleave should seem quite conventional but obviously I cannot take her with me to Hove – I must make a clean break, so I must send her home, but she is very young and too inexperienced to travel alone".

"I can deal with that for you", said Mr Whitney, "I have made up my mind to pay a visit to Cleave to see that everything is satisfactorily arranged and your maid can travel with me. I will arrange things at my office and set off on Monday. How will you travel to Hove?"

"I thought I would take the stage to Brighton – I can get a hackney to Hove".

"Not alone!" exclaimed Mr Whitney, "It is not fitting!" He thought …. "I have it! My senior clerk, Johnson, shall accompany you to Brighton and see you into a hackney – that will be best", and he beamed in satisfaction.

"Oh thank you, Mr Whitney, I own I was rather dreading the journey", said Jane.

"Then that is settled. If you will bring Elsie to my office by ten o'clock on Monday you and Johnson can take the eleven o'clock coach from Town". He looked at his watch, "I must be on my way. You need have no fear, Jane, all will proceed as you would wish", and he took his leave, already planning to deal with Lisette, whom he had never liked, despite her beautiful face and engaging manners.

Jane went to seek her hostess. She had not confided in Miss Duke, merely said that she wanted to travel a little to recover from her father's death and to that end had arranged matters with Mr Whitney. She thanked her governess for a delightful visit and said that she and Elsie must leave for Town early on Monday morning. She thought perhaps that she would stay for a while in the capital and visit places of interest and go to a theatre or two.

Miss Duke agreed that such a plan would be beneficial and that Jane must pay her a longer visit next time. She was so kind that Jane felt guilty at deceiving her but justified the deception to herself. She must cover her tracks so that only Mr Whitney knew of her whereabouts and her new identify.

On Monday morning Jane said goodbye to a tearful Elsie who was overawed by Mr Whitney's professional manner but impressed by his travelling coach, far finer than the one from Cheltenham.

CHAPTER 4

Mr Johnson, who was to convey Jane to Brighton, proved to be a quiet, middle-aged man. He whiled away the journey by commenting on the different equipages that used the busy London to Brighton road and pointing out some well-known travellers. On their arrival in the Steyne she thanked him warmly for his care of her and confessed that she had had no idea that in Stage Coaches one had to sit so closely with other passengers. "I am so glad you, and not some stranger, occupied the seat next to me."

He saw her into a hackney for the short journey to Hove and it seemed to Jane that in no time at all they turned into a quiet road leading from the sea front and stopped before a tall house in the middle of a terrace of similar houses. All other details went unregarded. As the hackney stopped the door opened and there was Becky, beaming a welcome. One look at Jane and her old nurse took charge.

"My dear child, you are worn to a thread! Upstairs with you this very instant minute!" and she swept Jane along the hall to a narrow staircase. Waiting at the foot was a pleasant, middle-aged woman bearing a strong resemblance to Becky.

"My sister, Sarah," said Becky, "You can meet her properly later". To her sister she said, "She's to go to bed at once – will you see that some broth is sent up in about half an hour?"

"Yes, Beck", replied her sister placidly and turned to go down the basement stairs to the kitchen.

Jane felt as if she were back in the nursery again and all at once the burden she had carried since she had discovered Lisette and Lucian in the pavilion was lifted and she burst into tears of relief.

She had driven herself hard to take the steps necessary to cope with her disastrous situation and now she had reached a safe haven the release from strain expressed itself in a storm of tears which she was unable to check. Becky made no attempt to stop her nurseling's weeping but undressed her as if she were the child she had cared for and when Jane was in bed she brought a cool cloth and said, "That's enough now – hold this to your face, it will soothe it."

Jane took the cloth and her sobs began to lesson. They ceased when she had sipped the water Becky brought and as she gave back the glass she said, "You must think me mad, Becky, I've nothing to cry for now".

"Those tears have been waiting to be shed for many a long day", and she unpinned Jane's hair and brushed it gently.

There was a tap on the door and a neat maid came in with a tray bearing a bowl of soup and some wafer thin bread and butter.

"This is Mary", said Becky, "She will look after you, Miss Jane, seeing as you've not brought your maid". She took the tray and placed it on Jane's knees.

"Thank you, Mary" said Jane, "This smells delicious".

Mary gave a bob and a smile, "It's Mrs Brown's special – every so nourishing, it is." She looked at Becky who said, "Thank Mrs Brown – that will be all for now, Mary. Miss Jane will send for you later."

Mary said, "Yes, Mrs Linton," and left the room.

Jane had discovered that she was hungry and was making short work of the soup, but now she paused. "Becky – I will explain everything later – but I have decided to be known while I am here as Jane Darcy."

Becky looked at her shrewdly, "I knew there was something up! That Lisette, I'll be bound! Well, if you want to be Jane Darcy, you've every right – it's your name after all. I'll remember Miss Jane – or maybe I should call you Miss Darcy, now?"

"What nonsense", replied Jane, "But try to remember Darcy, won't you?" She gave a huge yawn, "I'll tell you all about it, Becky .." she yawned again.

"Not today you won't! Sleep's what you need." She took the tray away and turned at the door, "Now settle down – morning'll come too soon."

Jane answered drowsily, "That's what you always said ..." and fell asleep as she spoke.

Becky looked lovingly at her erstwhile nursling and closed the door softly.

Morning came, but not until noon for Jane. She woke feeling the contented weakness one feels when recovering after a long illness. It took a few moments for her to realise where she was and just as she was about to get out of bed the door opened quietly and Becky looked in.

"Awake are you, Miss Jane? I thought I'd let you have your sleep out. When you are dressed there'll be a nuncheon in your parlour – though there," and she indicated a door in the left-hand wall. "I'll send Mary up with the hot water." She waited for no reply but closed the door.

Jane realised how deep had been her sleep when she found that her unpacking had been done and a gown laid out for her. As she opened the deep-blue curtains, which matched the carpet she saw, through the crisp lace which veiled the window, a small garden with a plot of grass surrounded by narrow flowerbeds just coming into bloom.

A tap on the door and Mary entered with a brass can of hot water. "Good morning ma'am, I hope you slept well", and she put the can on the marble-topped wash-hand stand and said, "Shall I help you to dress, ma'am?"

"Thank you, Mary, I shall manage very well and you must be very busy."

"Not so much yet, ma'am, it's early in the year. When it's the season and all our rooms is full there's a lot to do. Well, if I can't help you I'll go and get your nuncheon," and she gave Jane a beaming smile and left.

Jane hurried over her toilet and went into the next room. It was charming. Two easy chairs, upholstered, like the window-seat in the curved window, in flowered satin-chintz, faced each other across the small fireplace. A round table with four dining chairs stood in the centre of the room and there was a small desk against the wall opposite the door by which she had entered. The sun shone and was reflected in the mirror above the fireplace and drew Jane to the window. The view here was of the street and across the road could be seen a terrace of tall houses – replicas of the one in which she stood. Black ironwork like lace framed the little balconies on all the three storeys and was also used for the railings protecting the basement and the two pillars upholding a small zinc canopy over the shallow steps leading to the front door. The terrace was recently built and its cream façade shone in the spring sunlight, unmarred as yet by dust and soot.

One or two smart carriages passed up and down the street as Jane watched and on the flagways a number of fashionably dressed people were making their way.

When Mary set out an appetising light meal Jane was quite ready to leave the window and satisfy her hunger. She said cheerfully to Becky who had come with Mary, "It must be the sea air – I find I have quite an appetite!"

"Good," replied Becky approvingly, "You need feeding up, then you must have a nice rest."

"Oh, no, I feel quite energetic, I believe I'll walk down to the sea. As I remember from my drive, it is very near."

"Just through the Square – turn left as you go out. I'll tell Mary to be ready," and she turned to go.

"Surely I may go alone," protested Jane. "After all this is not London."

"It might as well be," replied Becky darkly, "We get enough of the Bucks and Beaux. No, Miss Jane it wouldn't be proper for you to be unaccompanied. Mary will be ready in a few minutes," and she closed the door on further argument.

Jane resigned herself and found Mary to be a pleasant companion. Her first real view of the sea was literally breathtaking. The tide was coming in and a stiff breeze fluttered their skirts and made them hold on to their bonnets. It was noisy too. The waves, Mary assured Jane, were "not huge like we get in the winter," but their drag over the pebble beach kept up a rattle like a roll of kettledrums.

Jane found it exhilarating and was with difficulty persuaded by Mary not to attempt to walk to the chain pier at Brighton, which appeared so near seen through the clear air.

"It's farther than you think, Ma'am, p'raps tomorrow you could drive into Brighton and see the Pier and the shops."

Jane allowed herself to be persuaded and they made their way home almost carried along by the strong wind at their backs.

The next day Jane and Mary went in an open carriage to Brighton. Everywhere there was building going on, mainly centred round the Prince Regent's Paladin villa in East Street, now rapidly being transformed into the exotic Indian/Chinese Pavilion. The Royal Stables and the Riding House in the Pavilion grounds already dwarfed every other building around, and as far as the eye could see terrace after terrace had been built to the East as far as Kemp Town.

What interested Jane more, however, was the fashionable throng crowding the Steyne. She was glad to be unknown and pleased to have brought only a modest wardrobe from Cleave. She saw that she looked hopelessly dowdy and provincial and now that she was no longer in the shadow of Lisette she determined to remedy the matter. She said to herself, "Plain Jane I may be but my clothes shall be beautiful!"

She was surprised to find that there were few modistes among the excellent shops and could only purchase a walking dress and a new bonnet to replace the one she was wearing which was quite outmoded.

There were some very good stationers and book shops and she was fortunate to acquire an up-to-date copy of La Belle Assemblée, for she had made up her mind to create her own dresses. Her last call was at one of the Libraries and she paid her subscription and chose a novel, 'Northanger Abbey' whose author, Jane Austen, shared her name and was highly recommended by Miss Duke.

Quite wearied by the noise and bustle she was glad to return to the peace of her parlour and spent the evening with Becky and her sister studying the fashion plates in La Belle Assemblée and deciding on the materials she would purchase the following day – Miss Austen would have to wait!

Becky urged her to sign her name in the visitors' Book at the principal Library then the Master of Ceremonies would call and provide invitations to the various Assemblies – for example the

Monday Ball at the Castle Inn and the Thursday Ball at the Ship as well as the Card Assemblies and …..

Jane interrupted this catalogue, "But, Becky, I am not planning to enter society here, I wish to remain unnoticed – besides I know no-one who would sponsor me. In any case I have been thinking about what to do with my time and I have decided to become a modiste. There seems to be a sad lack of really select establishments here – it is very strange."

"No, it isn't", replied Becky. "Most of the town are only visitors and patronise their own modistes in London, they buy very little here." She looked at Jane anxiously. "Miss Jane, you're surely not planning to go into trade! What would your father say?"

"He is dead, so we will never know," replied Jane dryly, "And I must do something with my time or die of boredom. Dressmaking is my one talent and I am sure I shall be successful – luckily I shall not have to reply on my efforts to keep myself – you will help me, won't you Becky?" she said coaxingly, "Until I can get started and can find myself a shop and one or two seamstresses."

Becky had listened in stunned astonishment, now she found her voice, "Keep a shop! You should be taking your place in society now Lisette's not here to take the shine out of you. You make too little of yourself, Miss Jane. Properly dressed, you'd hold your own with the best – your fortune would see to that!"

"Don't you see, Becky? That is just what I don't want! Lucian would have married me for my money and put up with my plain face and mousy ways," she said bitterly. "In any case, I have no taste for the emptiness of society. This way people will take me on my own merits and I shall be exercising my one talent and getting a great deal of satisfaction out of it." She added firmly, "Now no further argument! I intend to look for suitable premises immediately and make up a few gowns in readiness with or without your help – but you will help, won't you, Becky, I've always relied on you."

Becky looked at the anxious face and, although her heart misgave her, could not resist its pleading – besides she had not seen Jane looking so animated since her extreme youth before the advent of Lisette.

"I don't like it, but if that's what you're set on doing, I'll help all I can."

Jane hugged her in gratitude and went to bed well pleased.

CHAPTER 5

The next days were so busy that, for the first time, Jane forgot the scene in the pavilion, which had had a habit of stealing into her mind in any unoccupied moment.

In Becky's sewing room she made a walking dress of pale, sherry coloured crepe with a spencer of slightly darker grosgrain, made striking by the border of intricate embroidery round the neck and hem of the dress and the edge of the spencer. It was to be worn with a bonnet of burnt straw.

Becky and her sister had had a hand in making the outfit, and they exclaimed in admiration when Jane first appeared in it ready to drive to Brighton to consult an agent about possible shop premises.

Indeed it was a transformed Jane. It had not been apparent before but her figure was slender and beautifully proportioned and she carried herself well (Becky's early training had seen to that!) and her newly discovered self-confidence gave her poise. She was still undeniably plain but her eyes were brighter and her whole face more animated.

"Miss Jane – you look a picture," exclaimed Becky.

"Yes, it has turned out rather well has it not? Let us hope it impresses the agent. I shall bring back more material with me, Becky, and perhaps you and Mrs Carlton (Becky and her sister had both assumed brevet titles of matrimony though neither had been married), would discuss where I might find seamstresses – I would rather have them recommended personally than obtain them from an agency."

"My sister will know," replied Becky as she closed the door on the fashionable woman who she hardly recognised as the self-effacing, dowdy girl she had known at Cleeve.

Jane found Mr Blythe, the agent she met by appointment to be a cheerful, helpful fellow.

"Blythe by name and blithe by nature!" he smiled in greeting. "Now how can I serve you, Ma'am?"

Jane explained that she wished to rent a shop suitable for a modiste's establishment in as central a position as possible.

Mr Blythe's face looked less merry, he took in Jane's elegant appearance and her youth and said doubtfully, "Premises in the centre of the town come high —in fact if you had asked me a few week hence I should have had to disappoint you. Once the season starts there will be nothing available.

"Perhaps some other agent would have something available now?" said Jane rising and drawing on her gloves.

Mr Blythe said hastily, "Wait if you please, Ma'am, I have two possible properties, but, as I said, they come high."

"Let us see them, and rents can be discussion if either is suitable."

"By all means," said Mr Blythe, beginning to revise his opinion as to Jane's business acumen. "They are both within a short walk, one in North Street and one in Church Street", and he ushered Jane and Mary out of his office, calling to his assistant to take charge in his absence.

After viewing both empty shops Jane was quite decided that the one in North Street, just round the corner from the Theatre Royal, was the most suitable for her purpose. Unlike the one in Church Street, the rooms above it were empty and would be ideal for work and storerooms.

Mr Blythe became his sunny self when Jane gave Mr Whitney's name as a reference and as the lawyer who would deal with matters concerning the lease. Meanwhile she wanted immediate access and asked Mr Blythe to recommend a reliable firm who would adapt the premises to her requirements.

"Porter and Porter are the people you want, Miss Darcy. They are highly thought of and have been employed by his Highness for work at 55 Old Steyne," he looked knowingly Jane, "Where Mrs Fitzherbert lives."

Jane was aware of the gossip about the Regent and his mistress, Mrs Fitzherbert, and that he had recently broken off relations with her, but she replied formally, "That is certainly a recommendation. I should like Mr Porter to wait on me at ten-thirty tomorrow at North Street. And now may I have the key."

Mr Blythe was only too anxious to oblige, "I will send a message to Mr Porter, senior and he will wait upon you tomorrow morning."

"Thank you, Mr Blythe," said Jane, putting the key in her reticule. "You have been most helpful. Good day," and she and Mary left the beaming Mr Blythe to go to the silk warehouse where Becky had said the best materials were to be found.

Jane was amazed to discover how little fatigued she felt after her exertions, and she spent a profitable evening planning her showroom and the workrooms above ready for her meeting with Mr Porter.

She was surprised to find a young man waiting outside the shop the next day. If this were Mr Porter senior his son must be a schoolboy! As she hesitated he advanced and raised his hat.

"Miss Darcy? My name is Porter – Mr Blythe got in touch with us yesterday."

"But you cannot be Mr Porter senior whom I was expecting to meet."

"No, he is my father, but I am sorry to say gout has laid him low and I have come in his stead." He answered her doubtful look. "I assure you I am quite competent, Miss Darcy – I have worked with my father for years and he will make sure that anything I undertake matches his own very high standards." He looked at her anxiously but with an underlying confidence.

Jane was impressed by his manner and mode of speech, superior to that of the average artisan, and made up her mind. She liked him and, realising that she would have to work closely with whoever undertook the work, she decided that young Mr Porter would be an agreeable colleague. She never had reason to regret her choice of the junior partner, not only did he carry out her wishes, however unorthodox, but gave such good advice that many of her plans were modified to great advantage. He was valuable too in knowing the best tradesmen to be employed and in very short order Jane's shop and workrooms were ready for her.

Upstairs were three rooms, one for the seamstresses, warmed by a small range on the top of which irons could be heated and a kettle for steaming velvet and so on. The second room had ample storage space and was fitted with rails and shelves and cupboards; the third room had water laid on and a sink where the women could wash their hands and dampen pressing cloths. There was a very small range for simple cooking at dinnertime and for tea and cocoa making.

Mr Porter was much impressed by the care taken for the comfort of the workers, but Jane pointed out that the long hours from eight in the morning to six at night meant that, with facilities on the premises, time need not be lost while women went home for dinner and also that a hot drink was very welcome in cold weather.

"I shall expect value for the wages I pay, have no fear, Mr Porter, but in my experience people work better when they are comfortable."

Downstairs silver-grey curtains and reseda green woodwork provided a neutral background to the gowns Jane intended to display and the small window was lined with grey velvet. In the fitting room behind the shop grey hangings alternated with floor length mirrors in which the customer could see rear and profile as well as front views. The room at the back gave on to a small yard with a privy and access to an alley for deliveries. The room was fitted with shelves and rails on which garments could be hung and accessories stored.

There had been many discussions between Jane and the two sisters about a name for the shop. Becky favoured 'Modes' while Sarah thought 'Louise' would sound more welcoming.

Suddenly Jane said, "Isabelle – Modes et Manteaux!'"" French always sounds better in the world of fashion and Isabelle was my aunt's name – she taught me all I know about dressmaking and embroidery and deserves to be remembered." The sisters were impressed and the name was written in silver in flowing copperplate over the shop.

The problem, which had been exercising Jane's, mind of how to find competent and reliable employees was in a fair way to be solved. Sarah had a friend who did dressmaking. Mrs Gibbs was a childless widow and made a reasonable living with her needle but when approached over tea in Sarah's parlour was pleased with the terms offered her to take charge of the workroom at Isabelle's.

"It will be steady work," she said. "My work comes and goes – sometimes I've nothing to do and sometimes I'm so busy I wouldn't know where to turn if it wasn't for my sister's girl – she has a lame leg but she sews beautifully and embroiders too."

Jane spoke eagerly, "Do you think she would work for me as well, Mrs Gibbs?"

"I'm sure she would ma'am. She's lonely at home being the only one and she'd have company in the workroom. If I may ask, how many women are you looking for, ma'am?"

"I think I could usefully employ four – yourself for cutting and fitting, someone for embroidery and beadwork and two more for plain stitching. I thought of asking at the employment agency."

"Don't do that, ma'am," said Mrs Gibbs earnestly, "Some of the folk they send are useless, it's better to have a personal recommendation. Please don't think I'm pushing myself forward, but being in the trade so to speak I know most good workers and many of them would like a steady position instead of casual work. I can think of two this minute."

"Oh, can you, Mrs Gibbs? That would be splendid." Jane had taken to Mrs Gibbs. The first impression one had of her was of a solemn, long faced woman almost excessively neat and clean who looked as if she would never unbend until you saw the gleam of humour in her small grey eyes.

"Well, if you'd like I could have a word with them and send them round to see you – they're as different as chalk from cheese – one of them's a bit young – but they both sew well – they've done work for me and I'm hard to please. When would you like them to come, ma'am?"

"Could they come tomorrow afternoon? I shall be busy in the morning," replied Jane.

"I'll send them round at about three o'clock, if that will suit," said Mrs Gibbs.

"Yes, that will be convenient, thank you Mrs Gibbs," answered Jane.

"Very well, then I'd best be on my way and make arrangements with them. Good afternoon, ma'am. Thank you for the tea, Sarah, I can see myself out."

When she had gone Jane said, "Oh, thank you, Sarah, she's a treasure isn't she?"

"There's many that don't take to her on sight," answered Sarah, "She looks a bit forbidding like."

"But she isn't, is she? She's got a twinkle in her eye – oh, I do think I'm lucky."

Becky looked at her. Her animated face and manner and modish clothes had affected an extraordinary transformation. Few who had known Jane Gascoigne would have recognised Jane Darcy at first glance.

"There's one thing you haven't thought about, Miss Jane," said Becky, "Who is to sell the clothes in the shop?"

"Why, I am, of course," replied Jane.

"You, Miss Jane!" cried both sisters in unison. "It's not suitable," Becky went on. "Besides you don't like meeting lots of people and customers aren't easy."

"Jane Gascoigne didn't, but Jane Darcy does!" replied Jane mischievously. "I have come out of my shell, or, perhaps more like a moth from its chrysalis and now I want to try my wings!"

"Well, mind you don't get scorched," said Becky warningly.

"I'll take care," laughed Jane on her way to the door. "It's going to be a great adventure!" How much of an adventure she was not to know – for that day she was happy and fulfilled as never before, feeling that at last she was free of the shadow of Lisette.

Becky and Sarah talked long and anxiously after Jane had gone.

"She doesn't realise that after the shop is open she'll be tied there all day," said Sarah.

"And she had no idea how hard it is to be always bright nor how to put up with downright rudeness from twitchy customers," answered Becky.

Sarah looked at her sister in dismay, "It'll never do, Becky."

"I know, but she'll have to find out for herself! Miss Jane can be led but never pushed – I should know! She's got a stubborn streak for all her gentle ways. It's as well she can afford to lose the money for I doubt she'll succeed," Becky said. She got up and began to put the room to rights and went on, "But, Sarah, I wouldn't put a rub in her way for all the world. You don't know what a difference there is in her! Let her go her way – we'll help all we can, won't we?"

Sarah nodded assent and they went to bed resigned to let matters take their course.

CHAPTER 6

Could she have been in Bath, Jane would have found much to interest her. Lucian, as she had suspected, had joined Lisette, but his visit was not altogether pleasurable. He found himself competing for Lisette's favours. She was able to choose between a number of attractive men ready to escort her to routs, card parties – almost any social gathering short of balls – which Lady Amelia would not permit while Lisette was still in half-mourning. Her favoured escorts were two French émigrés, Raoul de Monforet and Jacques de Beauchamps, both claiming the title of Count and neither appearing to be short of money. After a few days of playing third fiddle to the personable Frenchmen Lucian went back to Cleave in a huff determined to make sure of Jane. He found her gone from home and what seemed to him a conspiracy of silence about her whereabouts. None of the servants could or would tell him where she was to be found and it had been obvious that Lisette had not known of her cousin's disappearance so, finally, he posted off to London to see Mr Whitney as the only person who might know where Jane had got to.

At first, Mr Whitney was adamant in his refusal to supply the information. He would not even admit to knowing anything about Jane, but when Lucian announced that he was going to Bow Street – Jane might have had an accident, she might even be dead, he declared passionately – Mr Whitney had second thoughts.

The lawyer could not allow such enquiries to be made so he reluctantly admitted that he knew where Jane was but he was pledged not to reveal her whereabouts even to Lisette.

"She must have run mad!" Lucian cried furiously, "She ...."

"If ever there was a sane woman, that woman is Jane Gascoigne," snapped Mr Whitney. He could barely bring himself to talk to this conniver, as to betraying Jane, it was out of the question. "Miss Gascoigne has every right to go where she chooses! She needs to ask no one's permission! I have no more to say – good day to you, Mr Chancellor," and he held the door of his office signifying that the interview was at an end.

Lucian snatched up his hat and left without replying.

Had he not been in such a rage he might have noticed one of the clerks in the outer office giving him a considering look. Most of what had been said in Mr Whitney's room had been overheard – the door had a faulty catch and had not quite closed and the voices of the two men had been raised.

The clerk, Jesson, was disgruntled. He was under notice having been careless and unpunctual for some time so that Mr Johnson, the chief clerk who had escorted Jane to Brighton, had asked Mr Whitney to dismiss him.

It was not until two days later that Lucian's gloves were found in the back of the brown leather chair against which they had been almost invisible. Mr Whitney could not at first identify the owner, then he thought of Lucian. He told Mr Johnson to have them taken round to the Poultney where Mr Chancellor might still be staying. Jesson was the most easily spared and was given the errand.

He found that Lucian was still residing at the hotel but was out. Jesson had been thinking on the way and he decided not to mention the gloves saying he would call again. When he returned to the office he said quite truthfully that Mr Chancellor had been out and quite untruthfully that he had left the gloves.

On his way home he called again at the hotel. This time he was successful and when Lucian had taken the gloves and offered him a tip Jesson said, "No, thank you, Mr Chancellor, I may have something of more worth to you than a pair of gloves."

Puzzled, Lucian said, "I don't understand you."

Coming straight to the point, Jesson asked, "You want Miss Gascoigne's address, don't you Sir?"

"Yes, of course, I do, she is my fiancée. If you know it you'd better let me have it," and he withdrew a sovereign from his pocket.

"Well, Sir, I've not got it yet, but I can get it sometime in the next fortnight …. if it's worth my while?"

"How much?" said Lucian, bluntly.

"Shall we say, ten guineas? After all I shall be risking my job." No need to say that it was lost already!

"You come high, don't you?" said Lucian unpleasantly. He hesitated. "Very well – you'd best send it to my address in Gloucestershire, I am leaving Town tomorrow."

"Then how shall I get my money?" protested the clerk.

"You'll get it – half now and half when you supply the address," and he added four more guineas to the one in his hand. He thought it worthwhile to risk five guineas for such a valuable prize – besides he felt sure the fellow would want the rest.

Jesson thought rapidly. He was pretty sure that he stood to lose the second instalment of his bribe, but a bird in the hand ……

"Very well, Mr Chancellor, make it six and I'm on – I will forward the address before the fortnight is out – I'm trusting you to do right by me!"

He accepted the six guineas and the address and took his leave.

In point of fact the two men haggled by post for many weeks. Jesson never got his money and took his revenge by writing 'Brightlingsea' instead of 'Brighton' – and Lucian went off on a wild goose chase to Essex. He was at his wits' end – his affairs were in a parlous state and the debtors' prison loomed. As he racked his brains for some clue as to Jane's whereabouts and looked in disgust at Jesson's sheet of paper, which was much folded and rubbed, the work 'Bright' stood out. His mind completed the work 'Brighton' and immediately he believed that he had hit on the solution to his dilemma. As quickly as he could he made his way to the resort.

CHAPTER 7

Jane was hard put to it not to smile when she met Mrs Gibbs and the two seamstresses. The one was very tall and thin and the other plump and shorter by more than a head with flaming red hair. At Mrs Gibb's instigation both had brought samples of their work.

Charlotte Formby, the tall one, was quiet and reserved in manner and when Jane had told her the terms and conditions of the work she was offering said only, "Thank you, ma'am, I should like to work for you."

Jane had hardly time to turn to Phoebe Wright, she of the red hair, before the girl said brightly, "And so should I, ma'am. I've always wanted to work with other girls."

"To chatter, no doubt," put in Mrs Gibbs. "You'll only chatter in the workroom within reason, Phoebe, you'll not hinder the work, mind!"

Phoebe looked a little dashed and Mrs Gibbs said to Jane, "Her tongue's as long as her thread, ma'am but she's a good worker for all that."

Jane looked at the irrepressible Phoebe and thought that she would be a good foil for the silent Charlotte. In any case she had every confidence in Mrs Gibbs' ability to rule her underlings.

When both girls had gone, Phoebe in full spate as soon as she was outside the door, Mrs Gibbs said, "I've taken the liberty of bringing my niece to see you ma'am, if it's convenient. She's waiting in the kitchen, but I can bring her another day if you'd like.

"Oh, do bring her in, Mrs Gibbs. I should like to see her, although I am perfectly prepared to engage her on your recommendation."

"Thank you, ma'am, replied Mrs Gibbs, "But," with a twinkle, "It doesn't do to buy a pig in a poke, does it?" and she went to fetch her niece.

At the sight of the frail creature with a diffident manner who limped into the room Jane's heart was touched. Although she had been told that Ellie was older by a year than herself she looked like a child.

"Please sit down," said Jane to the two women. She turn to Ellie, "Your name is Ellie, is it not?"

"Yes, ma'am," the girl replied in a soft voice. "I've brought some of my work, if you'd like to see it, ma'am," and she proffered a parcel wrapped in clean calico.

Jane opened it and gasped. The most exquisite embroidery she had every seen met her gaze – a border of leaves and flowers so perfect that one expected perfume to arise from them. They glowed like the illuminated borders in a medieval missal.

As Jane gazed, speechless with admiration, Ellie said hesitantly, "You can look at the back, ma'am, that's the real test of embroidery, isn't it?"

As in a trance Jane turned the material over, there was nothing to show where a thread began or ended, the wrong side of the work was a perfect as the right.

Jane found her voice, "It is exquisite, Ellie, I have never seen such perfect work!"

As the girl blushed at the praise, Jane turned anxiously to Mrs Gibbs. "Will Ellie be strong enough? She should not work beyond her strength – such a talent should be preserved.

Before her aunt could reply Ellie said eagerly, "I'm very strong, ma'am, although I don't look it – it's walking and standing that tires me and doing this means I'm sitting down all day."

"She's right, ma'am," agreed Mrs Gibbs. "She looks frail but she never ails. She will be perfectly able for the work if you decide to employ her."

"I shall be very glad to do so and count myself fortunate." She looked seriously at the two women, "What I am to say now I wish you to keep to yourselves. I propose to pay Ellie more than the two seamstresses who will be doing much less intricate work, but I think it is not necessary for them to know this – jealously is so easily aroused."

Mrs Gibbs nodded. "You have a head on your shoulders ma'am, if you don't think I'm impertinent to say so. Ellie and me won't say a word."

Ellie looked almost with awe at Jane and said, "if you think it's fair, ma'am, thank you, oh, thank you," and she seemed ready to burst into tears.

To check any display of emotion Jane said briskly, "Then that is settled. The workrooms are ready and I should like to prepare a stock of garments before we open the shop. I shall expect you all at eight o'clock sharp on Monday. Perhaps you would let Charlotte and Phoebe know, Mrs Gibbs and, if you can manage it, I would like to see you at Isabelle's tomorrow, Friday, at ten o'clock to go over the premises with me. I am expecting deliveries of materials and equipment then."

"I shall be there, ma'am," replied Mrs Gibbs. She and Ellie rose and said their goodbyes and Jane was left to catch her breath after the headlong pace of recent days and assimilate the fact that she was launched on a business venture for which she acknowledged, but only to herself, she had no experience whatever.

The next day Mrs Gibbs was impressed by her tour of Isabelle's and Jane left her contentedly viewing the details of the workrooms while she received deliveries of materials and saw to it that the load of coal was put tidily in the small coal house in the yard.

When the men had gone she showed Mrs Gibbs the way out through the alleyway and said that that was where she wished the women to enter rather than through the shop. She gave Mrs Gibbs keys to the gate and the back door and said, "This means that you will have to arrive first to let in the others."

"I understand, ma'am – I'll be there," and she stowed the keys away in her capacious bag.

"That is all then," said Jane. Can I take you back with me to Hove, Mrs Gibbs?"

That's kind of you, ma'am, thank you."

On the short journey she spoke tentatively, "Miss Darcy – I'm not one to push myself but ….. have you thought of the cleaning?"

Jane looked aghast. "Oh, no, Mrs Gibbs, I must own that it never occurred to me! Thank you for mentioning it."

Well ma'am, you can reply on me and the girls to keep the workrooms but scrubbing and such roughens their hands."

"I do agree – it would be wrong for them to do other than the work for which they have been hired. We must get a woman to do the cleaning – from the agency, perhaps?" she frowned in perplexity.

"You'd do better to ask Mrs Carlton, ma'am, she's sure to know some good cleaners." As she spoke the carriage drew up at Becky's house.

"Would you come in, Mrs Gibbs, and speak to Mrs Carlton? I am sure you will be able to explain what we need much better than I can." Jane had realised that domestic mysteries had been left to Mrs Reynolds at Cleave and she herself was woefully ignorant.

Sarah and Mrs Gibbs discussed cleaners over a pot of tea in the kitchen and came to give Jane the result of their debate.

"We think Mrs Medley would be best for you, Miss Jane," said Sarah, "She works in the best houses during the season and would be glad of work to keep her going all the year. She'd still be able to do other work when she could fit it in."

"I know I shall do well to employ anyone you two ladies recommend. How can we let Mrs ...?"

"Mrs Medley," interpolated Mrs Gibbs as Jane hesitated. "She lives not far from me and if you'd like I can ask her to come to see you."

"Oh, that won't be necessary, Mrs Gibbs. If she can undertake the work I will leave it to you to engage her and explain what has to be done and you will know what we should pay her."

Sarah said approvingly, "You can safely leave all that to Mrs Gibbs, Miss Jane, she'll make all the arrangements."

"Well thank you again," said Jane. "I don't know what I should do without your help and advice."

The two women smiled in appreciation and left Jane thinking ruefully that her overnight fears of her inadequacies bid fair to be proved true!

She had no time to reflect on her shortcomings in the days that followed, she was too busy designing gowns, pelisses and spencers. Mrs Gibbs proved to be a jewel – she could even make the fashionable redingote which was rapidly coming into favour with the ton.

Everyone of Jane's little force worked with a will and the stock of garments increased daily. Jane approached a milliner in the New Road who supplied her with hats to be sold on commission and with a recommendation to the milliner's establishment. Other accessories were laid by in Jane's stockrooms and at last Jane felt ready to open Isabelle to a waiting world. Mrs Medley had proved to be treasure and had given an extra polish to the mirrors and the shop window where one of Jane's most original gowns was displayed, a creation in oyster satin with a border of Ellie's superb embroidery edging the fronts which opened over a deep coral underdress, a lovely fan of silk with pierced ivory sticks and painted with a design to match the gown lay beside the dress with a pair of coral coloured Grecian slippers to complete the ensemble.

The season had barely begun and, although many paused to gaze, Jane spent the whole day without a customer crossing the threshold. When at last she returned to Hove she had never felt so tired in all her life. After the bustle and enthusiasm of the days before the opening she could have wept with fatigue and discouragement. Whatever was she going to do if she had committed herself to spending day after day shut in a box, however beautiful, with no occupation and no company except that of her work-women?"

She toyed with the idea of abandoning Isabelle and all that it entailed. After all she didn't need to earn her living – and that thought stopped her in her tracks. She didn't rely on Isabelle for her livelihood but five others did – six if she included Mrs Medley. What was she to do? "Keep on," answered Jane's stronger self to her weaker alter ego. The trait that Becky labelled as obstinacy but that Jane would have called determination stiffened her resolve, and, after a disturbed night, she set out for Isabelle's telling herself to have faith in her enterprise – things must become better – they couldn't be worse!

It seemed that faith was to be justified. She had not been half an hour in the shop when her first customer entered – a large lady of commanding appearance.

"You are new," she stated rather than asked. "That gown in the window – I should like to see it!" and she sat down with a regal air.

Jane was taken aback. The gown, made for a much younger, slimmer figure was wholly unsuitable for the large well-covered frame of the customer.

Before she could think of a tactful way to explain this the woman went on "It is an exclusive model, I collect? I shall not see it on back of any of my acquaintances I trust?"

Jane was able to speak for the first time. "All my models are originals, ma'am …" she got no further.

"Your ladyship" Lady Emily Fortescue!" I do not patronise only Brighton establishments as a rule but I need a new gown in a hurry."

"I understand, your ladyship," said Jane, inwardly amused at the pretentious female, "But I fear the gown in the window is not your …." She was going to say, 'size' but hastily substituted, 'fitting'.

"Nevertheless I will try it," replied her ladyship. "Pray bring it to your fitting room – you have a fitting room?"

"Through here, your ladyship – I will call my fitter," and she left her customer viewing herself in the mirrors and obviously approving of the sight.

Jane had not time to do more than whisper to Mrs Gibbs, "It's hopeless, she's far too big!" before they reached her ladyship. Mrs Gibbs helped her to remove her outer garments to reveal one of the newly fashionable corsets which did little to shape the figure it failed to control.

Jane appeared with the gown. It was clear at the first attempt that the underdress would not possibly fit.

Mrs Gibbs said quietly, "Perhaps madam would like the blue satin, ma'am, it is more in her style?"

"It is this gown or nothing!" declared Lady Fortescue. "Surely it can be altered? I'll try the overdress."

But Jane had had enough. To attempt to cram her ladyship into the exquisite creation was sure to damage it. She turned to Mrs Gibbs, "Pray return this gown to the window, Mrs Gibbs." To the customer she said, "I regret that, as you can see, the gown is far too small. If I cannot interest you in something larger ….?"

"You cannot! I have never been so insulted! My figure is the admiration of all my friends. How dare a mere modiste put herself forward to contradict them." She was scrambling into her clothes. "Fasten my dress!" Jane did so. "My hat!" Mrs Gibbs had returned and handed it to her. She pulled it on and swept past them.

I shall see that none of my acquaintances darken your doors!" and she slammed it after her.

Jane sat down limply and Mrs Gibbs said, "Good riddance!"

"But what shall I do?" asked Jane, in despair, "She will tell everyone!"

"But no one who matters," replied Mrs Gibbs. "She's a jumped up cit unless I my guess – her friends are not the kind we want. A figure like her's is no advertisement. Don't worry, ma'am, I'll bring you a cup of tea and you'll feel better in a trice."

The cup of tea did help, but a more effective cure came in the shape of two ladies who entered the shop some minutes later. They were obviously mother and daughter and had a well-bred air.

"Good morning," said the mother, "I am looking for a gown for my daughter, she is not yet out but is to attend her first dance – quite a small affair. Such a gown as the exquisite one in your window would, of course, be too elaborate. I wonder have you something more jeune fille – and not too expensive?" she ended with a smile.

Jane had been studying the young girl, she had quite good features and pretty brown hair. Her figure was immature but her carriage was good. Jane liked what she saw and replied to the mother, "I think I have the very thing, ma'am, please be seated, I will call my fitter." She returned with Mrs Gibbs carrying a silk-muslin gown in a delicate shade of shell pink.

The mother exclaimed, "What a becoming colour! So many young girls appear in white – so trying!"

"I do agree," replied Jane, "Perhaps you would come into the fitting room," and she led the way.

The girl turned to her mother, "Mamma, look at the lovely forget-me-nots embroidered on the scallops – oh, I <u>do</u> hope I may have it!"

"As to that we will see, my dear," her mother answered, "It may not fit and it may be too dear."

Mrs Gibbs helped the girl into the dress saying, "I think, ma'am, that there will be little alteration needed," as she spoke she finished fastening the dress.

The girl looked at herself reflected on all sides, the small puffed sleeves flattered her rather thin arms and the subtle shade of pink enhanced the slight flush in her cheeks.

She turned to her mother, "Oh, Mamma!"

Her mother smiled ruefully. She knew the gown was an exquisite model – the embroidery alone a work of art. "I am afraid, my dear, it will be more than we can afford."

Jane said impulsively, "Ma'am, you are my first real customer and I should like to mark the occasion by offering the gown at cost price," and she mentioned a sum which raised Mrs Gibbs' eyebrows. She knew that it barely covered the cost of the materials.

Jane went on smoothly, "I must ask you not to divulge this to your friends – they might expect similar privileges!" and she smiled conspiratorially at her customer.

"You are too generous, Madame. I am not sure I should accept …"

"<u>Please</u>, Mamma!" The girl looked beseechingly at her mother and in the face of the picture her daughter presented in the lovely gown, her mother capitulated.

She turned to Jane. "Sara looks so well in it I cannot refuse. Thank you very much, Madame, be sure that we shall respect your confidence as to the price, but we shall tell all enquirers where we purchased such a creation," and she went with Jane into the showroom while Mrs Gibbs helped Sara into her own clothes and took the gown, which had needed no alternation. For the first time, the silver-grey box signed 'Isabelle' was used to pack it in layers of tissue paper.

When the delighted pair had left Mrs Gibbs turned to Jane in dismay.

"Ma'am! You have hardly covered the cost of the materials – you charged nothing for the work!"

"I know, Mrs Gibbs, but did you see Sara's face? And her mother was finding it so hard to deny her daughter but she was sincere in her determination to keep within her means – I could respect that – as well, she was so … so loving!"

Mrs Gibbs was not to know that memories of her own bleak girlhood had, in some measure, prompted Jane's gesture plus a certain reaction from the earlier unpleasant encounter with 'her ladyship'.

On her way back to Hove Jane still felt elated by the memory of the pleasure she had brought to Sara and her mother. Later in the evening, however, her doubts returned about her ability to continue with her great adventure. Would it not be better to find someone to manage Isabelle's and confine her activities to designing? Should she not go back to Cleave? As long as she did not marry, Lisette was no threat – she would make it clear to her cousin that she would not benefit by her death – that should make her safe. She went to bed depressed at the thought of a loveless unwedded future dwindling into a spinsterish old age.

CHAPTER 8

The next morning Jane took a fat letter received from Mr Whitney to the shop with her, thinking it would serve to while away the boring, customerless hours. It contained news of Lisette and Lucian. The latter's visit to Mr Whitney's office was related in great indignation and ended in some satisfaction that "the villain had been sent packing!"

Lisette, he went on to report, had applied for more money and Mr Whitney wanted Jane's word as to whether he should refuse or grant the request. Lisette had said that Lady Amelia would chaperone her to London for the Season, but, as usual, Lisette needed a new wardrobe and extra pin money.

Mr Whitney had been obliged to tell Lisette that Jane had left Cleave and that her request must be forwarded to her cousin for her approval. Lisette had flown into one of her tantrums and demanded to know Jane's whereabouts. When she found Mr Whitney unmoved by her histrionics she calmed down and urged that Jane's consent be sought with the utmost despatch.

"So you see," Mr Whitney concluded his letter, "I am obliging the little baggage and would be glad if you would let me have your instructions in the matter." There was a P.S. to the letter but Jane had not time to read it before the shop door opened and she was forced to consider whether she was see double.

Two girls came in, the image of each other, dressed alike in neat but shabby clothes. They were of average height and build and their pale faces looked tired. They had not the look of customers and advanced hesitantly. One of them spoke.

"Good morning, ma'am. May we ask if you are in charge here?" Her voice was pleasant in tone with a slight Cockney accent.

"Why, yes," replied Jane. "What can I do for you?"

"We are looking for employment," the girl answered. "We …."

Before she could go on Jane interrupted. "I am very sorry but I have all the seamstresses I required."

"We're not seamstresses, ma'am, we're vendeuses." She brought out the word with pride – 'saleswomen' would not have had the same ring!" "We have been employed in one of the best Modiste's in Town – Cerisette's."

Jane noticed the silent twin who was pale to begin with turning every whiter – "Your sister looks unwell – should she not sit down?"

The first girl turned in alarm. "Maisie! Hold up, do!" and she guided her sister to a chair. She explained, "We came out without breakfast, ma'am, I expect that's it – we're both quite strong, really," she assured Jane.

"No breakfast!" exclaimed Jane.

"No, you see we have been looking for a place and our money will not last much longer so we try to save a little." She spoke in a matter of fact way, not as one asking for pity.

Jane made up her mind. "Sit down and tell me all about it," she said and took a seat herself and prepared to listen.

The girl who had done all the talking said her name was Doreen – Doreen Betts. She and her sister had been employed by Cerisette for the past six years – since they were 17 in fact, but now the shop was to close – Cerisette was to retire. Maisie had not been well – although she was not ill, not really – Doreen assured Jane anxiously, but the doctor had said she would benefit from 'Doctor Brighton's sea air', so they decided to try for positions in the resort. They had good references – she pulled some papers out of her reticule and said Cerisette had promised to speak for them, her address was on the references. So far, however, they had found only one establishment which was prepared to take one of them, "And, ma'am," said Doreen, "We've never been parted, but I doubt I'll have to take the place, we must earn something or go back to London."

The other twin sat silent throughout this recital – it was clear that Doreen was the dominant partner.

Jane had been observing the girls closely. Although shabby, they were presentable, and, if their story was true, and she believed it was, they were the very workers Jane needed. True, she only wanted one saleswoman but to employ two would mean that even if one were ill at any time the other could manage alone, otherwise Jane herself would have to step into the breach.

As the girl finished speaking Jane said, "Well, Miss Betts, as you will see I have just opened the shop and would have been looking for an assistant in a few days. Your experience in the work is in your favour and, although I really need only one person I am prepared to stretch a point and employ you both, subject to your reference proving satisfactory."

"Oh, ma'am, you'll never regret it!" and she handed the papers to Jane.

Tears of relief streamed down Maisie's face, but she dried her eyes and blew her nose when her sister adjured her not to be silly.

Jane took the papers and said, "I will send these to my lawyer in London and he will verify them in good time. He should let me know by the end of the week and, if all goes well, you could begin next Monday."

"He'll find them all in order," replied Doreen confidently, "And we'll have time to freshen up our shop gowns – they are dark blue, ma'am, and quite smart."

"Yes, well," answered Jane, "I may ask you to dress in pale grey with white fichus, but we can consider that if you are employed here. Meanwhile, if you will come upstairs into the kitchen I am sure we can find a hot drink and something to eat – your sister should not go further before breaking her fast."

"We wouldn't impose, ma'am, we can manage now," protested Doreen.

"I am sure you can," replied Jane, "But, as seems likely, you are to work here, it will be a good idea for you to meet Mrs Gibbs who is in charge of the workrooms. Come along!" and she shepherded them upstairs into the little kitchen. Having explained rapidly to Mrs Gibbs she left the girls in her charge and went down to the shop.

Before looking at the references she sat down to read Mr Whitney's P.S.

"I must not close without enquiring into your business venture. So far your enthusiastic accounts show that you are finding great satisfaction in your project. I have settled the accounts which have come in and will hope to receive some income from 'Isabelle' in time! Of course, it is early days yet and you can well afford the expenditure you have undertaken, nevertheless, as your accountant, I shall be glad to see some return for your investment! I wish 'Isabelle' every good fortune."

Jane smiled to herself. As her father's daughter she wanted the business to thrive and now there was prospect of freedom from the shop she could look forward to putting her energies into making it pay. She read the references supplied by Doreen and, if true, they portrayed the girls as excellent, experienced saleswomen. A second reference was from a clergyman, the vicar of their local church, who spoke well of them as regular attenders and of fine character.

Thinking that no one would be likely to speak in such terms of Lisette, Jane decided to agree to her cousin's demands. It might be that, with a second season, Lisette would achieve the kind of marriage she was set upon and so cease to be a problem to her cousin.

Before she left the shop the twins came down from the kitchen. Maisie looked less wan and Doreen expressed their thanks for Jane's kindness. Then she hesitated and added, "Ma'am, I don't want to presume, but Mrs Gibbs showed us some of the work that's been done. It is beautiful – but in a way too fine. If you could include some simpler, less expensive gowns and accessories you could attract a wider clientele. Of course, the work would be of as good quality but less time would have to be spent and the materials could be less expensive as well."

Jane was a little taken aback but she recognised the girl's earnestness and goodwill.

"Why, I had never thought – I suppose all the garments are such as I would buy myself."

"That's just it, ma'am, and you are as fine as fine – but lot of people can't afford such clothes. Why, even that lovely dress in the window could only be bought by a lady of the first stare." Her eager tongue flattered and a deep blush mantled her face. "I'm sorry, ma'am, I shouldn't have presumed."

Her sister had been tugging her sleeve and now looked anxiously at Jane. "She means well, ma'am, but she gets carried away, does Doreen."

"She shows great good sense," replied Jane reassuringly. "I am new to shop-keeping and had never thought out the matter clearly. I shall take your sister's advice – thank you, Miss Betts. Please come at nine o'clock on Monday, I shall have heard from London by then," and she smiled as the sisters made their adieux and left the shop with Maisie, once outside, talking earnestly to Doreen.

Jane wrote express to Mr Whitney and asked for an urgent reply, although she had made up her mind to take the sisters on trust. The time had passed quickly but with no customers and Jane could only hope, as she thought of the day before she slept, that more customers would arrive – but not before Monday! – so that she would not have to deal with them.

Her wish was not granted. The following morning she had scarcely begun, in response to Doreen's suggestions, on the choice of a gown to replace the one now on display in the window, when her attention was distracted.

An open landau with a crest on its panel drew up outside the door. A groom hurried to let down the step and a tall man alighted to hand down an elderly lady who came barely up to his shoulder.

Jane, looking through the glass panel in the door, stood as if transfixed. Here was the hero of her secret dreams – private fantasies when either, miraculously, she was beautiful and a tall, dashing lover begged for her favour, or, she was still plain but was loved for herself alone by the same gallant suitor. She had never expected to see her ideal in the flesh, but here he was! Alas, the everyday Jane knew full well that fairy tales remained inside the covers of a book and had nothing to do with the real world.

She was slow to recover and in those moments heard his voice. It had all the depth and music she ascribed to her hero, even when uttering such commonplaces as, "In half an hour then, Grandmamma, John knows when to return." He ushered the lady into the shop and, with a slight bow, left her. The carriage was already driving away down the street.

Mrs Gibbs placed a chair for the lady and by the time she was seated Jane had come to herself.

"Good morning, ma'am!"

"Good morning," replied the lady, "I understand that you create your own designs."

"Yes, all our models are originals," said Jane.

"So, Mrs Frobisher told me," nodded the lady, "When I complimented her on her daughter's gown last evening."

Jane smiled inwardly, she had cast her bread upon the waters to some purpose!

"I shall require several gowns – in fact, a complete outfit for my granddaughter who is much of an age with Miss Frobisher. She is to make her debut next year but I have decided to introduce her in a limited way to local society in preparation for her come-out."

"I understand, ma'am," said Jane, "I will have a selection ready for your granddaughter when she visits us."

"Nothing of the sort!" replied the lady decisively. In spite of her abruptness she was not offensive, merely a great lady accustomed to speaking her mind.

"I should like you to come to the Manor with some samples of materials and make a few sketches when you have met Althea. Can you do that? I will send the carriage – we live near Ditchling."

After the slight shock of the abrupt reply Jane had decided to fall in with her customer's wishes but to asset her independence a little.

"I could wait upon you next Monday, ma'am, if that would be convenient, at about eleven o'clock."

"Not before?"

Jane shook her head.

"Ah well, it will have to do. While I am waiting for my carriage, perhaps you will show me some of your gowns – I was greatly taken with the one in the window but did not look at it closely."

Jane said, "I will bring it to you, ma'am. Mrs Gibbs, will you fetch down a selection of gowns suitable for a young lady?"

"Yes ma'am," replied Mrs Gibbs and left while Jane took the ivory and coral creation from the window.

The lady inspected it closely through her lorgnette and said, "It is lovely – the embroidery is particularly fine." She looked at Jane, "You are new to this shop-keeping, are you not?"

"Yes, ma'am, this is my first venture," replied Jane.

"Come down in the world, I should imagine – you are a lady," stated her customer, "So may I give you a word of advice – do not display your models in the window – reply on recommendations from satisfied customers. No woman of quality would wear a gown previously displayed to the whole world. This is too beautiful for such treatment."

Luckily Mrs Gibbs returned at this point since Jane did not know how to reply.

The lady inspected the several gowns displayed – a walking dress in cream crepe, a lace evening gown, a ball dress in silver net over white taffetas, and a redingote in deep blue grosgrain – all of them deceptively simple and subtly elegant. The customer approved of them all and was still examining the walking dress when her grandson entered as the landau drew up outside.

"Ready, Grandmamma?" He put up his glass and looked at the array of garments. "Great Scot! You are not buying the whole stock, are you?"

Taking the opportunity for a closer look at her beau ideal Jane saw that there was a hint of temper in the set of the well-cut lips and in the dark brows ready to frown. However there were laughter lines at the corners of the lips and grey eyes which softened his countenance. Jane could find no fault in the splendid figure from the brown of his dark hair to his gleaming hessians. He laughed at this grandmother, ignoring Jane.

"Of course not, you foolish boy, I was passing the time until you came. I have arranged for Miss ....? She looked enquiringly at Jane.

"Darcy," supplied Jane.

"For Miss Darcy to come to the Manor next Monday to bring some samples and take Althea's measurements." She rose, took a card case from her reticule, and gave a card to Jane. "I will send the carriage at ten thirty on Monday. Come Dominic – good day Miss Darcy!"

He opened the door and ushered his grandmother out and Jane had barely recovered from her slight courtesy before he had leapt into the landau and it was rattling off down the street.

"I might have been a piece of furniture!" Jane thought indignantly and she took herself to task for indulging in romantic musings as she helped Mrs Gibbs to return the garments to the storeroom, including the ivory satin creation. Her common sense told her that the lady's advice had been good and the dress was not to be returned to the window.

The fan, laid on a gilt chair and a bewitching parasol leaning against it, looked attractive and when they had been displayed to the best advantage, Jane sat down to look at the card. It was engraved and read:

The Dowager Lady Delamere

Templeton Manor

Ditchling

Sussex

Jane put it in her reticule and sent Phoebe, always ready for a break in her work, to the livery stables to order the carriage to be sent round immediately – earlier than usual – to take her back to Hove. She told Mrs Gibbs, quite truthfully, that she had a headache and would close the shop early.

"We will choose some patterns of material tomorrow for me to take to Lady Delamere on Monday and you shall instruct me as to how to take measurements. I must be sure to do it correctly!"

"Very good, ma'am," replied Mrs Gibbs. "If you don't mind my saying so, Miss Darcy, you should rest tonight, this has been a very trying week for one not used to commerce."

"It has, has it not?" said Jane. "I shall take your advice, Mrs Gibbs – good afternoon," and she went thankfully to take the short ride to Hove.

The fresh breeze did little to calm her agitation and when she reached Becky's house she explained her early return – a slight headache. No, she did not want a tisane nor to bathe her temples in aromatic vinegar. She would rest quietly on her bed until dinnertime and would be complete restored.

Becky agreed 'a quiet lay-down would be best'. She knew from experience that when her nursling was upset she hated a fuss, so at last Jane gained the privacy of her room.

At first, as she sat by the window looking out at the little garden, her mind was in a turmoil and she could not order her thoughts. She had read of love at first sight – it had been portrayed as a deliriously happy experience – not this torment of pain. As she grew calmer Jane could only explain her state by acknowledging that, hopelessly plain as she was and moreover set in a background of trade, she scarcely existed to the object of her desire. She had not even the hope that he might become aware of her presence as a person so she determined to cease to indulge in her romantic fancies and treat them as the daydreams they were. Instead, after dinner, she made a few preliminary sketches in readiness for her visit on Monday.

Part of the next day was spent in selecting swatches of materials for Lady Delamere's consideration and in being instructed by Mrs Gibbs in the professional niceties of taking measurements. Luckily no customers appeared to interrupt these activities.

The text at church the next day was, 'Whatsoever thy hand findeth to do, do it with thy might'. Jane never heard the sermon, the text set her off thinking that she had certainly obeyed the precept of Ecclesiastics, but to what end she was not sure.

In the afternoon she sat in the little garden. The sun shone warmly and it was sheltered from the cool breeze off the sea. As she sat lazily reflecting she was coming rapidly to the conclusion that Lisette and Lucian had done her a favour. They had caused her to leave Cleave where her life had been uneventful and dull to the point of extinction and where she had been rapidly settling into an old-maidish existence.

By now, by a series of coincidences, she had widened her circle and discovered in herself a latent talent for dress design and business management. It was true that she was inexperienced but, with a smile to herself, time would remedy that! Life was becoming more interesting day by day, and tomorrow, tomorrow she might see him again! It was of no use to tell herself to be sensible – she <u>was</u>. She knew that nothing could come of it, but oh! she longed to see him.

Her wish was to be granted if not in the manner in which she could have wished!

On Monday the early post brought confirmation from Mr Whitney that the twins' references were authentic and Jane was able to engage them to their great delight. She had just time to arrange for Mrs Gibbs to give them any help required and to gather the parcel of samples and her sketching block before the landau arrived and she began her journey to Ditchling.

CHAPTER 9

When they had left the bustle of the Steyne behind and passed the imposing church of St Peter's, they reached the Ditchling Road. Jane had asked Becky and Sarah about Ditchling but, beyond mentioning the Beacon, which they had never visited, they could tell her little, so she settled back to enjoy the fine bursts of country as they left the town behind and climbed the slope of the Downs. On her right she saw, on the highest point, a great pile of timber and realised that this must be the Beacon. A little farther on they turned right into a much narrower road and passed through the small village of Clayton.

They had travelled about a mile beyond the village when they entered between some imposing gates, which were closed after them by a lodge-keeper, and swept up a long avenue bordered by wide lawns to come to a halt on a gravelled carriage sweep before the impressive entrance of a large, gracious house.

Jane had no time to take note of the building before the groom had let down the step, and, gathering up her parcel and sketch block, she alighted from the carriage and began to mount the steps leading to the wide double doors. She had reached the third step when the door flew open and a young girl in riding dress rushed out and called back over her shoulder, "I will, I will!" as she collided with Jane who had no chance to avoid her. The girl kept her feet and sped on – the carriage had driven away immediately so there was no obstacle in her way now she had disposed of Jane, who sprawled on the gravel in an undignified heap.

She had no time to discover if she were hurt before she was lifted in two strong arms and carried quickly up the steps and across the hall. She felt the vibration in the chest beneath her ear as the deep voice said to a footman, "Collect Miss Darcy's things and bring them to the morning room," and then she was deposited on a sofa, rather like a parcel, she thought later indignantly, and the voice said, "Brat!" She saw the dark brows drawn together and the lines of temper tighten round the closed lips before her rescuer turned away, tossing over his shoulder, "I'll send someone," and he was gone.

Jane had just realised that the epithet had not been addressed to her and was beginning to feel her hands smarting and to find her gloves in ruins, when an elderly woman in a snowy cap and apron came hurriedly into the room.

"Why, whatever's happened, Miss?" She took Jane's hands gently in her own and clicked her tongue, "We'll need to bathe these," and she drew off the ruined gloves saying, "I'm afraid these are past mending. Where else is hurting?"

"I don't know," replied Jane faintly, "Only bruised I think." She was feeling very shaken and lay back with her eyes closed. She was not aware that the woman had gone and returned with a maid carrying a tray with a bowl, a glass, and some linen on it.

"Shall I put it here, Nurse?"

"Yes," and the maid set the tray down on a small table drawn up to the sofa on which Jane lay.

Nurse began to bathe Jane's hands and said, "her ladyship will be very upset, and his lordship is annoyed too." She smiled at Jane, "But his temper don't last long – I've nursed him from his birth and he has a sweet nature."

Jane would not have thought so! She was beginning to feel sick and dizzy and Nurse picked up the glass of water and poured in a few drops from the bottle she took from her pocket.

"Drink this, my dear, sal volatile is a wonderful steadier," and she held the glass to Jane's lips.

The draught revived her and she thanked Nurse, who began to smear some ointment on the linen and to bandage Jane's hands. "They'll feel easier soon, they're only scratched and there are no deep cuts, but I daresay they are painful enough. Take the tray away, Annie."

As the maid reached the door it opened and she stepped aside as Lady Delamere came in.

"What is all this, Nurse? Dominic has just stormed out of the house looking like a thunder cloud!"

"After Lady Althea, I expect, your ladyship. She ran out and knocked this poor young lady down the steps. It has shaken her up but she says she is only bruised and I've seen to her hands – they were scraped on the gravel – it's destroyed her gloves, though."

Lady Delamere came to the sofa and said, "Miss Darcy, I am deeply concerned. Should we not summon the doctor to be sure you have suffered no serious injury?"

Jane was feeling much better although her various bruises were making themselves felt. It was time, she thought, that she spoke for herself. She sat up and, swinging her feet to the floor, arranged her skirts.

"No, indeed, your ladyship, your nurse has made my hands feel very comfortable and, apart from a few bruises, I feel quite myself."

The door opened and a footman entered. "The lady's reticule and parcel, your ladyship."

"Thank you Thomas, - put them on the table. Ask Lister to bring some ratafia and biscuits."

He bowed and left and Nurse said, "I think Miss Darcy will be quite recovered when she has rested a while, your ladyship," and she too went to the door.

"Thank you, Nurse," said Lady Delamere and sat down near Jane's sofa.

The butler appeared with the refreshments and retired, having served the two ladies.

"Can you manage the glass, Miss Darcy?" her ladyship enquired.

"Yes, thank you, my fingers are quite free – it is only my palms which are scratched." Jane took a reviving drink of the cordial. "Shall we look at the patterns, your ladyship? Fortunately the wrappings are stout and they will have come to no harm," and she made to rise to fetch the parcel.

"Are you sure you feel well enough?" asked Lady Delamere.

"Quite sure, perhaps we could sit at the table, the materials could be spread out," and she went to the table.

Her ladyship followed and opened the parcel saying, "I am sure I can manage this better than you."

The sight of the two ladies absorbed in comparing swatches of material halted Dominic on the threshold when he entered the room a few minutes later.

"Grandmamma! I should have thought Miss Darcy should be resting."

"She is made of sterner stuff, Dominic – nothing missish about her. Where is Althea? She must apologise for her dreadful behaviour."

"I have sent her to change from her habit – then she is to come down to you and explain herself and made her apologies." He turned to Jane, "My young sister is spoilt, I am afraid, and still behaves like a naughty child."

Growing up is a difficult time," said Jane. "I expect she will surprise you and become a young lady overnight."

Up till now Dominic had been going through a formal routine of courtesy. He had hardly looked at Jane, but now her soft voice arrested his attention – it was low and clear and she spoke calmly – he had expected an agitated outburst. However, he was disappointed to find her plain face had little attraction.

"You are very forbearing ma'am," he said, and turned as the door opened. "Ah, here is the culprit!"

Dominic and his sister had the same dark hair, although her's had auburn glints where the sun caught it, but there the resemblance ceased. Her slight and graceful form came well short of his shoulder and, indeed, Jane marvelled that Althea had had sufficient weight to overset her.

If Dominic could be accounted handsome, Althea was lovely and, with maturity, would be beautiful. An oval face with a creamy complexion was enhanced by deep blue eyes shaded by thick, curling lashes and her red lips invited kisses.

She stood for a moment and then ran impetuously to her grandmother.

"Oh, Grandmamma, I am so sorry – but Dominic put me in a passion."

"That is no excuse, my child, and it is not to me but to Miss Darcy that you should make your apologies. It is fortunate that her hurts are not serious and that she is courageously making light of them!"

Althea turned to Jane, looking more like a child who had been naughty than a young lady.

"Miss Darcy, I am indeed very sorry – I just did not see you – I was so enraged." She saw Jane's bandaged hands and her own flew to her mouth. "Oh, your poor hands – did I do that?" she asked in consternation.

"I rather think it was the gravel that did the damage," replied Jane with a smile.

"But I caused it!" cried Althea, tears starting in her eyes. "Oh, please forgive me!"

"You are forgiven," replied Jane. "The damage is quite superficial."

"That is very generous of Miss Darcy," said Lady Delamere, "But these outbursts must cease, Althea! What brought on this one?"

"Dominic, of course," said the girl, sending a mutinous look at her brother. "He forbade me to ride to the village!"

"Inaccurate!" snapped Dominic. "I forbade you to ride unaccompanied!"

"But I always used to ride alone before I went to school to be finished!"

"And came back very <u>un</u>finished!" replied her brother.

"That is enough!" interposed Lady Delamere authoritatively. "Miss Darcy can have no interest in family squabbles … Althea, you are to practice for an hour, Mr Brice was very dissatisfied with your playing last week – see that he is better pleased tomorrow!"

Althea recognised the stern tone and replied meekly, "Yes, Grandmamma," and made her escape.

Dominic was inwardly furious that he had been betrayed into childish bickering with his sister and said, "If you will excuse me, Grandmother, I must see Frazer. Good day, Miss Darcy, I hope you will suffer no lasting ill effects from my sister's hoydenish behaviour!" and he executed a slight bow and left the room.

Lady Delamere sighed, "I feel that this is my fault, I have let Althea get out of hand."

"She will settle down soon, I am sure, your ladyship. She was genuinely sorry for the accident," said Jane soothingly.

Later, the older woman could never explain to herself why she, usually reticent about her problems, should confide in a stranger. Perhaps it was the understanding sympathy she sensed in Jane.

She found herself going on, "I should have come here years ago when Althea's mother died but my son assured me that the governess was capable of taking charge and that she and Althea were friends. Dominic was in the army then, of course. Then, just over a year ago, my son died and there was no one. I came and found Althea quite out of hand, so I dismissed the governess and packed my granddaughter off to school". She sighed, "To add to my anxieties Dominic was severely wounded at Albuera and was invalided home. He is not completed recovered now and is fretting to rejoin his regiment – that is why he is so impatient with Althea, although he is very fond of her." She broke off. "I should not confide all this, I know, Miss Darcy, but I feel you are owed some explanation for Althea's sorry behaviour." She did not add, perhaps because she did not recognise it, her need to tell her troubles to a sympathetic ear.

Jane said reassuringly, "His lordship seems to be making a good recovery and men always make bad invalids, do they not? As for Lady Althea – perhaps if we could interest her in the choice of her new gowns and dwell on the prospect of parties in the near future, she will not feel so rebellious – I expect she is a trifle bored – too old for the school room but not yet involved in Society."

Lady Delamere smiled, "You show great good sense, Miss Darcy. Would you tell me how old you are – you look so young to sound so mature."

"I am over nineteen, Lady Delamere, but my father said some years ago that I had a head on my shoulders!"

"He is dead now, I collect, and you have to make your own way in the world – you are not born to trade, I feel sure."

"No, but I am learning." She paused and then continued, "I am afraid I shall not be able to take Lady Althea's measurements today, or to make sketches, but we might decide on the garments you would like to order and suitable materials for them." Jane hoped that she had distracted her hostess from further enquiries into her background.

Lady Delamere agreed. "If you are sure you are feeling well enough?"

Jane nodded and took out her block and pencil. "I can manage to make a note of your choices," she said and the two ladies settled down to make a selection of materials.

As they finished Jane said tentatively, "Do you think, your ladyship, that Lady Althea might see what you have chosen and might it be possible for her to suggest alternatives, subject to your approval, of course?"

Lady Delamere looked somewhat taken aback but then she nodded thoughtfully. "You are right, Miss Darcy. I have been remiss – we should arouse her interest," and she rang the bell. "I am afraid I am so used to ordering matters that I rarely consult."

To the footman who answered the bell, "Ask Lady Althea to come to me – she is in the music room." She went back to Jane. "You are what I need, Miss Darcy, someone to put forward another point of view."

Althea came in and was delighted to look at the patterns and daring enough to suggest alternatives in one or two cases. Then it was time for Jane to leave and the carriage was ordered.

"When would you be able to come to take measurements and make sketches, Miss Darcy?" asked Lady Delamere.

"I am sure my hands will be healed in a few days," replied Jane, "I can make some sketches before I come and you can then approve or reject them. Shall we say Friday morning, your ladyship?"

"That will be very convenient – at the same time? I do hope your hands are not too painful."

Jane shook her head.

"Then good day, Miss Darcy," said her ladyship.

"I will help you down the steps," offered Althea eagerly.

"Thank you," replied Jane. "I own I am a little stiff," and the two girls went slowly out to the carriage and Jane was waved off by a smiling girl very different from the virago of their first encounter.

As she drove home Jane's thoughts were all of Dominic and Althea. Lisette and Lucian had been relegated to the past.

CHAPTER 10

Unfortunately, this was not true in Lucian's case. Some few days before, he had arrived in Brighton in pursuit of his quarry. Jane's guardian angel must have been extra vigilant for on several occasions in the next few weeks she and Lucian had only been streets apart though neither had seen the other.

After a day spent being cosseted by Becky, Jane went back to Isabelle's. She found the twins jubilant: Mrs Frobisher had told many of her acquaintances about the new modiste and the original creations to be found there and the twins had been kept busy. They reported to Jane that several satisfied customers had declared their intention of recommending Isabelle's, although one or two wished to keep the find to themselves.

Mrs Gibbs had several orders to fulfil and was glad that Jane had returned to approve the designs she had selected. She exclaimed over Jane's hands although they were well on the mend and she and Jane set aside the materials chosen by Lady Delamere. Jane looked round the workroom and had a few words with everyone there. The busy hum reminded Jane of a contented beehive and she returned to Hove happily sure that Isabelle's was in safe hands.

She worked on some new designs trying to drive out thoughts of Dominic from her mind to no avail. She asked herself why she could not be sensible? It was madness to indulge in dreams of a man who did not even notice her. Plain Jane, in her saner moments, knew that she was unlikely to find a lover and would be obliged to settle for second best in marriage if ever the chance should come her way.

When Friday came she did not know whether to hope or fear that she might see Dominic again. In the event she need not have troubled herself – he was away.

Lady Delamere and Althea were charmed with the designs she submitted and Jane, profiting from Mrs Gibbs' tuition, made a note of Althea's measurements, then Lady Delamere insisted that Jane partake of a nuncheon before returning to Brighton. Excited by the prospect of a new 'grown-up' wardrobe Althea talked eagerly of the evening parties she was to attend, but still bewailed the fact that Dominic would not squire her to a ball at the Castle or the Ship.

Jane said, "I am persuaded that you would not enjoy it – the balls are very crowded with a mixed sort of company I am told, and you and your gowns would not be seen to advantage. Besides, surely you do not want to spoil the delightful surprise that you will give the ton on your come-out. Be sure there will be some of the beau-monde at the public balls who would see you as a jeune fille not yet out and not worth their regard."

It became clear that this cautionary speech made an impression on Althea and she replied doubtfully, "Perhaps you are right, Miss Darcy, I do so want to be a success at my come-out and first impressions are important, are they not?"

"Indeed they are, and now, if you will excuse me, Lady Delamere, I must return to Isabelle's and put this work in hand."

Lady Delamere rose, "Althea, order the carriage," and she joined Jane in the hall. "Thank you, Miss Darcy for talking sense to that flibbertigibbet. When do you think that you will be ready for the first fittings?"

"Mrs Gibbs should have the gowns ready by this time next week. Could Lady Althea come to Isabelle's next Friday morning?"

"Yes, I will bring her myself. Ah, here is the carriage – good day Miss Darcy."

CHAPTER 11

Mrs Gibbs and her helpers worked hard throughout the following week and by Friday Althea's new wardrobe was ready when Lady Delamere and Althea arrived for the fitting.

After a while, Lady Delamere grew bored and decided to go to the Library where she might meet some friends – Althea could walk there with her maid, it was only round the corner into New Road and then another turn into Church Street.

Althea left Isabelle's delighted with her new gowns – they were more beautiful than she had expected – and it was in a daze of pleasure that she approach the New Road corner. Lucian, hurrying to Castle Square, took the corner too quickly and knocked Althea's reticule out of her hand. He restored it to her and apologised profoundly, introducing himself as Leslie Crawford, an alias he had adopted in order that Jane should not be on her guard if she were in Brighton and should hear of the present of Lucian Chancellor.

His charming manner and debonair appearance captivated Althea, and she was just wishing that she could prolong the encounter when she was hailed by Barney Langford, a playmate from childhood. She introduced the two men and said she must hurry away – her grandmother would be getting impatient, but hoped to meet Mr Crawford again.

"Less violently, I hope!" replied Lucian with a bow and a smile.

Barney said, "I say, Althea, he could come to m'sister's party – she would be glad of an extra man for the dancing, you know." He turned to Lucian, "It is for next Wednesday evening – Roman Court – anyone will direct you," and he tipped his hat and went on his way. His impulsive invitation had been given in the erroneous belief that Lucian was an acquaintance of Althea's accepted by her family.

Lucian/Leslie could hardly believe his luck – the blushing Althea was very much to his taste!

"Until next Wednesday, ma'am," and, bowing gracefully, went on down North Street while Althea, hoping that her grandmother would not hear of the incident, charged her maid not to mention the matter on pain of her mistress' displeasure.

"I won't, my lady." Althea's maid, a romantic at heart, thought the encounter was just out of one of her favourite love stories.

Fate was not done with Lucian. As he went on down North Street a female came out of a shop a little ahead of him. Although she was walking away from him Lucian knew that walk! "Good God, Jane!" he said to himself and hurried to overtake her. He passed her and turned.

"Jane! I have looked for you everywhere!"

The shock nearly overset her but she drew a deep breath and said, "I have nothing to say to you – let me pass!"

"But, Jane, I love you!" he said ardently.

"You love my money!" she riposted. "Lucian, let me pass!" She made to side-step him and he put a detaining hand on her arm.

There were few people about but Jane, dreading a scene, tried to turn back but his hold was too strong.

Suddenly a voice behind her said quietly, "Take your hand from this lady's arm, Sir!"

Dominic had been walking on the flagway opposite on his way to meet his grandmother when his attention was drawn to the little scene and he recognised Jane. It was clear that she was in difficulties and he crossed the road to be of help.

Lucian glared at him furiously, "This lady is my fiancée, Sir! I will thank you not to interfere!"

Jane was thunderstruck – how dared Lucian! "You lie! We were never engaged!"

"May I repeat – take your hand away!" Dominic from his greater height looked down on the seething Lucian and there was that in his look which caused the shorter man to drop his hand.

"We will settle this matter later – in private!" he snarled at Jane, "With no meddler to interfere!" and he strode off down the street.

Unperturbed, Dominic turned to Jane. "Miss Darcy, may I escort you to my grandmother?" and he offered his arm, which she accepted gratefully.

She was trembling and, as they reached Isabelle's, Dominic said, "Miss Darcy, I am persuaded that you should rest before meeting my grandmother." He opened the shop door and ushered her in, Jane was too agitated to resist.

The twins came forward and he said, "Miss Darcy is a little faint – would you bring some water?" and he seated Jane while Maisie hurried off to fetch the water.

When he had taken a few reviving sips Jane looked round at Dominic, she felt confused and embarrassed, wondering how to explain the confrontation.

"Lord Delamere," she began. He had been standing gazing round the shop in a detached manner giving her time to recover, but turned as she spoke.

"Thank you for your help – I must explain …."

"There is no need, Miss Darcy, the man was obviously annoying you. If he gives you more trouble you should report him to the authorities." His withdrawn manner and cool tones were like having the rest of the cold water flung in her face.

"Pray accept my thanks, nevertheless." She rose. "I am quite recovered now. My carriage should be arriving soon and I will return to Hove. Pray make my excuses to Lady Delamere."

She still looked pale and Dominic's code of manners would not permit him to leave her without an escort. "I will do so after I have seen you safely home, and here, if I mistake not, is your carriage."

It drew up as he spoke and, under the interested gaze of the twins, he escorted Jane to the carriage and seated himself beside her. Jane was feeling wretched. She sat back and cudgelled her brains as to how she was to extract herself from this coil

Dominic had much to engage his thoughts too. While Jane had aroused little interest in him till now he had noted with approval her steadying influence on Althea and how his grandmother treated Miss Darcy – quite unlike her usual manner to trades people. Now he was worried, there was obviously some mystery attached to the modiste. He did not want his sister and grandmother involved in an unsavoury affair and he had formed a very poor opinion of Lucian. He had come to no conclusion by the time they arrive at Becky's house and he escorted Jane to the door and saw her admitted.

On the way back to Brighton he decided to say nothing to his family at present but to keep a very watchful eye on Miss Darcy.

As for Jane, she managed to reach her room without encountering Becky and resolutely turned her mind from worrying about Dominic's part in the recent encounter and began to consider what steps she could take to elude Lucian. She wrote to Mr Whitney to acquaint him with the latest development and spent a wretched night unable to think of a way out of her dilemma.

In the morning she sent a message to Isabelle's to say that she would not visit the shop until Monday and received a note enclosing an invitation from Lady Delamere to spend a few days at the Manor. There was also a note from Althea begging her to come so that she might see her arrayed for the first time in her 'grown-up finery'.

Althea's wardrobe was to be delivered on Monday, and Jane saw in the invitation an opportunity for a breathing space safe from Lucian, so she accepted gratefully.

The two days spent in sanctuary at Hove steadied Jane and on Sunday evening she found herself asking why fear Lucian? It was true that his importunities were unpleasant but he had no power to affect her life. She went to bed in a calmer frame of mind and arrived at the Manor next day with Althea's wardrobe and Mrs Gibbs to attend to any last minute adjustments. To her great relief, Dominic was away. In spite of having come to terms with the problem of Lucian she felt embarrassed at the prospect of meeting her rescuer and was glad not to be put to the test.

There was very little adjustment to be made to Althea's gowns and Mrs Gibbs went back to Isabelle's well satisfied.

Althea's delight in her new clothes seemed a little extreme to Jane. After all the girl had not been badly dressed before but when, that afternoon, she was taken to explore the gardens, she discovered the real reason for Althea's high spirits. At the party on Wednesday she was to meet again a Mr Crawford. "He is so handsome and well-bred I am sure he is used to London society.

He is so much more polished than boys like Barney Langford – he, Mr Crawford I mean, is older, of course, just enough to make him different!"

Jane listened indulgently to these outpourings and replied that the charming Mr Crawford would seem to be quite an acquisition to local society.

I collect you are to have your hair styled on Wednesday, Lady Althea?" she said to cut short the girl's outpourings.

"Yes, M'sieur Jacques is coming from Brighton in the afternoon. Miss Darcy," she went on eagerly, "Do you ride?"

Jane thought nostalgically of long days in the saddle in the Cotswolds and said, "Yes, I love riding but have had no opportunity here."

"But you have your habit with you, have you not?"

"It is at my lodging in Hove."

"But, I want to show you the view from the Beacon – it is not so fine as from Chanctonbury but that will be too far for our ride tomorrow. Do say that you will come."

Jane felt she must explain to Althea that she was not to be treated as a usual guest – her position was equivocal – she was now, after all, in trade.

Althea listened to Jane's somewhat halting protests and then burst out impatiently, "But you are my friend and Grandmamma said you are a lady – forced to earn your living – so that need not concern us! Do send for your habit and ride with me tomorrow!"

"If Lady Delamere approves," Jane assented weakly. After all she would not be accompanying Althea on a social occasion and she longed to become Miss Gascoigne of Cleave again if only for a few hours.

The next day was one of the happiest Jane had spent for weeks. She and Althea, accompanied by a groom, rode over the Downs through a sparkling morning. They dismounted when they reached the Beacon and Jane was presented with a view that rivalled the best that the Cotswolds could offer. The Downs rolled for miles with here and there a farm or a small village while clumps of trees threw pools of shade over the close cropped turf. A silvery blue ribbon to the South showed where the sea fretted the shore and Jane exclaimed with pleasure.

Althea said, "We must take you to Poynings to the Devil's Dyke and to Chanctonbury of course. You will see the dew pond there, they were made in pre-historic times it is said."

She talked of the ring of trees in Chanctonbury and of other Sussex beauty spots as they strolled over the sheep-cropped turf. A lark sang high above them and small blue butterflies danced over scabious and harebells making a symphony of blue. Althea said, "I think scabious is a horrid name for such a lovely flower, lady's pincushion is much more poetic, do not you agree?" Jane assented as she watched cloud-shadows chasing each other across the rolling sea of turf, she felt free of all the troubles which had beset her and would have stayed in this euphoric state for hours but the groom came up to them and touched his hat.

"Your ladyship, there's a storm a'coming up – see?" and he pointed to where a bank of cloud was rushing towards them – Jane was not to know how symbolic it was! They could see rain falling although it was miles away and the sun still shone above them.

"Goodness Sam, so there is!" exclaimed Althea. "We had best hurry." She and Jane were mounted by the groom and began to ride rapidly back to the Manor with the groom in close pursuit.

The storm caught them while they were still some distance from shelter and they were soaked, Jane in even worse case than Althea for she had lost her hat in her final dash and her hair was dripping down her back.

Nevertheless it had been an invigorating experience and when Althea came to Jane's room she was in high spirits and had a lovely colour.

Jane had rubbed her long hair almost dry. It had become badly tangled and she was trying to brush it into some sort of order.

Althea said, "Let me do that – I can manage at the back better than you."

As she brushed the soft, silky tresses she exclaimed, "You have lovely hair, Miss Darcy, it is like a polished hazel-nut and so soft."

Jane replied ruefully, "My mother called it mousy – plain, like my face!"

Althea was shocked. "That is not so," she checked. "Perhaps I should not contradict your mother, but indeed you have an.. an interesting face – your eyes smile and your mouth is made for laughter – when you smiled upon the Downs you showed such pretty teeth and your whole face lighted up."

This encomium quite embarrassed Jane. "Lady Althea, you put me to the blush! You are too kind."

"I say what I think," said Althea. " I do not mean to be rude – please pardon me and to show you forgive me will you let me put up your hair?"

"I should be glad," replied Jane and so far forgot here role as an impoverished gentlewoman as to add, "Without my maid I find it such a nuisance, I have been thinking of having it cropped."

"Please don't," said Althea, not noticing Jane's slip, "It makes you look quite out of the common. Why not let M'sieur Jacques advise you when he comes tomorrow to style my hair?" As she talked she was weaving Jane's luxuriant hair into a heavy plait which she pinned securely round Jane's head like a coronet. She stood back to appraise the result.

"There! You see you carry your head so gracefully and have a lovely neck and shoulders and beautiful ears – now they show to advantage."

Jane looked at herself in the mirror and could hardly believe what she saw. Althea had effected a transformation: All Jane's understated and hitherto hidden features were now displayed to advantage.

She rose, "I scarcely know myself – thank you, Lady Althea, you are a magician!"

Althea laughed and disclaimed and the two went down to join Lady Delamere who was most complimentary and endorsed Althea' opinion that Miss Darcy should consult M'sieur Jacques next day.

Far away in Bath Lisette was writing an urgent letter to Jane. She needed money, she said, everything cost so much and it was nearly time for her to go with Lady Amelia to London for the Season and she simply must have new gowns and fripperies – her last pair of silk stockings were torn and her hats were too frumpish for the beau monde – the catalogue went on and on. Would dear Jane be extra generous?

After all she had received no legacy from her uncle although she was sure he would have provided for her had he known he was going to die. What she did not tell Jane was that her gaming debts were beyond her resources and she was panic stricken at the thought of Lady Amelia getting to know of her folly if she could not settle what she owed.

She dispatched the letter under cover to Mr Whitney urging him to forward it without delay, then, with a light mind – she never considered the possibility of a refusal – she went to meet the authors of her predicament. The two Frenchmen still paid extravagant court to her. It was in their company that she had been introduced into a fast gambling set. She had been flattered to mingle with the sophisticated crowd and at first had had some lucky wins but soon she began to lose steadily. When she would have withdrawn her escorts urged her to go on playing, assuring her that her luck would turn. It didn't! However, the Frenchmen came to her rescue and took over her vowels. They were charming and said that she could take her time to redeem them. As far as it was possible for such a shallow brain, Lisette was worried, but when a young attaché from the Foreign Office became épris she put aside her worries and enjoyed his company with zest. Strangely the Frenchmen seemed not to be offended at being supplanted as her regular escorts.

Lisette continued to live for the day and gathered its rosebuds with a careless hand, only taking care to please Lady Amelia on whom her London Season depended.

At Ditchling Manor the little Frenchman achieved a coiffure for Althea which more than satisfied her desire to look grown-up. Pearls were threaded through her piled-up curls and one glossy ringlet was allowed to rest on her shoulder forming a dusky background to the pearl-drop earrings which she was to wear for the first time.

He made no demur when asked to dress the nut-brown hair of Lady Delamere's protégée – her ladyship's patronage was valuable. For some minutes he studied Jane and held her heavy tresses at all angles, exclaiming at its luxuriance.

"But, as you see, M'sieur, it is absolutely straight and nothing will make it curl," said Jane. "I fear it is impossible to make anything of it."

"Mam'selle, for Jacques nothing is impossible – we shall contrive!" and he drew the hair to the crown of her head and pinned it securely in a glossy knot allowing the last five inches or so to fall in a silky plume down the back of her head. It should have looked quite odd, but instead it looked becoming, revealing as it did Jane's beautifully poised head and neck and her pretty, well-set ears.

"Voila!" exclaimed M'sieur Jacques, "When Mam'selle is en grande tenue she should thread strings of brilliants to match her jewels in the fall of her hair."

Lady Delamere said rather hesitantly, "The style is most unusual and becomes you, Miss Darcy. You should certainly wear your hair so in the evenings and in the plaited coronet for the daytime," and she congratulated the beaming M'sieur Jacques.

Before getting dressed for her party Althea begged Jane to dress up for dinner. She was like a child with a new doll, thought Jane, but had not the heart to deny the young girl the extra pleasure.

So it was that when Lady Delamere and Althea, charming in a gown of soft blue crepe clasped down the front with pearl clusters and with pearl earrings and pearls threaded through her sophisticated coiffure, left for Roman Court, Jane too was in full fig. Her plume of hair was threaded with a fine gold chain and she wore a gown of changeable silk of grey and violet with long gold and amethyst earrings dangling from her well-set ears.

When the ladies had gone Jane was free to explore the house. Lady Delamere had said she might go where she wished. Her first choice was the notable state drawing room – a truly magnificent apartment with a wonderful ceiling divided into octagonal panels with clusters of different flowers in each; the walls were panelled in eau-de-nil silk framed in ivory. The room was vast and three large Chinese carpets were islanded on a gleaming parquet floor. Two marble fireplaces faced each other across the room and three huge chandeliers carrying innumerable candles were matched by silver girandoles placed at intervals round the walls.

Rare objects d'art were displayed on occasional tables of inlaid walnut and chairs and sofas in the same wood were upholstered in floral silk to match the carpets.

Jane found such magnificence overwhelming and turned with relief to the library. She could see that it was in constant use. Chairs were drawn up to desks and tables and books from the shelves were open here and there. A huge globe attracted her and deep leather armchairs invited the reader to settle comfortably.

But it was the music room across the hall that halted her wanderings. It was such a room that she would dearly have liked at Cleave if her family had had any turn for music. There were many instruments displayed, including a harp, but what drew her irresistibly was one of the new square pianos. She succumbed to temptation and, seating herself, began to play the Mozart sonata upon the rack.

Jane had been well-taught and had found solace at the piano in many a dull, sad hour at Cleave, but she had never played on such a magnificent instrument. From Mozart she strayed through many of her favourite pieces quite oblivious of the passage of time.

Dominic, returning late and entering the house by a side-door, heard the music but did not stay to discover the performer. He made his way unobtrusively to his room and hastily washed and changed from his grimy, shabby clothes into more orthodox garments.

His valet entered in the middle of this activity and said in reproachful accents, "Your lordship should have rung!"

"And let the world know a down-at-heel ruffian was in the house? Someone else might have answered the bell had you not been available. Get rid of this rubbish, John, and then ask Lister to send some wine and sandwiches to the library."

As the man was collecting the discarded clothes Dominic asked, "Do I need a shave or will I pass for tonight?"

John looked critically at his master. "You've got a bit of a shadow, Sir, but the ladies are out so it won't matter. Anyway you look more fit for your bed – a bad crossing was it?"

"Thick fog – we were hours late into Shoreham."

"And you've ridden hell for leather, I'll be bound, when you've no business on a horse with that shoulder!"

"That is enough, John!"

Dominic's valet had been his batman and they had shared many tight corners and John felt privileged to take his master to task when he thought that that gentleman was being foolhardy.

"By the way," Dominic enquired as John prepared to leave the room, "Who is in the music room?"

"That Miss Darcy – she needn't bother you, sir," disapproving John left, taking the rejected garments with him.

Dominic went downstairs but on his way to the library paused to listen to the charming air that was being played. The music room door was ajar and he looked in quietly.

Seated at the piano with her back to him was a graceful figure. The queenly head with its fall of softly shining hair set upon a beautiful neck and shoulders was no-one he knew. The light from the tapers on each side of the music rack threw a golden nimbus around her enhancing the sheen of her creamy skin.

Dominic thought, "John said it was Miss Darcy – but this is not that plain mouse!" Intrigued, he went into the room and, in a pause in the melody, said quietly, "Good evening."

It would be difficult to say which of the two was the more astonished.

Dominic saw a graceful girl rise to face him and realised it was indeed the 'plain mouse'.

Jane turned to see the object of her dreams, whom she had thought far away, standing within a pace of her looking very tired and slightly less immaculate than usual.

She hurried into speech. "It is such a beautiful instrument, I could not resist."

"Your playing matched it. Althea has not your touch. That was a charming piece I interrupted – I have not heard it before – please go on with it."

68

"It is a nocturne by John Field, an Irish composer, but he had lived for some time in Russia, I believe."

"Not the best place to be at the moment, I should imagine. But do continue Miss Darcy, would you mind if I stayed to listen?" he asked. The shadowed peace of the music room appeared very soothing to the tired man.

Before she could reply, Lister appeared in the doorway. "I have taken your refreshments to the library, my lord."

Greatly daring, Jane asked, "Why not enjoy them in here, if you would like to hear the rest of the piece?"

"Would you mind? I own it would be much more pleasant." At her shake of the head she murmured, "If you would prefer it. That chair over there would be comfortable," indicating a deep armchair.

Dominic turned to Lister and said, "Bring the tray in here, Lister. I am to have music with my supper!"

The butler brought in the tray and, as Jane seated herself at the piano, poured a glass of wine for his master and left the room thinking, "Not quite the thing, but she's only in trade, after all – not one of us!"

Jane, at first a little nervous, began the nocturne over again and Dominic in the shadows enjoyed his wine and thought what a pleasant picture she made – in profile she was not nearly so plain.

He had been travelling continuously for over twenty-four hours with very little pause for rest and only managed one sandwich before sleep began to overcome him. The tranquil music helped and when, at the conclusion of the nocturne no sound came from him, Jane went on to a Mozart adagio, not realising that her listener slept and longing to prolong this blissful interlude.

Some time later when she ventured to look towards Dominic she was struck by his absolute stillness. She played a few idle chords and then said softly, "My lord ...?" No reply, so she went over to his chair. He was sunk so deep in sleep that a half-eaten sandwich had dropped from his hand.

For a few moments Jane gave herself the exquisite pleasure of studying his sleeping face then, regretfully, went quietly to the piano and, carefully closing it, took a taper and lit a candle in the candelabra on the table before snuffing the ones on the piano.

She allowed herself one last look at the weary face and softly left the room.

As she prepared for bed the pain of unrequited love seemed more than she could bear but, "At least," she whispered to herself, "I have had this last hour," and, dwelling on the rapturous memory, at last she fell asleep.

CHAPTER 12

Jane was awakened by a maid bringing her chocolate and a note addressed to Miss Darcy in strong black script. She was about to break the wafer when there was a scratch on the door and, obeying she knew not what impulse, she hid the billet under her pillow.

Althea ran in, still in her wrapper with tumbled curls and a conspiratorial air.

"I waited till they brought your chocolate but I must tell you about last night, Miss Darcy – he was there!"

"Mr Crawford, I collect?" said Jane smiling, "Was he as wonderful as you expected?"

Althea plumped herself down on the bed. "More wonderful – and he danced with me twice! Of course, we could not be partners a third time – people would think I was fast – but we were in the same set for most of the country dances! I wish we had had the waltz, but Mrs Langford is too rustic!"

"You would not have been able to participate even had it been played until you have made your début," reminded Jane.

"That is true and I should have hated to see Lillian Langford waltz with him – fancy – she has been out for two seasons! But Mary Osborne says she did not take!"

"I am sure you will take," said Jane reassuringly, "I expect you will be much admired. Whom did you dance with besides the dashing Mr Crawford?"

"Oh, all the usual boys, but they did not count!" Returning to her obsession she went on, "He – Mr Crawford – said I looked charmingly and said my gown was the equal of anything he had seen in Town, so you see you played a part in my success – nearly all the ladies asked about my dress and I told them it was an exclusive model from Isabelle!"

Jane laughed, "Thank you for the advertisement! Shall you see Mr Crawford in Town?"

"I shall see him before that! Grandmamma had taken a liking to him and has invited him to our dancing evening next week. Won't it be wonderful!" She gazed besottedly into space then came to with a start. "Miss Darcy – I have had a great idea!

Why should you not come to our party, then you could meet Mr. Crawford!" This with the air of one who promised a presentation to the Regent, no less.

"Thank you for the honour," replied Jane. "But it would not be fitting."

"Well, I asked Grandmamma on the way home and she said 'Why not? You are not known as Isabelle – only by Mrs Frobisher and her daughter and they are abroad."

"It is still not suitable," protested Jane.

"Well, Grandmamma said it was time you had a little pleasure – she said you are too young to be deprived of all gaiety. Do say yes, Miss Darcy."

Seeking for a final objection Jane said, "But I am persuaded that Lord Delamere would not agree."

"Oh, he agrees with anything Grandmamma suggests for me – in any case he will not be there. He is to pester the Horse Guards for the next fortnight.

Jane capitulated and Althea ran off, triumphant at having got her own way. Until she met Jane her own sex had had little appeal for her but she found Jane's personality attractive and she thought the older girl's circumstances romantic. What clinched the matter was that she still felt some compunction over the injuries she had inflicted at their first tempestuous meeting.

Alone, Jane did not immediately begin to consider the possible consequences of agreeing to Althea's suggestion, instead she took out the note from beneath her pillow and broke the wafer.

There were only a few lines in the black, decisive handwriting:

'Dear Miss Darcy

This is to apologise for falling asleep while you were playing so delightfully. Please pardon my unmannerly behaviour and give me the pleasure of hearing you perform when I return to show that you have forgiven me.

Delamere'

As a first letter from the loved one Jane could not but feel it lacked warmth! But to touch the paper his hand had touched gave her exquisite pleasure. She hoped that the episode in the music room would not come to Lady Delamere's ears. She need not have worried. John and Lister had always conspired to allow no hint of their master's unorthodox activities to become common knowledge and Dominic had been roused to go to bed by his man and Lister had removed the tray from the music room the previous evening.

The next few days were filled for Jane with the routines connected with the shop which was beginning to become quite well-known. She rarely visited the premises preferring to stay in Hove and produce more designs for Mrs Gibbs.

When she thought of the forthcoming party at the Manor her feelings were ambivalent. She was, after all, not quite twenty, and looked forward with pleasure to a pleasant social evening, but at the back of her mind there was a reluctance to become more involved in Dominic's circle. The slight contact between them had given her such rapture that common-sense dictated that she should see no more of him and so avoid further heartbreak, then she remembered that he would not be at the party and so she could safely indulge herself on this one occasion.

Becky was pressed into service and threaded Jane's hair with strings of pale topazes which matched her earrings and pendant. The low neckline of her gown of ivory lace displayed her lovely neck and shoulders to perfection. With a velvet cloak of slightly darker shade than her jewels Jane looked so charming as she set off on the drive to the Manor that Becky's eyes filled with sentimental tears.

To her great pleasure Jane discovered that her dinner partner knew the Cotswolds and had frequently stayed with friends for the hunting. They were able to enjoy spirited arguments as to which were the best runs and marvel that they had previously never met.

Jane was prepared for the magnificence of the great drawing room but to see it cleared for dancing with hundreds of candles shedding brilliant light on masses of flowers was breathtaking. There was a small orchestra on a dais at the end of the room and

Lady Delamere and Althea stood just inside the double doors to welcome their guests.

Chairs and sofas were arranged round the walls and Jane made her way to the far end of the room where she might listen to the soft music. Her dinner partner joined her and she turned slightly away from the door where a steam of guests was now entering, thus she did not see Lucian bending over Lady Delamere's hand and holding Althea's a fraction too long as he begged for the first minuet when dancing should begin.

It was not until all but a few stragglers had arrived that Althea was permitted by her grandmother to join the guests now scattered in small groups about the room.

She soon found Lucian and said, "I want you to meet a great friend of mine, you are tall, can you see her, she is wearing ivory lace.

Lucian looked about and saw a girl in a lace gown half-turned to speak to her companion. He had no premonition, Jane had never looked like this graceful, fashionably dressed girl and, unsuspecting, he allowed himself to be drawn by Althea to the end of the room.

She exclaimed, "Miss Darcy, may I present Mr Crawford?"

Jane looked up and it was as well that she was sitting down – her legs would not have supported her.

Lucian turned white and for a moment could not find his voice, then he said, "I am delighted, Miss Darcy. Do you know you remind me strongly of a former acquaintance – a Miss Gascoigne – is she by chance a relative of yours?"

His impudent speech gave Jane a few moments breathing space in which her thoughts raced. Should she confront him and expose his duplicity? But to do so would be to reveal her own secret, Lucian would see to that! She could not do it! She must have time for reflection.

Althea was gazing in a puzzled fashion from one to the other but before the pause became too long Jane pulled herself together.

"I do not believe so, Mr Crawford – of course, she may be a remote connection." She held out her hand and was pleased to see that it did not tremble as Lucian bowed over it.

Fortunately neither of the antagonists was called upon to prolong the conversation for the orchestra struck a series of chords as a signal that dancing was about to begin and Lucian turned to Althea.

"Lady Althea, you promised me this dance – servant, Miss Darcy," and he led his partner away.

Jane's companion, Henry Graham, asked her to dance and she was glad to escape for a time from the need to think of some way out of her dilemma. Deliberately she put the problem to the back of her mind and danced and chattered through the evening of which later she had no recollection.

She was to stay overnight at the Manor and was very relieved when Lady Delamere said goodnight and, turning to Althea said, "Now, no bothering Miss Darcy with chatter tonight – she looks very tired – you can talk over the evening tomorrow."

Althea who, unlike Jane, treasured every moment of her evening spent with Mr Crawford and longed to talk it over, knew that her grandmother must be obeyed and said submissively, "Yes, Grandmamma. Goodnight Miss Darcy, we will have a long cose tomorrow if you will," and ran lightly upstairs as fresh as if she had not danced every dance.

On reaching her room Jane found that the meeting with Althea was not the only one promised for the morrow. The maid who was waiting to help her to bed said, "There is a note for you, Miss Darcy – the gentleman told me to give it to you in your room," and she gave Jane a folded note with a sentimental look – it was obviously a romantic affair – the gentleman had been as generous as he was handsome!

She was disappointed when Jane dropped it casually on the table and said coolly, "I will read it lately. Perhaps you will help me with my hair, these topazes are apt to get tangled in it," and from then on she said little. However, she was no longer calm when the maid had left but impatiently tore open the note. It was brief:

'We must meet. I will be at the Library at three tomorrow – do not fail.
L'

Although she had intended, when once alone, to decide on her course of action, Jane was so exhausted by the strain of the evening that she fell asleep as soon as she had snuffed her candle and woke the next morning to face her meeting with Althea with no idea as to how to solve the problem. Her impulse was to disclose the whole matter to Lady Delamere, but she was faced with a glowing Althea asking did she not think that Mr Crawford was wonderful? She had seen that her friend had been stunned into momentary silence by his elegance of form and manner which Jane must agree put all the other men present in the shade, and Jane could not bring herself to expose Lucian to a young girl in the throes of first love.

It was dishonest, it was cowardly not to denounce Lucian there and then Jane acknowledged to herself, but her courage was not equal to blighting the naïve pleasure of the young girl so cruelly and the moment passed.

As she travelled home she admitted the fact that an added reason for her silence was that she could not face the thought of confessing her own deception and so exposing herself to the contempt of Althea and her grandmother and ... and ..... but she would not think of Dominic.

By the time she reached Hove she was so wretched that she was almost ready to pack up and rush back to Cleave. Strangely, it was the thought of Dominic that made her hesitate. She feared that Althea might become more deeply infatuated with Lucian and he might persuade her into some illicit liaison. He had no scruples she knew and Althea was too innocent and inexperienced to recognise such a conniver. Could she allow the young sister of the man she loved to be so betrayed! Her courage rose to meet the challenge and she decided that even if it meant exposing herself to the scorn of Dominic and his family she must force Lucian to withdraw. Althea, no doubt, would feel that her heart was broken but she was young and would soon find distraction in the excitement of her first season.

Firmly resolved, she went to her rendezvous with Lucian. He suggested that they stroll by the sea. The day was fine and the breeze light and Jane would have enjoyed the walk under other circumstances. As it was she ignored the light-hearted scene and began abruptly.

"Lucian, you must take final leave of Lady Althea and quit Brighton."

"Oh, I must, must I? And what of you, Miss Darcy? I don't know what your game is, but if you attempt to queer my pitch I'll see to it that your fine friends know how you have tricked them. I cannot think why you are masquerading under a false name but they are sure to believe that there is some unsavoury reason – the world always jumps to the worst conclusion!"

His voice and manner and the very phrases he used showed a side of him that Jane had never suspected. He seemed to have deteriorated since the days at Cleave.

"My reasons are my business. They are quite innocent and if you force me to I shall confess my deception and reveal yours!"

The firmness of her tone startled Lucian; if she thought that he had changed he was astonished at her decisive calmness. Where was the mousy, diffident Jane of Cleave! Her appearance was as changed as her manner and Lucian eyed her with growing admiration. He felt he had been a fool not to make sure of her before being distracted by Lisette.

He spoke in conciliatory tones, "It is your fault, Jane. When you disappeared I was distraught and that fool Whitney would not give me your direction. I have searched everywhere for you. I gave a different name here so that you would not disappear again before I could tell you of my love. You know I have always wanted you ever since we began to grow up."

"You want my money, you mean! It is of no use, Lucian, I shall never marry you – that is final! And now let us end this discussion. I will give you until this time next week to make your excuses to the Delamere's, but, if you do not, I shall confess all."

He was about to protest but she said sharply, "No more, Lucian!" and turned on her heel and made her way back to the Steyne and the livery stable which supplied her carriage.

She saw nothing of Lucian or the Delameres for several days and went about her business with the shop in an outwardly normal manner which concealed a feeling that the sword of Damocles hung over her.

Could she have know how Lucian was spending his time she would have had reason to be alarmed. He had thought long and hard after his talk with Jane. His affairs were approaching crisis. If somehow he could announce his forthcoming marriage to a rich woman his creditors would hold their hands. He <u>must</u> make sure of Jane – Althea was useless to him – she would not succeed to her inheritance for several years and he could place no reliance on being accepted by her family as her suitor. No, Jane it must be! If only he could compromise her in some way that she would be forced to marry him – he began to plan.

First, he sent his man, Judson, to rent a small cottage off the beaten track behind Portslade. Judson had spent his childhood in the shadow of St Michael's Church in the village – his father had been the sexton. As a youth Judson had narrowly escaped the Press Gang and he had run away to get as far from the sea as possible. Finally his wanderings, living by casual labour and petty thievery, brought him to Cheltenham. He was a personable man and had the good fortune to ingratiate himself with a well-to-do family when, suspecting he was about to be denounced as a thief – he had prigged the father's purse – he turned the situation to his own advantage by restoring the purse to the grateful owner, claiming to have seen the gentleman drop it. Saying he was looking for employment he was taken into the gentleman's household first as a footman and by devious ways getting himself promoted to valet to the young son of the house who had reached the age of requiring one.

He should have been settled for life but the flaws in his character were too ingrained. He seduced one of the maids and was summarily dismissed.

Unable to find any but the poorest type of labouring work Judson reverted to thievery and grew bold as he became successful – too bold! He waylaid Lucian late one night and met his match.

A strange rapport spring up between the two men. At first Lucian was for handing Judson over to the authorities but the man's impudence, when he suggested that Lucian would never miss the stolen money, appealed to him. Lucian's present valet – passed on by his father – was too old. He sensed that this fellow would aid and abet him in the dubious pursuits he indulged in from time to time. He took his precautions – before engaging Judson he wrote out an account of the man's attempted crime and said that he would add spurious accounts of other misdeeds if the need arose. Then he told Judson that if he wanted to be taken on as valet he must sign the confession which would be deposited with Lucian's bankers to be used if necessary.

Faced with the choice of a prison sentence with hard labour at the very least or a comfortable life with one whom he recognised as a kindred spirit – Judson signed.

Since them, although to outward appearance they were gentleman and valet, they had shared many dubious adventures.

The cottage Judson rented was almost derelict but its walls were sound even though the thatched roof leaked. The one bedroom up the rickety stairs contained a broken-down bed and a small chest. The lattice window was narrow and the ceiling was the cobweb-hung thatch.

Lucian, meanwhile, had not been idle. He had continued to be one of Althea's circle secure in Jane's pledge to give him a week to withdraw. He had commented on the absence of her friend, Miss Darcy, whom he had thought to be staying at the Manor.

"Oh no, she has lodgings with her old nurse in Norfolk Street in Hove, but of course she stays here often. She does not keep her own carriage so she uses ours when she comes."

"She must find it difficult without a carriage at other times," commented Lucian.

"Oh, she hires one regularly from the livery stable, she says they serve her well."

"I am afraid she may have felt I was remiss the other night," said Lucian. "I barely acknowledged her – in truth I was so impatient for our dance ...." And he smiled ruefully.

Althea returned his smile, "I am sure you did all that was proper. In any event you may be more attentive at the concert on Wednesday, although she is not staying at the Manor but returning home afterwards.

Content with this information Lucian went on to pay Althea practised compliments and Miss Darcy was forgotten. Then Lucian had only to wait for Wednesday night.

Jane did not notice that the driver of the carriage which took her to the concert was not the usual man. Judson had struck up a drinking acquaintance with him and had doctored the man's drink and taken his place.

After the concert, at which Jane's pleasure had been destroyed by seeing Althea escorted by Lucian, she sank back in her carriage and closed her eyes in despair. It seemed that Lucian was going to brazen it out.

She sat up suddenly – surely they should have arrived at Becky's. The night was lit intermittently by the moon, hidden at times by scurrying clouds, and she could see little but, as the sky cleared for a few moments, she saw nothing she could recognise from the racing carriage. They seemed to be passing through a deserted countryside.

She tried to attract the coachman's attention thinking he had mistaken the direction and she was becoming alarmed at their headlong pace. If he heard her he took no notice and Jane became more frightened as they turned off the pike road into a narrow, ill-paved lane.

After a short, bumpy ride the carriage halted and a man standing in the shadows by his tethered horse stepped forward and opened the carriage door.

"I am afraid you must walk the rest of the way, Miss Gascoigne."

The light was too poor to recognise the speaker but the voice was only too familiar.

"Lucian! Desire the man to return to Hove immediately!"

"He would think me run mad, my dear Jane, since I told him to come here!" replied Lucian. "Come now, out with you, or would you rather be carried?"

Jane thought for a moment of staying obstinately in the vehicle but realised that she was no match for two men.

She stepped down, therefore, and looked about her. The fugitive moonlight showed her an overgrown track leading to a tumbled-down cottage overshadowed by a clump of ragged trees.

"And don't think that screaming will help you – this is known as Dead Man's Coppice, where murder was done and the locals would not come near it after dark for a fortune – they say it's haunted!"

As he spoke Lucian grasped her arm and urged her towards the cottage.

"But why bring me here?" asked Jane, "You surely do not intend to demand a ransom for my release?" She was dreadfully afraid but determined not to give Lucian the satisfaction of knowing it.

"Oh, no – I am not playing for a mere ransom – I want you and all your money – I want your hand in marriage!" he replied.

"You cannot believe that such behaviour advances you in my regard? Marry you! I would sooner die!" Even as she spoke Jane regretted that she had been betrayed into such Gothic utterances – quite out of a tale by Mrs Radcliffe.

"When it is known that we have spent a night together you will be glad to marry me!" By this time he had pushed her on to one of the broken-backed chairs in the filthy hovel.

He turned to Judson who had followed them with a lantern. "Best get back to the stables – explain the delay – lame one of the horses when you are nearly there."

The man said, "Right, sir," put down the lantern and went. Soon the carriage was heard to drive away.

During this brief interlude Jane had been trying to gather her courage and she now addressed her captor.

"Lucian, if it is money you want I will pay you an agreed sum if you restore me to my lodgings and cease acquaintance with Lady Althea."

"An agreed sum! I want it all and you, Jane. You've turned into a woman to be proud of. Never fear, I shall treat you well when we are married."

"And when you are ready, arrange a little accident, I collect!"

She was almost sick with fright – she feared he meant to rape her and kept talking to hold her fears at bay.

Lucian started, hearing the echo of his words with Lisette. "Enough of this! Up with you," and he dragged her from the chair and pushed her towards the stairs.

She hung back and tried to break his grip but with an oath he picked her up and stumbled up the dark steps.

He dumped her on the bed and before she could recover had fetched the lantern from below.

She sat braced for the worst when he said, "I do not wish to go to extremes unless you force me to – I'll leave you to think things over tonight. As far as the world knows we are together – sweet dreams, my love," he added ironically and she heard the key being turned in the lock and his fumbling descent of the stairs.

She sat trembling on the edge of the filthy bed almost sick with relief that her worst fears had not been realised. She thought it was not some remnant of decency that had prevented Lucian from inflicting the ultimate violation, rather it was a strand of weakness that made him finally ineffective even in villainy. Whatever the reason she resolved to turn the respite to good advantage and as soon as her knees would support her she stood up and, taking the lantern, examined her prison.

The dirt encrusted window was not made to open and was too narrow and heavily leaded to afford a way of escape. She wasted no time on the door, at first glance she could see that it was too strong to be broken.

For a brief moment she even wondered whether to try to make a hole in the thatch which came down nearly to the floor but she had nothing with which to attack it – besides she would still be faced with an unknown drop to the ground.

By this time she was almost light-headed with fear – she must escape before Lucian returned but there seemed no hope of deliverance. She sank down on the bed and stared hopelessly at the lantern that she had placed on the chest and saw to her horror that the candle had only an inch or two left. The thought of spending the rest of the night in the dark drove her to her feet again and she went once more to examine the door. She tried pushing to see if she could jerk the tongue from the lock but only succeeded in bruising her hands and she leant against the wall almost resigned to her fate. The wall! She had never thought of looking at it closely – now she saw it was just lath and plaster and crumbling at that if only she had a tool to make a breech!

Desperation sharpened her wits and she took one of the small drawers from the chest and began to batter the wall near the door with its sharp corner. She soon realised that to make a hole big enough for her to pass through was beyond her powers, already she was beginning to feel exhausted. Hope died, but then her scurrying mind suggested another possibility. If she could make a hole near the lock sufficient to get her arm through she could perhaps reach the key – if the key had been left in the lock her tired thoughts reminded her!

She refused to be discouraged and casting aside the drawer she had almost destroyed took another from the chest and went to work with such vigour that a hole large enough to take her arm was made. The lantern was burning low but Jane forced herself to wait and still her nerves so that her hand would be steady, then she pressed close to the wall and felt along the outside of the door – the key was there! Her joy was premature however, she found that there was not sufficient purchase for her to turn the key in the stiff lock.

So near to victory – she could not acknowledge defeat. The door could be unlocked from the inside if only she could take out the key and bring it back through the hole.

She had to push her arm right through to the shoulder to get the right angle to withdraw the key and was terrified that her numb fingers would drop it. With infinite care she managed to draw it out and bring it safely inside.

As if in a scene from a Gothic horror tale, at that moment, the candle expired! For a moment of complete despair Jane stood in the dark, then a gleam of moonlight shone through the grimy window and she was able just to make out the keyhole. She needed two hands to turn the key and then she was free!

New energy swept through her and she wasted no time but caught up the cloak which she had discarded and felt her way cautiously down the narrow stairs; to her great relief the door there was unlocked.

The moon was still playing hide and seek but was low in the sky and Jane thought that it would not be long till daybreak.

She made her way as quickly as the uncertain light would allow until she reached the place where the carriage had halted and then was able to make better progress along the rutted track to the pike road.

There she paused, above all else her exhausted body longed to sink down on the grass verge but her mind warned her that she needed to get home to refute Lucian's slanderous accusations ….. Which way to go? To her left the sky was already paling to the dawn and she thought back to the beginning of her disastrous journey. At first they had driven in the usual direction from the concert hall towards Hove, westwards, and she was sure that they had made no deviation from the road until they had turned off to the cottage. That meant that if she walked East towards the rising sun she would be making for Hove … She turned left and began walking along the grass verge which was easier for her feet in her flimsy slippers. She had pulled up the hood of her cloak and hope it would conceal her dishevelled state.

When she heard rapid hoof-beats at first she was alarmed. Could it be Lucian? Then she realised that the horse was coming up behind her and Lucian would be coming towards her. She drew her cloak more closely round her and tried to walk as normally as possible.

The rider drew alongside and passed her and then pulled up and turned. "You seem to be in some difficulty, ma'am, may I be of assistance?"

Great Heavens, it was Dominic! Of all the unlucky chances!

In the growing light he bent to look more closely. "Good God, it is Miss Darcy! How do you come to be in such a plight?"

Jane could not speak, she swayed and he was out of the saddle in an instant and supporting her.

"You are ill – this is not time to talk – that is for later." He thought rapidly. His horse Dancer would never allow him to put Jane in the saddle while he walked beside her, in any case she was not dressed to ride. With his cursed shoulder he could not mount and lift her before him, and then, as she stared ahead while he thought, he saw a stile a few yards away.

"Miss Darcy, could you reach that stile? From there you could mount before me and I could take you to your lodging."

A low, "Yes," answered him and they were soon riding steadily towards Hove.

By this time Jane was barely conscious. With the arrival of someone who had taken command she had lapsed into a state of automatic obedience and only roused when Dominic's quiet voice said, "You are home, Miss Darcy, and are obviously anxiously awaited."

It was true. Lights shone from Becky's house and she and her sister and Mary came running down the steps.

"Oh, Miss Jane, Miss Jane, whatever has happened?" cried Becky.

"There has been an accident," replied Dominic, "But Miss Darcy is too spent for questions – she should be in her bed." As he spoke he lowered her carefully into the waiting arms of the women, then, waiting for no more than a brief, "I will call tomorrow to see how she does," clattered off down the street.

All the way home he puzzled about the mystery of Miss Darcy. The scene in the street – this extraordinary encounter on the Portslade Road. He was determined the puzzle should be resolved the next day unless the lady was too unwell to be visited.

He was so weary by the time he dismounted at the Manor and made his side door entrance that he went straight to bed and put all thoughts of the Darcy conundrum out of his head until the morrow.

In Hove, Becky had wasted no time in seeing that Jane had a hot bath and was put to bed with nothing said except a fierce aside to her sister, "I knew she'd not go off to spend the night at the Manor without sending word – bring some of your salve for her hands – they're that cut and bruised."

Jane herself was beyond speech and thought and fell into so deep a sleep that no nightmare had power to trouble her.

CHAPTER 13

Jane slept late into the morning and woke sore and stiff but insisted on getting up. The day being fine, she sat in the little garden to think seriously about what explanation she could offer to Dominic. She had put Becky off by saying that she would tell her all very soon but did not want to talk about it now and with that Becky had to be content.

Her problem was still not resolved by mid-afternoon when the dreaded interview with Dominic was upon her. The Delamere carriage drew up and Dominic sent in his card with a request that he might call upon Miss Darcy were she well enough to receive him.

He was admitted and found Jane pale, but composed.

"I trust you are not too shaken by your experiences Miss Darcy," said Dominic, "Should you have left your bed?"

"I am tired but quite well," replied Jane. "Lord Delamere, I must thank you for your help last night – this morning rather," she corrected herself. "My predicament – you must have wondered …" she faltered and came to a halt.

"I did wonder and if you are sure you are well enough I think you must bring yourself to explain."

She looked so forlorn that he felt himself to be a brute but he owed it to his grandmother and Althea to clear up the mystery. As well he found himself wishing to help this plain little creature who looked once more like the mouse he had first thought her.

He spoke gently, "Would you feel better in the carriage? The air would do you good."

"Oh yes," replied gratefully. She feared that at any moment Becky, with the best of intentions, might interrupt them.

"I will await you then, Miss Darcy – pray do not hurry yourself," and he bowed and returned to the carriage.

She did not keep him waiting long putting aside Becky's protests and stepping into the carriage with the air of an aristocrat on the way to the guillotine.

Dominic tucked a rug carefully round her and then sat back as the carriage moved off and said in encouraging tones, "Now, Miss Darcy!"

As she remained silent but looked expressively at John who was driving at a steady pace, Dominic went on, "Do not mind John – he is unlikely to hear us, and in any case is discretion itself, that is why I brought him – he has my entire confidence."

"But not necessarily mine!" she replied with the first show of spirit she had displayed.

"I will engage his silence, never fear. Now, Miss Darcy," he repeated, "I ask for an explanation not from vulgar curiosity – but you must realise that I have a duty to my grandmother and sister, they must not be touched by scandal connected with one who has enjoyed their hospitality."

Jane plumbed the depths of despair. She recognised his duty to his family and was aware of the base construction that could be placed upon the various situations in which he had come upon her. All day she had tried to decide on how little she need divulge but now she realised that a partial revelation would only lead to further deception and she could bear no more.

"Very well, Lord Delamere. It is a long story but I must beg you not to interrupt or I shall be unable to continue," and having taken the plunge she began with an account of the events which had led to her flight from Cleave and her subsequent decision to make a new life for herself, there she paused.

By this time they were well up into the Downs and her hearer looked in amazement at the indomitable little figure whose story, told in such a matter of fact manner, betrayed so much of loneliness and steadfast courage in confronting her difficulties.

"And that fellow who accosted you – was that Lucian?"

"Yes," she acknowledged, "But worse than that, he is passing himself off as Leslie Crawford and has made the acquaintance of Lady Althea."

"And you said nothing about it?" he demanded indignantly.

"I did not know until the night of the party at the Manor."

"But you still did not denounce him! That was ill done of you, Miss Darcy, or is that not your name?"

"It is – they are two of my names. I am Jane Elizabeth Darcy Gascoigne." She took a steadying breath and went on. "I did not confront him at the Manor, I shrank from creating a scene, but I saw him next day and gave him a week to withdraw." She turned piteously to Dominic. "My motives were mixed. Lady Althea had begun to form an attachment for him and I thought of how mortified she would be by a public denouement. As well he had threatened to reveal my deception and I shrank from the contempt that Lady Delamere and Lady Althea would feel for me." She buried her face in her hands, then she looked up, "But indeed I was prepared to tell all if he had not withdrawn."

"So you say," he cried harshly. He was finding it difficult not to sympathise with her, caught as she was in such a coil.

"I promise you I meant it, but last night …"

"Yes, last night – what happened?"

"He abducted me and locked me in a derelict cottage not far from where you found me. He was to spread it abroad that we had spent the night together so that I would be compromised and forced to marry him." The strain of the recital was beginning to tell and she broke down in tears.

Dominic was horrified and realised what a brute he had been to force this girl, little older than his sister, to undertake such a horrifying recital. He took the trembling figure into his arms and spoke soothingly as he would have to his sister.

"Come, now you have told me you need have no further fear – I will deal with Master Lucian," and with his handkerchief he gently dried her cheeks. As he did so a dreadful thought struck him.

"Miss Darcy, he did not … harm you?"

"No, that is what I feared – that is what made me determined to escape."

Although she found his arms so comforting she drew away into her own corner of the carriage.

"But how did you escape?"

She described how Lucian had left her alone 'to think things over' and her attempts to break out and how she had succeeded.

His reaction was divided between horror at the outrage she had suffered and admiration of the courage of this slight creature caught in such a perilous situation.

"That settles it!" he said with determination, "You must stay at the Manor where you can be protected!"

At her start of alarm, he went on reassuringly, "Do not fear, I shall not betray your confidence and I will make sure that Master Lucian removes himself from Sussex. Althea shall keep her dreams and if she suffers a little heartache, well, she is young enough to fall in love many times before she meets her match."

Jane could scarcely believe her ears after his harsh words. She felt almost faint with relief and closed her eyes in thankfulness only to open them as he said, "We will drive back to Hove and inform your nurse that you are to spend some weeks at the Manor – we will send for whatever you need tomorrow." He called, "John, back to Hove," and having settled matters to his satisfaction, Dominic sat back in his corner only rousing when they reached Hove to inform Becky of the arrangements.

Jane was too spent to protest at such high-handedness. In truth she was glad to have matters taken out of her hands. She was worn out, not only with the physical exertions of the previous hours. She remembered little of the rest of that day. Althea and Lady Delamere received her at the Manor with great kindness accepting Dominic's explanation of an accident to her carriage which, providentially, he had witnessed. He said Miss Darcy was shaken but unhurt but she needed time for rest and recuperation which he thought would be better spent in the quiet of Ditching than in the bustle of her nurse's guest house.

"That was well done, Dominic," approved Lady Delamere. "Miss Darcy looks fit for nothing but bed. Althea, ask Nurse to attend our guest," and in no time at all Jane was in bed and drinking a posset of Nurse's brewing. She sank into sleep feeling safe and cared for.

Dominic told his grandmother in confidence that he was sure that Miss Darcy's accident had been contrived and he wished her to stay securely at the Manor until he had investigated the matter. Lady Delamere was shocked but readily agreed that Jane, to whom she had taken a great fancy, should be kept under her wing.

Dominic then had a word with Lister and instructed him to tell Mr Crawford that Lady Delamere and Lady Athea were not at home should he call.

"There is no need to inform my grandmother or my sister of the matter," Dominic ended.

Lister replied with an expressionless face, "Very good, my lord." He had not taken to Mr Crawford!

CHAPTER 14

Lucian's feeling when he returned with Judson to the deserted cottage early in the morning after the abduction could not be expressed adequately even in the vilest language at his command. He and Judson searched the area and when no trace of Jane was found fear began to oust Lucian's rage as he realised in what danger he stood.

He was at the end of his resources in money and credit and could only see the bars of the debtors' prison ready to close on him. In his extremity he was driven to think of his last refuge – the family he had treated so shamefully.

He returned to his hotel, paid his shot, then he and Judson made tracks in his curricle, still unpaid for, for the Cotswolds. They arrived in the small hours of the morning, having paused only to change horses and snatch some refreshment.

Once home, Lucian threw himself on his father's mercy. He told him of his debts but not of his attempts on Jane and Sir Roderick listened with growing anger and dismay, thankful for the first time that his wife had died some years earlier and could be spared this sorry tale.

He dismissed Lucian to take a few hours' rest with orders to attend his father in his study promptly at nine o'clock. He himself spent the time in heartbroken contemplation of the mistakes of the past and of what steps he should now take for the future.

When Lucian appeared his father said, "I have given much thought to your future, Lucian – we had better not speak about your past! I suspect that you have not made a full confession of your mis-doings – you are still fearful of some consequences that I am unaware of. No!" as Lucian made to speak, "Do not utter more lies! Listen to what I have to say – you may sit down."

As Lucian obeyed he went on, "One of our ships is at Bristol, ready to sail. You will board her with that man of yours, leaving a complete list of your debts before you go. I will settle them for the last time. I am sending you to our plantation in Barbados – it is in a bad way and you can either work hard to restore it or go down with it – I care not! Take this money, it is the last you will have of me. When I die you will inherit what is entailed but nothing else – the rest will go to your cousin Gerard, I have already made my will to that effect."

Lucian sprang up in protest, "Sir ….."

His father held up his hand. "Not a word – and this is <u>my</u> last word to you, do not come back to England. If you do I shall hand you over to the authorities to answer for the crimes you have not confessed to me – oh, yes, I know of some of them. I have been a weak fool not to have handed you over before – but you are my son …" his voice broke. "Go, get out of my sight! See that you and your henchman are in Bristol by this evening!" and he turned his back.

Lucian glared at him in fury and, snatching up the roll of bills, stormed out of the room.

As the door slammed his father let the tears he had held back trickle through the fingers with which he had covered his face.

CHAPTER 15

For the first two days of her stay at the Manor Jane was content to live in a timeless limbo, cosseted by Nurse, in which she was called upon to make no physical, mental or emotional effort.

On the next day, however, she joined Lady Delamere and Althea at the breakfast table declaring herself fully recovered and saying how grateful she was for their kindness.

"We are very glad to see you looking so much better, my dear," replied Lady Delamere. "Now you must rest and forget your dreadful experience."

Jane looked at her – she could not believe that Dominic had betrayed her confidence. She was reassured by her hostess' placid demeanour and realised that she referred only to the supposed carriage accident.

Life became a tranquil round of riding and walking with Althea and reading and making music. One day Jane ventured into Brighton with Althea in the carriage and called at Isabelle's to make sure that all was well. Mrs Gibbs and the twins were well in control and the business was flourishing.

Dominic returned after a few days absence and took the first opportunity to tell Jane that Lucian and his henchman had decamped and his lordship thought that Jane's escape had caused her abductor to make himself scarce for fear of reprisals.

"We shall hear no more of him I am sure," said Dominic, "So your fears may be laid quite to rest."

"Thank you for all you have done," said Jane. "In that case I could go back to Hove and trouble Lady Delamere no longer …" Her feelings for Dominic were threatening to overwhelm her and she knew that her only hope for any kind of peace was to remain out of reach of his magnetism.

With Dominic it was otherwise. This girl, whom he had regarded at first with indifference and then with suspicion, now roused in him a desire to protect and shelter her – it puzzled him. Except when she was animated she had little attraction and he had yet to see her in a happy mood. Until now the women in his life had been personable – some even beautiful, full of gaiety and ready to offer pleasurable entertainment in the intervals of battle.

Impatiently Dominic put behind him thoughts of the little mouse and set out once again on his travels, leaving Jane under his orders to stay at the Manor at least until his return.

In his absence she was glad to do so. Only one thing troubled her. She hated the deception she was practising on Lady Delamere and Althea but could see no way to end it and tried to put the worry out of her mind.

She was helped by the arrival of seven year old Adrian who was to stay in Nurse's charge until his baby brother or sister had put in an appearance.

He confided to Jane, "My Mamma has gone to fetch a baby brother for me – at least she says I might have to make do with a baby sister." He looked doubtful and then brightened up, "But it will be something to play with!"

"Perhaps not at first," cautioned Jane. "Babies are too little to play with at first, you know. You will have to wait for a few years for it to grow big enough."

Adrian looked downcast, "Oh, yes – you are right – I remember my cousin's babies – they couldn't even talk and they couldn't walk or run either!" He looked so disconsolate that Jane, hoping to distract him, asked "What is your favourite sport?"

"Cricket! I can bowl – I can bat but I bowl better."

"Come along then," said Jane, "We will ask Lady Althea if there are such things as bats and balls."

Althea said that she was sure that in the games cupboard in the nursery there was a bat, smaller than full-size, that had been made for Dominic and some balls as well. These were discovered and borne in triumph to the small lawn enclosed by a yew hedge.

Althea excused herself, she hated to get hot and dishevelled, and Jane and Adrian were left to try their skill.

Adrian said doubtfully, "After all, you're only a girl."

"Yes, but I played with my friend (a fleeting thought of Lucian, whose slave she had been). He said I would make a good bat – you try me!"

She took up her stance and soon the battle was joined. They had found only two wickets and Adrian laid them low with his first two balls but then Jane got her eye in and hit him all over the lawn.

Dominic, home and crossing the garden in search of one of the men, was attracted by Adrian's shrieks and rounded the end of the hedge to receive a flush hit on his shoulder from a ball despatched by a triumphant Jane, a great rope of hair falling down her back and her whole face alight with laughter.

"Miss Darcy's a great gun, isn't she, Sir?" cried Adrian, "Not a bit like a lady!" and received his ball from Dominic with a twinkle and turn to Adrian. "Let us see if you can bat as well as Miss Darcy. I will give you an over before we go in to nuncheon and Miss Darcy will have time to collect herself. My grandmother has guests I believe."

The delighted boy ran to the wickets and Jane collapsed on to an oak seat deeply mortified at once again being taken at a disadvantage and reading reproof in his comment about Lady Delamere's guests.

She hunted in her reticule for the small lawn handkerchief to wipe her flushed face only to have him say, "This will be more serviceable, I think, Miss Darcy," and he dropped into her lap a large handkerchief as he turned away to bowl to the boy.

It was too much! Jane buried her face in the snowy linen as much to hide her tears of chagrin as to blot up the beads of perspiration. But, by the time six balls had been delivered under-arm to a wildly swinging Adrian, she had pulled herself together and accompanied the sportsmen back to the house with an outward appearance of calm.

In her room that night, before she put the handkerchief with the linen for laundering she buried her face once more in its folds, in joyful anguish cherishing something he had touched, and used it once more to soak up her tears as she cried herself to sleep.

Dominic shed no tears but smiled wryly as he prepared for bed. He could not get rid of the picture of the laughing girl he had surprised that morning. He would have been hard put to it to recall the features of any one of the ladies who had previously enjoyed his brief attentions but Jane's vivid face stayed with him and he determined that somehow he must rouse her to such animation more frequently, on which happy resolve he too slept.

When Jane discovered that Dominic was to go to a distant farm with his agent she fulfilled a promise to Adrian to visit his lordship's retriever, Bess, and her pups. This was an attempt to console the little boy. He had heard that he was to return home the next day to greet his newly arrived little sister.

"A girl," he exclaimed in disgust, "And Mamma told me that she wouldn't be able to send her back or exchange her for a boy! I don't want a sister – especially a baby!" and he wavered between tears and temper.

Jane said cajolingly, "Well, Adrian, I was a girl baby once and now I can play cricket – you will have to teach your sister to play as well as you when she is old enough, but for now come and choose which one of Bess' pups you are to take home with you – they can lap now," and she bore him off, all eagerness, to the spare loose-box in the stables where Bess' accouchement had taken place.

The pups were squealing bundles of mischief, except for one who kept nervously by his mother. Jane sat down in the straw and stroked Bess and praised her offspring and told her that they would not hurt her pups.

Adrian chose first one and then another of the puppies as his favourite until the most venturesome of them climbed on the squirming backs of his fellows and fell rather than jumped over the side of the box which cradled them. He picked himself up and planting his large paws unsteadily in the yielding straw set off to explore.

Bess looked anxious but Jane reassured her and Adrian followed the little fellow exclaiming, "This is the one! See, Miss Darcy, how brave he is!"

Dominic, making an unheralded return on foot to the stable yard heard the shrill voice. His mare had cast a shoe and he had left her at the smithy in the village and walked back to the Manor, leaving his agent to visit the farm.

He went quietly into the tack room next to the loose-box and was an unseen observer at a small window through which the head groom could keep an eye on the work in the stables.

Jane's narrow skirt had ridden up and revealed her ankles and Dominic saw with appreciation that they were beautifully turned and matched the fine delicacy of her wrists and hands that he had seen gliding over the keyboard.

It seemed that each unexpected view of Jane revealed yet another excellence. Her face was now lit with varying expressions, tenderness and reassurance for Bess and sparkling amusement at the antics of the pups.

"Miss Darcy, do you think I may have this one? I like him best."

"Lord Delamere said you might choose so I see no reason why the puppy should not be yours – what shall you call him?"

"Well, if I had had a baby brother we were going to call him Lancelot – I think it's a silly name, don't you? But that's what Mamma said – if it was a girl she was going to be Laura." He thought for a moment. "I know, I'll call him Lance – short for Lancelot, you see!"

"An excellent idea," applauded Jane and Adrian squatted down and snapped his fingers calling, "Lance, here boy – here," and the puppy, intrigued, ambled toward the boy and licked his fingers.

"See, Miss Darcy – he knows his name! Isn't he clever?"

"Above ordinarily intelligent," Jane agreed gravely.

"Can I take him now?" begged Adrian.

"I think I should give him back to his mother for today," replied Jane, "He can go with you tomorrow.

Regretfully the boy put Lance back in the box to the obvious relief of his mother, and Jane rose to her feet in one graceful movement.

"Come now, Adrian, we must tidy ourselves for nuncheon," and the two left the stable, unaware of the silent watcher. Dominic saw how well she moved, lightly and with dignity. How could he have thought her dull and unattractive! To use Shakespeare's phrase she had 'infinite variety' so different from the usual run of debutantes cast in the same boring mould of appearance and manner.

Next day both male members of the household left the Manor – Adrian to his home to meet his new sister, consoled by the company of his beloved Lance, and Dominic on one of his periodic journeys.

Lady Delamere and Althea accepted his explanation of pestering the Horse Guards to sanction his return to active duty. Jane was not so sure. She could not forget the meeting on the Portslade Road in the early hours, Dominic on horseback before he was supposed to be riding. His wound seemed now to be giving him no trouble, so why the delay in joining his regiment?

She thought regretfully that as one practised in deceit it could be that she was overly suspicious of others. To her distress her suspicions seemed to be in a fair way to be confirmed the day after he had left.

She was walking in the rose garden missing the lively companionship of Adrian and troubled by continuing under false colours to Lady Delamere and Althea and by the unremitting ache of her unrequited love for Dominic, when she was approached in a furtive manner by a rough looking man.

Alarmed, she would have hurried away but the man said hoarsely, "Don't you be afeard, ma'am, I'll not 'arm you. I got a message, see?" and he held out a grimy, much-folded paper. "It's for 'is lordship, but I must missed 'im."

"Yes, his lordship is away," said Jane. She looked more closely at the man. He seemed to be a rough kind of sailor so what was he doing so far from the sea?

"Yes, I told you – I missed 'im," replied the man, "But you know 'im – I've seen you with 'im."

"So you may have done, but why not hand the note in at the Manor - it will be given to his lordship when he returns."

"'Cause it's secret – nobody is to know. Come on, ma'am," he edged closer. "If you're 'is friend you could slip it to 'im unbeknownst. 'E's got to 'ave it – it's life or death! E'd ought to 'ave 'ad it before!"

His urgency persuaded Jane and she took the paper. "Whom shall I say brought it?" she asked.

"No names, no pack-drill," the man replied roughly. "What you don't know won't 'urt you – just you give it to 'im!" and he turned and made off so rapidly that Jane was left in the empty rose garden wondering whether she had dreamed it all. The paper in her hand was proof, however, and she looked at it distastefully. It was folded several times and there was no superscription.

She turned it about in her hands and, as the paper fell open, a line or two of writing became visible. At the sight her breath stopped and she sank down nervously on to a garden seat. It was in French! All her fears came back to torment her – Dominic was in contact with the enemy! Her heart said "No," her mind said, "It explains everything. His mysterious journeys – one to her knowledge certainly not from London, more likely from Shoreham back to Brighton on the Portslade Road."

She found herself unfolding the note. "Prenez-garde, ne quittez pas L'Angleterre, n'approchez pas à Lille. R."

Before she had time to take in the implications of the note she heard Althea calling.

"Miss Darcy – Miss Darcy."

"Here I am," answered Jane, surprised to find that her voice could obey her. She rose to meet Althea, pushing the paper securely into the pocket of her morning gown.

"Miss Darcy, Grandmamma has asked me to call at the Library in Brighton for some books she has ordered, she says it is too warm for her to go herself. I wondered if you would care to come too?"

Anything to distract herself from agonising over the bomb-shell in her pocket! Jane replied, "I should like that. I could call at Isabelle's while you are at the Library," and the two girls quickly made ready for the drive.

On the way, Althea, who for some days had alternated between gloom and somewhat feverish high spirits, turned to Jane.

"Miss Darcy, what do you think has happened to Mr Crawford? He departed so suddenly and left no message. Unless some accident had befallen him, it was ill-done of him?" and she looked ready to burst into tears.

Jane hesitated and then said, "We should have heard of an accident, I am sure. Perhaps he was called away so suddenly that he had no time to get in touch with his friends."

"He could have sent a note," protested Althea. "That would only have taken a few minutes and would have been only courteous!"

Jane had now made up her mind. "Please don't be offended, Lady Althea, at what I am about to say, but |I have heard that Mr Crawford was somewhat light-minded and was not constant in his attachments. In short, he pursued his pleasures for a time but soon tired and then moved on."

Althea stared at her indignantly, "How could you know that? He was not like that! He was sincere!"

"I am afraid not. Shortly after he left someone at Isabelle's remarked on Mr Crawford and his known reputation – indeed, she was a most reliable informant and no scandal-monger." Jane assuaged her conscience by mentally identifying herself with the unnamed intelligencer.

Althea's tears could not be held back. "It is a wicked lie!" she sobbed.

"Indeed no. I am sorry to have to tell you this, but the fact that Mr Crawford has not been heard from surely bears out the truth. Lady Althea, he is not worth one of these tears. Pray put him out of your mind and think of the success you will be in your first Season. You will meet many men in Town who will show Mr Crawford to be nothing but a farthing dip to a candle."

After a short while Althea sniffed and blew her nose and said with a watery smile. "I know in my heart that you are right, Miss Darcy. I have been so miserable because I was beginning to suspect the truth of what you say. Ah well," she sighed, "Mr Crawford has taught me a lesson – I shall not be so easily taken in another time!"

They drew up at the Library and dismissed the carriage telling the coach man to return in an hour's time, then they parted, promising to meet at the Library at the time appointed.

Jane received a warm welcome at the shop and asked Mrs Gibbs to join her in the stock room. During her stay at the Manor Jane had given serious thought to her future with

Isabelle's. She now realised that to confine herself to the running of a small shop, however exclusive, was misguided. The setting up of the shop had served its turn as an absorbing activity to tide her over the misery and uncertainty after her departure from Cleave. She was too responsible, however, to abandon the shop and all it represented to the people whose livelihood it was and had decided to make certain suggestions to Mrs Gibbs and then to the twins —Doreen in particular.

She opened the talk with Mrs Gibbs with no preamble. "Mrs Gibbs, how would you feel about becoming the manageress of Isabelle's – being responsible for the work room, as you already are, but as well ordering materials and goods as they are required and taking overall responsibility for the establishment?"

Mrs Gibbs' face was a study, "Miss Darcy," she gasped.

Jane interrupted her. "Pray do not give me an answer now. I realise you need to give the matter some thought. I need hardly say that you will be paid much more than at present. My man of business, Mr. Whitney, will help with financial matters and I shall continue to supply designs. If you approve I shall ask Doreen to be in charge of the shop itself in consultation, of course, with you. You get on well together do you not?"

"Very well," replied Mrs Gibbs. "She knows her business and has a very good manner with the customers … Miss Darcy, I must ask this …. Do you think I would be good enough for such a position? I've had some schooling and of course I managed my own small dressmaking business, but Isabelle is a much larger matter."

"I am quite sure you will be more than adequate to the task, Mrs Gibbs. Please think over my proposal and I will call again in a few days time for your answer. If you agree I will speak to Doreen then. Meanwhile, here are some designs ….. I must go – I promised to be at the Library … good day, Mrs Gibbs," and she left quickly before Mrs Gibbs could complete, "Good morning, Miss Darcy."

Once back at the Manor Jane managed to behave naturally through the rest of the day but once in her room that night she dismissed the maid and sat down to think.

What <u>was</u> the mystery surrounding Dominic? She could not believe that the man who held her heart and who, moreover, had fought for years for his country could be a traitor, but so many odd happenings called for some explanation.

She enquired casually at dinner when Dominic was expected to return and was told that, unless he said to the contrary, he was usually away for a week, that meant he would be back next day.

Jane made up her mind that, although she quailed at the thought, she would confront him with the note on his return and ask for an explanation. She shrank from the idea but knew she could have no peace of mind until the puzzle was solved. In any case, she had made up her mind to leave the Manor as soon as he came back so whatever his wrath she would not have to endure it for long.

She went to bed, having decided on her course of action, but had little sleep and spent a wretched day starting at every sound and sustaining boring conversations with afternoon callers expecting every new arrival to be Dominic.

Dinner came and went and he had not appeared. The thought of another day of suspense was not to be borne. Then she remembered that the time he had surprised her in the music room she had not heard the arrival of a carriage and, now that she knew the Manor more intimately, she realised that he must have come in by the side door which gave on to the back stairs. These emerged on the first floor landing by the sewing room so, when she was sure that everyone had retired, she made her way there and waited. The house was quiet. The occasional call of a hunting owl or the bark of a fox sounded loud in the silent night and the single candle burned ever lower.

Jane was about to give up her vigil when she heard a noise at the side door. It was quite loud and she started up in alarm, then, plucking up her courage, she went fearfully to the head of the stairs.

The dim flame of the small lamp left burning in the passage gave little light and all she could make out was a figure leaning against the wall at the bottom of the steps, she felt sure it was Dominic and went back to fetch her candle.

The man had not moved when she returned and she called softly, "My lord …" then more emphatically, "My lord!" and he raised his head.

"These stairs are devilish steep," he complained in a voice that was almost a groan. "They cannot be climbed," and with that he sank down on the steps.

Jane went down quickly. Her candle showed him to be only half-conscious and she said anxiously, "Sir, you are hurt – come I will help you," and she blew out her candle and tried to get him to his feet. She knew she should call for help but something stopped her from doing so, his return was obviously intended to be secret. All her efforts, however, failed to get him upright and she was in despair until she thought of John. Dominic had said the man had his entire confidence.

Leaving him, Jane went to Dominic's room, which was in a wing away from those of Lady Delamere's and Althea's, hoping that John would be waiting up for his master. He was, and looked astonished at the appearance of a guest fully dressed at such an hour, but Jane spoke with authority.

"Lord Delamere is hurt – he is at the bottom of the back stairs and I cannot manage alone."

He wasted no time in questions but hurried with her to his master. With some difficulty, between them, they got Dominic up the stairs and to his room.

As they laid him on his bed he put up a hand and groaned, "My head … oh my head!"

Jane looked at the side of his head as his blood-stained hand fell away and found a shallow cut and a large lump.

John looked and said, "No real damage, ma'am – scalp wounds always look ugly, but it's not deep, a cold compress'll work wonders."

"I'll see to that," said Jane and wrung out a towel in cold water from the pitcher while John removed his master's boots.

She held the compress against the wound and wrapped another towel round to hold it in place.

John said, "Thank you, ma'am, I can manage now," and obviously expected her to leave.

Jane stood her ground and asked worriedly, "Should we not send for the doctor?"

"No, ma'am. His lordship doesn't like his doings known. Don't fret, Miss Darcy, I've seen him through worse than this. I know he would ask you to say nothing and," he looked at her anxiously, "He doesn't like his grandmother to be worried."

"I understand," said Jane. "I shall say nothing," and with a lingering look at the figure on the bed she went quietly from the room.

Once in bed, after two broken nights, she was too tired to keep awake and her sleep was too deep for dreams.

CHAPTER 16

Jane slept late and when she woke longed to know how Dominic had fared but could make no direct enquiry. She joined Lady Delamere and Althea at nuncheon to find her hostess saying in some irritation, "I knew how it would be! Dominic is as stubborn as his father! He was told not to ride so of course he came off his horse and has a nasty bump on his head which he might expect, riding home so late."

Althea exclaimed. "Oh, it is not serious," her grandmother assured her, "But he is keeping to his room today – partly I think to stay out of my way – I gave him a piece of my mind!" she added with a satisfied smile.

"I thought Lord Delamere's wound was healed," said Jane. "He has been riding about the estate recently."

"The wound is healed – it was in his right shoulder, and his arm is still weak. There is some damage to the nerves and he cannot grip a sword properly so naturally the army will not accept him for active duty, and if he was not so pig-headed he would give up trying to persuade them and settle down to marry and manage his estates – it is high time!" declared his grandmother. "But let us leave the subject of my tedious grandson. I have something to discuss with you, Miss Darcy."

"About my come-out?" exclaimed Althea eagerly.

"Yes, my child, we must prepare your wardrobe and be in Town next month." She turned to Jane, "Would you undertake the task, Miss Darcy? Your designs and workmanship are the equal of any London modiste, indeed they far surpass many of them."

In her relief at hearing that Dominic was not badly hurt Jane had not taken in what Lady Delamere had been saying. She flushed and said, "I am afraid I do not properly understand you, Lady Delamere."

"It is clear enough," Lady Delamere replied brusquely, her temper still a little ruffled by her passage with her grandson. "Are you able to supply a complete wardrobe – including a Court dress, in time for Althea's debut?"

Jane was overwhelmed, "Your ladyship …."

Althea broke in, "Do say you will, Miss Darcy. I like your designs so much – better than those we bought in Town last year. Besides they would be exclusive – all specially designed for me," she added smugly.

"I should be honoured, Lady Delamere," replied the astonished Jane. "I will submit some designs to you and Lady Althea in the next few days if you will supply me with a list of what you require. The work should go quickly as we have all Lady Althea's measurements and my women can concentrate on the order to the exclusion of all other work."

"Good," said Lady Delamere, "The Court dress will be the most important, it has to be white, of course."

"I will begin work on that today," said Jane. "Please excuse me," and she rose and hurried to her room to start on the prestigious order.

She finally settled down in the sewing room where the large table allowed her to spread out her materials. Lady Delamere and Althea had gone to make a promised visit to an old friend and Jane, her mind at ease for the moment about Dominic, concentrated on her work. She was so absorbed that she did not hear the door opening.

"So here you are," said Dominic. "I have come to thank you for your help last night," and then in an explosion of wrath, "What the devil do you mean by spying on me – lurking about the back stairs in the small hours!"

Jane's temper, fuelled by the hours of anxiety she had suffered, rose to match his.

She sprang to her feet. "That comes well from you, my lord. I could give you back the word spy with justice!"

"Of course, I am a spy," he declared with an effrontery which took Jane's breath away. "But it is no business of yours!"

"It is the business of every loyal citizen!" she snapped back. "Perhaps you can explain this!" and she took from her reticule the tattered piece of paper.

He snatched it from her. "How came you by this? I should have had it before I left. Who are you working for?" The questions came like bullets. "You can tell a good tale, Miss Darcy, but we'll have the truth now," and he took her angrily by the shoulders, looking as if he would rather have taken her by the neck.

She glared back at him, "It is your tale we should hear now, Sir – you have much to answer for!"

For several seconds they confronted each other then Dominic came to himself. He released her and she sank down nervously into her chair her surge of anger leaving her as swiftly as it had arisen.

Dominic too sat down and stared at the valiant David who had outfaced his Goliath.

They both spoke at once.

"Miss Darcy …"

"My lord …" and then both stopped in confusion.

Then he began again in a calmer tone. "Should we not talk quietly together? There seems to be a good deal of misunderstanding. Perhaps you will tell me first how you came by this note."

"It was given to me in the garden the day after you left by a rough looking man – a seaman I believe …"

"Jem," put in his lordship.

"Yes, well he said it should be given to you secretly but would answer no question."

"When I discovered it was in French …" she stopped.

"You? Go on," he urged.

"I thought you were in league with the enemy," she got out in a rush.

At his astonished look she went on hurriedly, "But only for a moment! But you can see, my lord, that I felt I must have an answer to the questions such a letter posed."

"I see," he answered thoughtfully. "How did you guess when to expect me and that it would be by the side door?"

"I thought of the side door when I remembered your visit to the music room and that there was no bustle attending your arrival. I was prepared to keep watch each night until you returned so as to confront you with the note."

He smiled, "Valiant Miss Darcy! Instead, you had to play the Good Samaritan for which I owe you most sincere thanks and for your discretion in not rousing the house."

"As to that, I realised that your return by such means and at such an hour must be for the sake of secrecy and that John must be in your confidence."

"And now I will repose my trust also in you if you will promise to continue to keep silent."

The deep voice was speaking to Jane's heart as well as to her mind. This man – this beloved man – could claim her allegiance no matter what devious work he was involved in. She nodded her agreement.

He smiled at her and completed her overthrow. "Sounds pompous, doesn't it? Well, when I found that I would not be seconded for active duty again I was about to send in my papers. Peace time soldiering held no appeal for me, but a friend at the Horse Guards asked me, after my last Medical Board, if I was prepared to help the war in another capacity – in short, to spy. At first, I was outraged but he pointed out that accurate intelligence was worth a division to Wellington and my command of French would be invaluable. He also pointed out that the work was not without it's risks and that decided me."

"But to spy!" protested Jane.

"My feelings exactly at first. Then I realised that spies, on whichever side, were the most valuable assets a country could possess and I was completely won over."

It was clear, too, that he was avoiding stressing the danger, but Jane was becoming aware that the work called for courage of a high order. To be alone in enemy territory without even the slender protection of a uniform and to pit not only one's body, as in battle, but one's wits against the foe required daring and resourceful men. She gazed at Dominic with increased admiration and respect.

"You have won me over too, Sir. I salute your courage!"

"Yes, well," he was embarrassed. "To cut a long story short, our agents are travelling all over the Continent sounding out the amount of support Napoleon might count upon if and when he succeeds in extricating himself from his ill-advised adventure into Russia. Deserters have told us of the terrible conditions during his retreat from Moscow. Now that we have a fair idea of how things stand and where we may expect the strongest resistance, Wellington can plan his strategy."

"Thanks to you and others like you," said Jane. "But why were you advised not to go to Rouen?"

"As I discovered, they had found me out, I have been there too often and they were waiting. I got away from them in Rouen but they caught up with me at Dieppe. Luckily Jem was waiting with his men at the safe house there and managed to get me to his boat. They had been hovering for days."

"He is a smuggler, I collect?"

Dominic laughed. "They call themselves Gentlemen in Sussex, Miss Darcy. Anyway they have been good friends to me and it is thanks to them I got back to Shoreham with only a sore head."

"I gather John knows of your work?" asked Jane.

"Yes, and Roberts, our head groom – he looked after Starlight when she brought me home. Luckily for me that mare can find her way to Ditchling under any circumstances. You are now the only other confidante of mine except for Lister."

As if on cue there was a tap at the door and Lister said, "There is a nuncheon laid in the breakfast room, your Lordship, Miss Darcy." His attitude to the latter had begun to change even before the stirring events of the previous night. All the servants had become aware that Jane was no mere modiste and was to be regarded as a friend of the family.

"Thank you, Lister. I believe my appetite is back." Lister permitted himself a slight smile and left the room.

Dominic turned to Jane. "May I escort you, Miss Darcy? But before we go I must tell you that you have a large smut on your nose!" he smiled mischievously as she began furiously to scrub at the smudge of charcoal with her handkerchief.

"No – there – allow me," and he took the handkerchief and said, "Spit!"

The childish command made her giggle but she did as she was told and he rubbed her nose gently and then discovered that her eyes were brimming with tears.

"Miss Darcy! I have not hurt you?" he exclaimed in distress.

"No," she said, taking back the handkerchief and blowing her nose. "Do not mind my tears they – they … you might have been killed – you were in such danger!"

"And you cared? My little dear," and he took her into his arms. "Come, you have been so brave standing up to me like an Amazon and you're only as high as my heart," and he bent his head and kissed her.

Heaven opened: passion so exquisite and pulsating consumed Jane. Her whole being responded – time and space were transcended. When Dominic's lips and exploring tongue left her mouth she felt like a parched creature denied life-giving water. Had his arms not still supported her she would have dropped where she stood.

Dominic, the experienced, was shaken. The impulse which had driven him so unexpectedly to give way to desire was prompted by no siren-song from a ravishing beauty. He only knew that at last he was in earnest. Here was no passing fancy but a woman of spirit to match his own and a passion that equalled his.

He became aware that she was trembling and put her gently into a chair. "Miss Darcy," he began formally enough, then "Jane – no dammit it does not suit you! I shall call you Elizabeth!"

Jane covered her hot face and whispered, "My lord …."

He ignored the interruption and swept on, "I shall not apologise! You feel as I do – you cannot deny it! Say that you know that we are meant for each other!"

This was going too far and too fast. Jane summoned all her resources, "You must think me shameless to …"

"To respond so honestly? No, no – your body spoke for you – I could not mistake!"

She rose, "My lord, you insult me! I am not one of your flirts to pass away a boring hour!" she said indignantly trying hard to regain her composure even though it meant denying what her heart was telling her.

"Indeed you are not! You are the woman I never hoped to find – the woman I want for my wife. Say you will marry me, dear, dear Elizabeth!" and he went to take her in his arms.

110

She avoided him, unable to take seriously his impetuous words. "You must be mad! The blow on the head … how can you wish to marry me? You hardly know me!"

"You are wrong! A kiss such as we have just exchanged opens all the secrets of your heart. Besides, you told me all about yourself the day after we me on the Portslade Road – don't you remember?" he said teasingly.

"Come now," and he gathered her in his arms, "Come now, give me your answer. It must be yes!"

To Jane it seemed as if the gates of Paradise were opening but she made one last effort before she agreed to pass through them.

"But your grandmother – she will never permit."

"What has she to say to anything? I am my own master! I own I would prefer her blessing but with or without it you must be mine!"

She gave a sigh of surrender and nestled closely in his embrace. "The commands of a masterful man must be obeyed," she said demurely and raised her face and returned the loving kiss he gave to seal their bargain.

"And now we must have nuncheon – I am devilish hungry and you should have a glass of wine …,"and he opened the door.

Jane's hands flew to her hair. "I must look a fright – I will go and tidy myself."

"You look charming and I am not letting you out of my sight!" He armed her through the door and down to the breakfast room.

Once he had poured wine for her and filled a plate for himself Jane was able to claim his attention.

"My Lord," she began.

"Dominic," he said with his mouth full.

"D .. Dom .. Dominic," she got out. "We must tell Lady Delamere and Althea my story. I cannot enter into an engagement based on deception."

"It isn't," he riposted. "I am not deceived!"

She gave an exasperated laugh. "You are impossible," she declared. We must tell your grandmother …… when?"

"We are dining en famille tonight, that will be a good time when they bring in the tea tray. Will that satisfy you my nagging wife to be?"

"Admirably.   And now I <u>must</u> tidy myself and finish my sketches." She rose and went to him, "Please, Dominic, no more teasing. I need to be alone for a little – don't hinder me."

He kissed her hand, "Your wish is my command, dear Elizabeth. I will finish my meal – you appear to live on air, I can see we shall keep an economic household!"

He sat down again and she went smiling to dwell on the complete reversal in her fortunes which had just taken place. Jane's sketches were pushed aside as she struggled to bring into the realm of everyday life the fairy tale through which she had just lived. Had anyone told her that in one flash of splendour all the reticences of an unwanted spinster's life would have been annihilated and that she would be capable of a display of passion that would previously have disgusted her to hear of and furthermore, that the experience had been so wonderful that she longed for it to be repeated, she would have laughed in disbelief. Dominic was right. At last she accepted it: she was no longer Jane, the plain, the undesired, but, Elizabeth, beloved of her beloved.

She collected her drawing materials and having completed her return to normalcy by washing her face in cold water and redressing her hair, settled down to consider the future of Isabelle's. She had not got far in planning before it was time to change for dinner ready for the moment of truth with Lady Delamere.

Dominic's high spirits throughout the meal were in sharp contrast to Jane's subdued manner and drew from Lady Delamere the dry comment, "You must fall from your horse more often, Dominic, since it puts you in such a cheerful mood!"

"Perhaps I should," replied her grandson, "I must say that the results are most pleasurable," and he shot a wicked glance at Jane.

Fortunately the meal came to an end on this note and Dominic added, "I believe I will join you for tea. I shall not take wine tonight, Lister," and he followed the ladies into the drawing room.

Lister lost no time in bringing in the tea-tray and only wished that he could have lingered instead of leaving the family to serve themselves.

When he had gone and Lady Delamere had poured and Dominic had handed tea, he put his aside and said abruptly, "Grandmamma, Elizabeth and I have something to tell you."

"Elizabeth?" exclaimed Althea, "Who is she?"

"You know her as Miss Darcy .... Jane," replied her brother with a twinkle.

"Grandmamma, make him talk sense," begged the bewildered Althea.

Jane, who had sat quietly while Dominic had his small joke, now said, "Perhaps I should explain. Please Lady Delamere and Lady Althea, understand that I did not want to deceive you. I have been longing to confess ever since I met you."

Dominic went to sit by her and took her hand in his but Lady Delamere's glance forbade Althea to comment.

As simply as she could, Jane told her story and her audience listened enthralled; some details were new even to Dominic and his love and admiration for his indomitable darling grew with every word.

Jane ended her story with her arrival at the Manor after her rescue by Dominic after her abduction and he interrupted Althea's exclamations of horror and amazement by say, "There is a postscript. Elizabeth and I are in love and she has consented to marry me!"

Both he and Jane had avoided any mention of his work in espionage – it was not their secret.

Lady Delamere was not unprepared for such a declaration. She had observed Dominic's protective attitude and his loving looks while Jane told her story and now she said, "Well, Dominic, I did not know you had so much good sense!"

Jane went over to her. "You do not mind – you do not object? You do think it is unsuitable and too sudden?"

Lady Delamere took her in her arms. "My dear, I have grown to value you this long time, your breeding speaks for itself. I was hoping that you would consent to stay with us but never dreamt that Dominic would make it possible. I am more than glad to welcome you, my dear." She kissed and released her. "You look worn to a thread and no wonder. Off to bed with you, we can talk further in the morning."

Jane, with tears of fatigue and relief in her eyes, said, "Thank you, - oh, thank you," and turned away to be seized by Althea.

"I think it is wonderful! You are to be my sister, what a lot we shall have to say to each other, dear Jane," and she kissed her.

"My turn!" said Dominic, taking Jane from her, "And her name is Elizabeth – Jane is buried forever!" and he kissed her soundly and opened the door for her to hurry to gain the sanctuary of her bedroom where the maid found her to be in a daze as she helped her to prepare for bed. Jane was asleep almost before the door of her room was closed.

CHAPTER 17

The next day was a busy one. Dominic left for London to report at the Horse Guards and to make sure that arrangements were well in hand for opening the Delamere Town House.

Several minor matters were settled out of hand by Lady Delamere. She decreed that Jane was to spend the Season with them as Miss Gascoigne of Cleeve, Donimic's betrothed. After a little argument, she agreed that Althea's wardrobe should be carried out as planned. She and her granddaughter chose a design of heavy white crepe with an overdress and train embroidered in crystal and silver for her Court dress. "I shall lend Althea my diamonds," said her grandmother. "I think the setting is delicate enough for a young girl." Althea was in enthusiastic agreement.

Jane explained that she felt she should not close Isabelle's on which so many of her loyal workpeople depended and her suggested arrangements for the future of the establishment were approved. Lady Delamere saw no reason why Jane should not continue to supply designs anonymously as and when she chose: her connection with the shop need not be disclosed.

Jane asked that Mr Whitney should wait on her at the Manor to discuss the many business details about the future of the shop and the estate at Cleeve.

Then she said, "Lady Delamere …"

She was interrupted, "A moment," said her ladyship, "We cannot have you using this formal address. You will not, I suspect, like to call me Grandmamma. As you may know, my name is Helena – why not Aunt Helena – a courtesy title?"

"You are very kind – I should like that … Aunt Helena!" and the two ladies exchanged a smile.

"Then that is agreed," nodded Lady Delamere with satisfaction. "Now what else is to be settled?" she asked, a rhetorical question which she answered immediately. "Dominic will attend to the notices in the journals and we can decide on a date for the wedding when he returns."

Jane blushed, this was going too fast for her. "Lady … Aunt Helena, may I order the carriage to visit Hove today? I have neglected my dear Becky and she should have my news in person so kind she has been to me. As well I could call at Isabelle's to make final arrangements with Mrs Gibbs and set the work of making Althea's wardrobe in hand."

"An excellent idea. That reminds me," said Lady Delamere. "You should arrange for your own wardrobe for the Season. I can see that Isabelle's is going to be busy!"

The meeting broke up and Jane set out for Hove.

Becky and her sister were delighted to see her and when she told them of her engagement they could scarcely find words to express their joy. For Becky to be at a loss was almost unheard of but she laughed and cried together and exclaimed over and over, "To think my nursling is to be married – and to a lord!"

The first excitement over, Jane cautioned them to keep the news to themselves until it was formally announced and took her leave, promising to make a longer visit and "Tell them all about it."

She sent the carriage away for an hour when she arrived at Isabelle's and was fortunate to find the only two customers leaving as she entered. She asked Doreen to put up the 'Closed' sign and sent Maisie to summon Mrs Gibbs.

When all four were seated, Jane asked Mrs Gibbs whether she was prepared to accept the management of the business.

Mrs Gibbs gave her a straight look. "I've thought it over carefully, Miss Darcy, and yes, if your man of business will help with the money side I should like to take it on."

The twins look round-eyed and Jane explained that she had not broached the matter to them until she had had Mrs Gibbs' answer. Then she asked Doreen if she would be prepared to manage the shop with Maisie's help and in close partnership with Mrs Gibbs.

Doreen did not hesitate, "Indeed I would, Miss Darcy, it will be like having a business of our own." Maisie nodded enthusiastically.

"Then that is settled," said Jane, heaving a sigh of relief, "I am glad. I shall still do some designing but all the rest of the ordering and so on will be in your hands, and that reminds me, I have brought an order and some designs for Lady Althea's wardrobe for her come-out. I assured Lady Delamere that we could undertake it, but it has to be completed in a month and I shall need some new gowns as well for I am to stay with her ladyship for the season."

Mrs Gibbs looked thoughtful. "In that case, Miss Darcy, would there by any objection to bringing in some temporary help?"

"That is entirely for you to decide, Mrs Gibbs. If you need more help you must get it. I should add that of course you will all be paid more for your extra responsibilities. I shall ask Mr Whitney to come to see you and arrange matters with you. And now I really must go, I have to call at the Receiving Office with an urgent letter." She rose and said with a smile, "I think Isabelle's can reopen for business now, under new management, don't you?"

The three women returned her smile and seemed almost shy in their farewells, still somewhat overcome by the thought of their changed status.

Jane hurried to the Receiving Office with her letter to Mr Whitney asking him to come to the Manor on the following Monday and to stay the night as she had much to discuss with him. Unless she heard to the contrary she would expect him. She arrived back at Isabelle's to find the carriage just pulling up and sat back, glad to have a brief respite after her busy day.

There followed two days in which Jane had leisure to come to terms with the amazing transformation in her life: she became more at ease with Aunt Helena and Althea and learned a great deal about Dominic from both of them. When he returned she looked at him with new eyes and loved him the more.

After dinner that night when he joined them for tea Lady Delamere said, "Well, Dominic, You have made sure that Delamere House is fit to live in, I hope?"

"Yes, Grandmamma, you can move in whenever you choose," he replied.

"And your other commission?" she ask archly.

"Successfully accomplished," he said with a grin and took from his pocket a small box and went to sit by Jane. Opening the box and taking her hand in his he kissed it and said, "My love, with this ring I give my pledge of devotion," and he placed a magnificent ruby and pearl ring on her finger.

Jane was speechless and Lady Delamere said, "It is the Templeton betrothal ring, my dear. Dominic had it cleaned at Rundle and Bridge and made sure it would fit – I lent him one of your gloves for the purpose.

Jane found her voice. "It is beautiful, Dominic – rubies are my favourite gems."

Dominic smiled at her fondly, "I am glad of that. The setting is antique but I am afraid that tradition dictates that it must be passed on to any Templeton bride unaltered. However, this is yours," and he drew a longer box from his pocket and took from it a ruby and pearl pendant on a chain set at intervals with small pearls and rubies.

There were grasps of admiration from the Dowager and Althea and Jane gazed in wonder at the jewel – the first that had ever been specially chosen for her.

Before she could speak Dominic said, "You may exchange it if you don't care for it. I had it made up to match the ring." He looked at her anxiously.

"I love it, as I love the giver," and Jane held it out. "Please put it on."

As Dominic fastened the chain with somewhat unsteady fingers, Lady Delamere said, "Althea, you look very tired and I am more than ready for bed, come my dear," and she rose with a commanding look at her granddaughter who had been watching entranced as her brother, previously not giving to displays of emotion, looked with such adoration at his beloved. She came to with a start and said tactfully, "Yes, I am tired, my bed will be welcome, too Grandmamma," and the two ladies left the lovers to tell each other all that was in their hearts before, at a scandalously late hour, they too retired.

CHAPTER 18

Mr Whitney was delighted to hear of Jane's engagement when he arrived at the Manor on Monday, and, before he settled down to discuss matters with his client, met the family over a pleasant nuncheon at which he impressed the formidable Dowager as a very good sort of man. He and Dominic got on well and they arranged that they should discuss settlements before Mr Whitney should leave the Manor. Jane had never though of such things, but both men assured her that, in the absence of a senior member of her family, it was proper for Mr Whitney to negotiate with her fiancé.

He had news to impart to them before he and Jane began to discuss her affairs. On a recent visit to Cleeve he had heard that Lucian had left for Jamaica to manage the family property there: Jane and Dominic exchanged glances and Mr Whitney was told of Lucian's attempt to abduct Jane. He was horrified but agreed that, with Lucian out of the country, it was best to let sleeping dogs lie, much as he and Dominic would have like to bring the villain to book.

Jane asked about Lisette and was told that she was still in Bath but preparing to go to London and, as usual, was never ending in her demands for money. Jane said that, if both men approved, she thought that Lisette should be given a Trust Fund, the principal of which could not be touched and which would revert to the estate on her death.

"What if she marries?" asked Mr Whitney, "Does she still enjoy the income?"

"Yes," replied Jane. She smiled at the two men, "She will have no such wise advisors as I have to arrange settlements – let the Fund be her dowry!" and so it was agreed.

Dominic left them and Jane explained about her plans for Isabelle's. Mr Whitney looked at her doubtfully then he appeared to make up his mind. "Jane," he said, "Have you discussed this with his lordship?"

"No," said Jane in surprise, "I assure he knows that I shall still be interested in the shop although, of course, it will be kept secret in the family. Why do you ask?"

"Because, my dear, you do not seem to realise that your money and property will pass to his lordship on your marriage. Remember Lucian hoped to marry you to get his hands on your fortune."

Jane was aghast. "Do you mean that Dominic can countermand any arrangements I may make?"

Jane rose agitatedly, "I had no idea," she exclaimed. "This must be settled at once," and she rang the bell. She told the footman who answered it to request his lordship to join herself and Mr Whitney as soon as possible, and then went on to pace the room restlessly.

Her unfortunate man of business wished he had held his tongue but reminded himself that he would have failed in his duty if he had not advised his client of the true state of affairs.

They did not have long to wait, Dominic came in looking puzzled. "You sent for me, my love?"

Jane turned, holding both hands tightly together in a way Mr Whitney recognised.

He rose and said, "With your permission, your Lordship, I will leave you for a while – I have some papers to prepare," and he left the room before either of them could reply.

Dominic went to Jane and took her hands in his. "What has so disturbed you, my dear? Our Mr Whitney looked quite frightened," he said teasingly.

"Did you know that you would acquire all my property when you married me?" she asked bluntly. "Was that why you ….." she became too upset to continue. The doubt sown by Lisette and Lucian's cruel words had gone deep, re-enforcing as they did her mother's previous denigration, and, although she was unaware of it, had festered in her mind ever since.

"What are you saying?" demanded Dominic. "Of course, I knew that your property would revert to me on our marriage, but surely you know that I stand in no need of it? As for my reasons for wanting you to be my bride …," he stopped speaking and crushed her to him and kissed her passionately. "My, very dear, how could you doubt my love?" and he put his hand beneath her chin and forced her to look at him. "In law I may be granted your fortune, but have you forgotten the marriage service, my darling? 'With my body I thee worship and with all my worldly goods I thee endow', and I assure you I am a man of my word and keep my promises – especially the first!" and he kissed her again.

Her tears overflowed, "It is only that Listette and Lucian were so sure that I had nothing to offer except my money …"

"You have yourself, my foolish darling, and that is a treasure beyond price. As for this nonsense about your property you will do with it as you wish and I will sign any papers necessary for you do so. Does that put your mind at rest?" He looked at her quizzically. "You know, I must take exception to your thinking me such a clutch-fisted fellow!" and he gently dried her tears.

"Oh, Dominic, I am such a fool, but I have loved you so much from the first moment I saw you that I cannot be sensible about you," and she smiled mistily at him.

"Knew my worth at once, did you? Than you showed more sense than I did. I only really saw you that night in the music room and only really loved you at the foot of the back stairs!"

They were both laughing helplessly at this nonsense when Mr Whitney put his head cautiously round the door.

"Well, I will leave you two to dispose of Miss Gascoigne's fortune," said Dominic with mock formality. "Let me know if there will be any left of me to squander!" and with this Parthian shot he left the room.

The details of the plans for Isabelle's were soon dealt with and as to Cleeve, Mr Whitney said that the property was being well managed under existing arrangements and these could easily continue.

After their business was concluded both Mr Whitney and Jane were glad to take a turn in the garden before dinner and the lawyer took the opportunity to say, "Since your father died I have tried in some measure to take his place and have so much admired your courage and good sense in the way you have faced your difficulties. I am very glad that now you will have someone to look after you. I am sure, were your father to be with us still, he would whole-heartedly approve your choice of husband. I have rarely met a man who has so impressed me. I am very happy for you, my dear Jane." He paused and said with a wry smile, "But I suppose such informality must cease when you become Countess Delamere!"

Jane stopped dead. "But ... but ..." she stammered.

"Did you not realise that that would be your title?" asked a puzzled Mr Whitney.

"I suppose I ought to have done but you see we have been so caught up with affairs and have met so recently that ... that ... In any case," said Jane recovering from the second shock she had received, "I shall always be Jane to you, Mr Whitney, even were I to become a Duchess! And now we must hurry. It will not do to keep the <u>Dowager</u> Countess waiting for dinner!" and she hurried off laughing leaving her lawyer to follow more slowly.

Mr Whitney and Dominic had an amicable discussion about settlements and, before he returned to London, the lawyer made careful arrangements for running Isabelle's with Mrs Gibbs and Doreen.

CHAPTER 19

At the end of the month there were so many bandboxes full of the new finery for Althea and Jane that an extra coach had to be used when they removed to Town.

During the first few days Jane felt she would never be able to live in such noise and bustle. All day and for most of the night wheels rumbled and hooves clattered and street cries penetrated even their exclusive square, but surprisingly soon she grew accustomed to the pandemonium.

The arrival in Town of the Earl of Delamere and his party and his engagement to Miss Elizabeth Gascoigne of Cleeve had been reported in the Journals and the Ton was agog to meet the unknown beauty who had captured one of the most eligible bachelors who had so far successfully avoided the snares of the accredited beauties and match-making mammas.

Invitations to balls, soirées and every possible social event came pouring in. Lady Delamere reciprocated and the ball she gave to introduce her granddaughter and Jane to society was such a squeeze that its success was assured.

Everyone was agog to meet the siren who had lured Dominic to the altar. It was unbelievable! One had to admit that Miss Gascoigne was the epitome of elegance – her clothes were the envy of all the ladies, but she had not the least claim to beauty! It was known that Dominic had no need to hang out for a rich wife, so what was the attraction?

After a short time the leaders of fashion decided that Miss Gascoigne was an original. She had an air of distinction and it was noticeable that men who counted for more than mere fops or fribbles or sporting-mad Corinthians were to be found in her company at most gatherings although no one could accuse her of being a blue-stocking.

At balls she more than held her own. Her grace and charm and lovely figure amply compensated for her lack of conventional beauty. In short, Dominic's fiancée was making a marked success of her first Season. Jane, when she had time to draw breath in the whirl of engagements, felt a little like

Cinderella at a perpetual ball and wondered occasionally when the clock would strike twelve.

Althea gave no thought to anything but the exhilarating moment and soon brought her grandmother to a state of exhaustion where she was willing to let Jane perform the part of chaperone at such staid gatherings as the Assemblies at Almack's to which exclusive portal they had been granted vouchers.

Dominic found his hands full as he escorted his ebullient sister and sought after fiancée from one function to another and it was some days before he could arrange for a quiet morning drive in the Park with Jane. In spite of having to bow and smile acknowledgements to their acquaintances they managed to discuss Dominic's more serious concerns.

To Jane's great relief he told her that for the immediate future he was to stay in Town and undertake no more missions to the Continent.

"Dearest, I am so relieved," she said. "Shall you mind not being assigned to any duties?"

"Far from it. My duty is here. We are getting very worried about Boney's agents – they are being too successful by half and stir up trouble from one end of the country to another and I have to unmask them if I can. We are sure their leaders are moving in the first circles and have their informants among the best people.

"Surely not. How could they persuade Englishmen to help that monster? In any case, what is there for them to discover? Napoleon is finished – we hear on all sides that his Grand Armée is being overtaken on the retreat from Moscow by the Russian winter and is being decimated. He cannot recover from such a disaster!"

"His pride and conceit is so great, love, that he does not recognise defeat, besides, he has the knack of winning men to his side and remember, too, that he is one of the most brilliant generals of all time.

Jane looked at him indignantly, "Dominic, how can you praise such a fiend? Think of the crimes he had committed!"

"I do not praise him – I just acknowledge his qualities as a leader. It does not do to underestimate the enemy, you know.

He has taken care to leave Russia ahead of the main army, bringing his best officers with him, and he is desperate to know what dispositions we and our allies are making to receive him. That is what his agents must find out and we must prevent them."

"I see," said Jane thoughtfully, "Of course, he has never yet met Wellington."

"No, and when he does he will want as much information as he can get and Wellington will need to have early news of Napoleon's movements in order to prepare his counter attack. It is not generally known, but Nelson was constantly given wrong and late information about the French Fleet and was very courageous to achieve such a wonderful victory at Trafalgar."

Jane was pensive during the drive home. How few of the sparkling throng at the daily and nightly festivities gave a thought, indeed were aware of the unremitting, secret struggle going on in their midst. After all it was only by chance that she herself knew of it. Even the dashing officers in their splendid uniforms seemed as carefree as the lovely ladies they squired to balls and routs. It was said that Wellington himself was often seen relaxing in the ball-room seemingly with not a care in the world, though in his case it must be a morale-boosting façade.

It was as well that no prophetic vision was vouchsafed to Jane of the summer in 1815 when Wellington, bedevilled by lack of intelligence, was to lose many of these light-hearted, gallant figures near the obscure village called Waterloo a few miles south of Brussels.

It was not long before Lisette was to meet the soignée Miss Gascoigne whose engagement had been announced and whom the gossip writers had made much of. She could scarcely believe that Elizabeth Gascoigne was her cousin Jane but to her knowledge there were no other Gascoignes in Cleeve.

They came face to face at Lady Hapgood's ball. She was an old acquaintance of the Dowager's who looked forward to hearing the latest on dits from Bath.

When Jane heard of the invitation her first impulse was to have a diplomatic headache so that she could be excused: she had second thoughts, however. It was inevitable that she and

Lisette would meet frequently during the Season and the sooner the first encounter was over the better.

Lisette, who had not looked through the acceptances to the ball, had no warning. She was receiving with Lady Amelia when the Major – domo announced 'The Dowager Countess and Earl of Delamere, Lady Althea Templeton, Miss Elizabeth Gascoigne." In the brief interval before she found herself curtseying to the Dowager and having Dominic bow over her hand she tried to prepare herself to meet Jane. She had no feeling of apprehension for she was unaware that Jane had overheard her incautious remarks in the pavilion. She barely saw Althea, her eyes were fixed unbelievingly on the graceful figure in a gown of oyster satin over a coral underdress with necklace and earrings of coral and diamonds. The unique arrangement of Jane's hair was enhanced by a string of coral and diamonds glinting through the shining plume.

The girls stared at each other as they made their formal curtseys but neither spoke. Lisette could scarcely believe that this elegant vision was the despised plain Jane and she was struck dumb with envy and fury as she realised that her mousy cousin had made the catch of the Season.

For her part Jane could find nothing to say to the stranger who epitomised all the misery of her early girlhood but to whom she now felt quite indifferent, and she moved away quickly to join Dominic and his sister. The Dowager was already making for the card room where she and her contemporaries could indulge in cards and gossip.

When the ball began Dominic could not bring himself to dance with Lisette as he remembered her heartless treatment of his beloved. Lisette took note of his omission and added it to her score against Jane. She did not lack for partners – the two Frenchmen and the Foreign Office attaché were assiduous in their attentions and the latter claimed her for the supper dance.

Dominic, from a nearby table, observed the obvious intimacy between the two and was sorry for it. Young Mark Howard was a brother of one of Dominic's close friends and he did not like to see the boy drawn into Lisette's circle which included the two Frenchmen.

CHAPTER 20

As the Season progressed Dominic grew more uneasy, the boy was clearly infatuated and there few occasions when he was not to be seen in Lisette's company. As for the Frenchmen, he was becoming surer as he pursued his investigations that they were impostors and the leaders in espionage on Napoleon's behalf.

Could he have been pleasant when the two men met in their Mount Street house for a private discussion he would have found his suspicions confirmed.

"We must move quickly," said Raoul."

"Yes," agreed Jacques. "Our masters are getting impatient. What is left of the Grande Armée is struggling back from Russia and the Emperor needs to know what alliances are being made against him before he can mount his offensive."

"You are right. It is an open question as to where the partners in this ill-matched Grande Alliance are to be deployed. Our petite coquette should make more use of that young idiot in the Foreign Office. So far she has had no success. We know, but not from her, that secret orders are to be sent to the Allies soon and we must get hold of them fast."

"Never fear, mon vieux, I am to stroll in the park with our so far useless Lisette this afternoon and will remind her that we still hold her vowels and make sure that she understands what she must do to redeem them!"

"And tell her that time is of the essence. I must work on the latest message. They have changed the cipher and that makes me slow."

"Au 'voir," called Jacques as he strolled off to keep his appointment with Listette.

At first she found the walk enjoyable. Jacques was a dashing escort and she made no objection when he guided her into a more secluded path.

"Ma chère, you grow more beautiful by the hour," he said caressingly in his quaintly accented English. "But you should use your beauty to more purpose."

"What do you suggest?" she asked demurely, every ready to respond to compliments.

"That you should find out from that young admirer of yours – M'sieur Howard – when the next despatches are to be sent to the Continent, by what courier and by what route."

Lisette came to a halt. She did not question the motive behind the order. The two Frenchmen had already promised that when Napoleon was again supreme she would have a rich reward and a secure place at the French Court so she was more than ready to oblige them, but she was not going to appear to agree to their demands too easily.

"And if I do not?" she enquired archly.

"Then regrettably," the r's rolled threateningly, "We shall have to demand that your debts be settled immediately!" There was not smile on his face although he spoke quite gently.

Listette paled. "You would not! It may not be possible – he may not know!"

"He will know – he and his clerk have a hand in preparing the documents, we know that. It is for you to do the rest! Come now, we do not ask much – there is no danger for you and a fine reward as we have promised." He and Raoul had no intention of honouring their pledges and, indeed, had no power to do so. They were of the petit bourgeoisie and had no entrée into Court circles.

The use of the stick and the carrot persuaded Lisette. "Very well, I will do my possible," she said sulkily.

"You must do more than that, you must succeed!" he said menacingly, "You know the consequences of failure!" and he drew her arm through his and led her back to the frequented paths and so to her home.

In the ensuing few days Dominic noticed with increasing uneasiness that Lisette and Mark Howard seemed scarcely ever to be out of each other's company and he decided that it was time to take a hand. As the Frenchmen had discovered, a vital despatch was being prepared and great secrecy and elaborate precautions were being taken to ensure its safe passage to the Allied Headquarters and Dominic had his part in this.

CHAPTER 21

To this end Dominic began to join Lisette's circle and to become better acquainted with Mark Howard. Jane watched with sick dismay the number of times Dominic made an excuse to leave her and join Lisette. It gave Lisette tremendous satisfaction, she thought her charms were outshining those of this new Jane as they had always done in the past and she began to slight Mark in favour of Dominic.

Jane was too proud and too hurt to reproach him and the ensuing days were the most agonising of her life. Was she never to feel secure? Was Lisette always to usurp her place in the affections of Father, Mother and, dearest of all, Dominic, who had like Pygmalion, caused Jane, his Galleatea, to awake to new life, to the ecstasy of being loved? She walked the treadmill of the social round but grew quieter and more depressed every day.

Mark Howard could have matched her in misery and bewilderment. Suddenly Lisette seemed to have no time to spend with him. He watched Dominic's growing intimacy with her with increasing anger and disillusionment.

One day, he walked aimlessly in the park so distraught that he was considering putting an end his existence, and leaving a note laying the blame for his suicide at Lisette's door. Then his natural good sense came to his aid and he began to smile at his histrionics. At this propitious moment he was hailed from a passing curricle.

"Howard! I say, Howard!" and he turned to see the author of his misfortunes pulling up a pair of fine greys who were on the fret to be off.

"Just the man I was hoping to see! A word with you, if you please – climb up, Caster and Pollux are too fresh to stand for long!"

Mark was of a mind to refuse the abrupt invitation, but to his surprise he found himself climbing into the curricle and before he could protest they were off. He blushed with fury at his tame capitulation and took a deep breath to speak his mind.

Before he could utter Dominic said drily, "Like to plant me a facer I am sure – I don't blame you, but, before you do, will you listen to me for a moment?"

"I could hardly resort to fisticuffs just now," said Mark sarcastically, "And in any case I should have small chance to get near you – Jackson says you could make your fortune in the ring if you chose," he added resentfully.

"Yes, well ….. I own you have a cause for grievance, but could we talk together first? Your brother is my close friend as you know and asked me to make your acquaintance."

"Oh, so he had put you up to this! I am out of short coats you know!" he snapped angrily, only too aware that so far in the interchange he had succeeded in sounding more like a sulky schoolboy than a man of the world.

"Oh, take a damper! He is far too busy in the Pyrenees to have time to spare for either of us. But what I have to say in some measure affects the Army, so will you sup with me at Delamere Manor at say, nine tonight? All the ladies will be at the Opera so that we shall be on our own and I give you leave to ignore the fact that you will be my guest and you may tell me precisely what you think of me!" and he smiled at his reluctant passenger.

Dominic's smile had won him many friends and it did not fail him now, if only in turning Mark's intended refusal into a reluctant acceptance.

"Very well," he said grudgingly, "At nine then."

"Thank you," replied Dominic, bringing his curricle to a stand still, he added, "Before you leave me, and at the risk of sounding like a Gothic mystery may I ask one more favour? It is that you tell no one of our coming meeting and enter the house by the back-door – I shall be on the watch for you."

Puzzled but intrigued, Mark nodded agreement. He repeated, "Very well," as he alighted and Dominic drove off.

He excused himself from attending the Opera on the score of business that had to be attended to without delay. "I never have time these days with all my escort duties!" he declared with a twinkle which raised no answering smile in Jane's eyes. His heart ached for the pain he was causing her but consoled himself that soon he would be able to put matters right.

"You need not flatter yourself that you are indispensable, we have an eager deputy in young Fitzallan, have we not, Althea?" said his grandmother.

Althea blushed, she was in no hurry publicly to proclaim her interest in any one of her coterie. She wished to be free to enjoy the attentions of all her swains with a fine impartiality, but she had confided in Jane that William Fitzallan ranked high above the rest.

William, the heir to one of the richest baronies in the country, had already spoken to Dominic of his hopes, but said indulgently, "I shall not hurry her, Sir. She is very young and will, I hope, come to be sure of her heart when she has enjoyed the success of her come-out to the full – she has led me to believe that she is not indifferent to me." He spoke with forced calm but it was easy to see that his feelings were deeply involved. Dominic was impressed by the good sense and maturity of a man some way short of thirty and willingly agreed to Fitzallan paying his addresses to his temperamental sister judging him to be the ideal husband for her.

*   *   *

After a day of puzzled resentment Mark arrived to keep his appointment and was admitted at the back-door by his host under the disapproving eyes of the butler and settled in the library. He refused the offer of refreshments.

Dominic smiled understandingly and said, "The fact that you are guest in my house need not prevent you, if you still wish to do so, from planting me a facer – I shall not retaliate!".

"I cannot imagine what we have to say to each other! I came because …"

His host interrupted, "It is rather what I have to say that is important and, much as you dislike me, may I have your word that what I tell you now will not be repeated to anyone – not even Miss Duclos?"

Mystified, Mark started at him. This was a close friend of his elder brother who respected him to the point of hero worship so he, Mark, must believe in his integrity. "Very well, I give you my word."

"Thank you. Will you indulge me further and hear me out without interruption before you comment?"

Mark nodded and Dominic began. His hearer found it difficult to keep silent when Dominic's first words were critical of Lisette.

"I want you to believe that I dislike speaking ill of a woman, but Lisette Duclos is using you. She is in league with two of Napoleon's agents and has been set on to obtain information from you owing to your position in the Foreign Office."

Mark moved protestingly but Dominic swept on.

"Think! She blows hot and cold does she not? Only when her masters urge her does she pay attention to you."

As Mark again made to speak, scarlet with anger, Dominic held up his hand.

"Wait! Consider! Has she not flattered you and asked questions about your work? I give you credit for being discreet but I am sure she has done her best to extract information from you."

Hot now with embarrassment, Mark remembered several occasions when Lisette had permitted liberties while murmuring, "Your work must be so interesting, so important! I expect you know all the plans that are made to defeat the monster. Tell me about them, it must be so exciting!"

He remembered thankfully that, though tempted to cut an important figure to impress her, he had not fallen into the trap. Dominic had judged rightly that though Mark was as young and as foolish as any boy overwhelmed by his first real passion, he was, at bottom, intelligent and sound and able to keep his head where the safety of his country was concerned. Lisette would find Dominic was so enamoured his scruples could easily be overcome – at least that was what he intended she should believe!

Now Mark said thickly, "She did not succeed!"

"Good! I was sure of that! Now we come to my part in this affair. I have set out to rouse her interest fairly sure that she would respond" he smiled deprecatingly. "Not only in order to show you how fickle she is but also to use her for my purposes."

"Which are?" asked Mark truculently. "It is a pretty blaguardly thing to do is it not? I never used her!"

"Where the safety of the country is concerned I use any tool that comes to hand – even to my own detriment!" replied Dominic, thinking with some bitterness of the increasing estrangement between himself and Elizabeth. "My aim is to give Lisette information – false, of course, I need hardly say – that she can pass on to her confederates and so mislead them."

In spite of his initial hostility Mark was now beginning to trust Dominic. "To what end?" he enquired.

"I do not need to tell you of the plans which are now almost complete and ready for despatch to Allied Headquarters."

"How did you know that?" interjected Mark. "Not that I confirm it," he added hastily. "Surely such matters are not your province? You are a soldier, not on the Staff, I expect you will be rejoining your Regiment in the near future."

Dominic shook his head ruefully, "I am afraid they will not pass me as fit for active duty – but the fact is not to be published abroad," he said warningly. "My work at the moment is in counter-espionage. I have taken care to see that our French friends know this."

"But, surely it is of the first importance not to betray yourself?" Mark asked in bewilderment.

"Normally, yes, but we are trying a double bluff. When the plans are ready I shall take a false set, leaving from Dover – if I ever get there – while the real courier with the genuine plans makes for Plymouth. He will leave after I have drawn off the pursuit and I shall do my best to evade capture for long enough for him to board the frigate to Dieppe and so on to Allied Headquarters.

"And you will let the Frenchmen know when you are leaving? How?"

"They are already watching me and I shall make sure that Lisette knows when I must absent myself from her side to undertake a mysterious journey to the Continent – that should do the trick!" He smiled at Mark and poured out some wine – he held the decanter over the second glass. "Talking makes me thirsty, will you join me?"

The younger man smiled back, "With great pleasure – listening is dry work!"

When they had sipped their wine and were making inroads on the sandwiches Mark enquired, "But why are you telling me? What can I do?!

"I am telling you so that you may keep up your guard now matters are coming to a head and also because I am anxious that my friend's brother is not involved in the debacle when the villains are exposed. Your part is to keep up the deception – continue to pursue Lisette and become enraged when I appear to be ousting you – then gradually draw off. On no account show any signs of friendship between us. Can you do this? It is vital that there is no obvious change in the situation."

"It will be difficult now that I know the truth, but I was good at amateur dramatics at school!

Dominic laughed, "Capital! Now I think you should leave – by the back door, if you please! It will arouse suspicion if any watcher knows that we have been closeted together for so long. After all – it should not have taken you long to knock me down!"

Mark grinned, "Small chance of that! Good luck sir – take care!" and the two men – one who had just been disillusioned in love and the other whose heart was torn when thinking of the hurt he was inflicting on his beloved – clasped hands, and Mark took his leave.

CHAPTER 22

In the days following the visit to the Opera Jane watched with increasing anguish Lisette's apparent conquest of Dominic. His grandmother had, so far, not heard the gossip which was beginning to couple the names of Lisette and Dominic, and Althea was too preoccupied in the delicious game of postponing her capitulation to William Fitzallan to be aware of it.

Jane was not so fortunate. Kind friends 'felt it their duty' to inform her of the number of times Lisette and Dominic were seen together.

"My dear, they are never apart! The Counts and Mark Howard are quite out of favour! She is your cousin, is she not, such a beautiful girl! I suppose you have asked him to pay her some attention, but he seems to be carrying it a little too far, does he not?"

The barbed remarks found their target and Jane writhed inwardly in humiliation, although she met every jibe with a composed smile.

Raoul and Jacques were pleased with the turn of events: Lisette reported snippets of information gleaned from Dominic, far more than she had extracted from Mark Howard, and she had a moment of triumph when she could inform them that Dominic was unable to escort her on a projected expedition to Richmond. His excuse was so lame! He said he was obliged to undertake an important journey – nothing else would have kept him from her side, he protested.

She asked, "Could you not postpone it? Surely a little delay would be of no consequence?"

"I am afraid it is out of my power to change the date – too much depends upon it," he said regretfully.

"But you will not be long away? Lady Hapgood's ball is only a sennight and I count on you," she said archly. "No one matches my steps so well as you." She felt so secure that she ventured on a show of temper when he shook his head.

"I see what it is, you do not <u>wish</u> to accompany me! Very well, Sir, you need not trouble! Others will be glad to take your place!"

Dominic managed to look crestfallen. "Indeed, Lisette," he pleaded, "I cannot help myself – I am under orders. I am afraid I cannot promise to be back in time for the ball. I shall have to spend a little time on the Continent ..." he stopped abruptly and looked at her anxiously. "Excuse me – I should not have said that – please do not heed what I said. I forgot to be cautious in my great disappointment and fear that I have angered you beyond forgiveness." He took her hand and pressed an ardent kiss upon her fingers, wondering as he did so how she could be taken in by so much flummery. "Forgive me!" Inwardly he was sickened by having to touch her but he must make sure that she had all the facts necessary for his purpose to pass on to her confederates. He went on, cajolingly, "Perhaps some French perfume would sweeten you – as long as you do not divulge how you came by it!"

"Wretched one! You grow more mysterious! When are you off to Newhaven – tomorrow?"

"Not for three days, and I sail from Dover. I shall leave at first light and you may be sure I shall make all haste to complete my mission and return to you, but I beg you to keep my journey secret – I should not have spoken of it."

"Do not fear – your secret is safe with me," she replied mendaciously. "But remember, I shall expect my reward!"

"You shall have it, I promise you," and he pressed another lingering kiss on her stubby fingers thinking the while of his Elizabeth's slender hands and marvelling at the credulity of this graceless creature.

Lisette drew her hand away and said playfully, "Come, Sir – unhand me! We must rejoin our friend," and she led the way from the secluded alcove to which they had retreated back to the supper room.

Be sure their absence had been noted and Jane had to call on all her pride to sustain her for the rest of the evening. She had little sleep that night and Dominic had none. He had spent the last weeks driven by his strong sense of duty to deny the impulses of his heart and now he was faced with a task which might well end in his death.

As a soldier he had always accepted that risk, but to die in the heat of battle seemed far less terrible than to face the lone death of a spy. He knew these feelings were morbid but he was haunted by the thought that he might die leaving Elizabeth, his beloved Elizabeth, to believe that he died unfaithful to her. He was determined to spare her that cruel blow and settled down to write to her assuring her of his love and asking her to meet Mark Howard who would, under pledge of secrecy, explain all. The letter was to be given to her after his death.

It was no use! No letter could convey the depth of his love and longing and he consigned yet another spoiled sheet to the fire. He paced the room reminding himself that the French might attack him to steal the plans but he gave them credit for sufficient intelligence to realise that if the plans failed to reach the Allies another stratagem would be plotted of which they would have no knowledge.

No, they would delay him and make a copy of the papers and do so without his knowledge, then let him complete his journey while they would be able to prepare a counter attack, although they would not know that it would be based on false information. These thoughts of death, he told himself, were the outcome of tiredness after weeks of strain, but still he could not rule out accidents, either brought about by the enemy or by natural causes. As dawn began to make his candle pale he came to a decision.

Elizabeth was already privy to his undercover work and her discretion was absolute. If he could trust Mark Howard surely he could trust his other self?

Now, how to contrive a tête-à-tête unremarked by friends and relatives? His pursuit of Lisette had become so public that suddenly to attach himself again to his fiancée would raise eyebrows and cause Lisette to question his enslavement. Ideas chased one another through his tired brain only to be discarded as impractical until, as he was almost in despair, the solution came to him and he sat down again to write to Elizabeth. It was a short note:

'Dear Elizabeth

*I <u>must</u> speak to you and we cannot be private here. I beg
you to make some excuse – to say perhaps that you have been
summoned to Brighton, an emergency at Isabelle's – and to meet
me at Hove at Mrs Lineton's, I know you keep your rooms there.
You might pretend that this note comes from Mrs Gibbs. I will
tell John to drive you, he will be discreet. Whatever your
feelings are for me now, I beg you not to fail me,*

Dominic

He sealed the note and addressed it to Miss E Gascoigne at the
London address and used his left hand so that his writing might
not be recognised.

It was now full light and the servants were stirring as he went
along to Jane's room and slipped the note beneath her door.
Then, returning to his room, he rang for John and changed
hastily as he gave him careful instructions, then, a quick cup of
coffee and he was in his curricle on his way to Hove.

Jane's maid picked up Dominic's note and brought it to her
mistress with her morning chocolate. The abrupt, disjointed
message seemed a fitting climax to her uneasy night.

At first she was tempted to consign it to the fire. Did Dominic
think that he could neglect her so shamefully and then expect her
to fall in with his wishes at his convenience? She crushed the
note in her hand, full of righteous anger, but the strangeness of
the message checked her before she threw it away and she
smoothed it out and read it again. Then she had it! He wanted to
end their engagement and had just sufficient grace to do so face
to face! Bitter tears rolled down her cheeks and she knew a
desolation that was almost unbearable. After a while she braced
herself. At least the meeting would put an end to an intolerable
situation and give her the opportunity to demand that she be the
one to break the engagement – he had humiliated her enough!

When she looked through her letters at breakfast with Althea
she put on a convincing show of surprise and wondered aloud

what emergency had cropped up at Isabelle's. She said she had been out of touch these last weeks and must pay a flying visit to Brighton. Would Althea present her excuses to her grandmother – she would stay the night at Hove – they had only an unimportant engagement that evening and Althea could offer her excuses there too.

Althea listened with only half an ear. She was pre-occupied with a letter from William Fitzallan and had little interest in Jane's affairs. She agreed to make any excuses necessary for Jane's absence and Jane left the breakfast table relieved that she could get away so unobtrusively.

The journey to Hove was accomplished smoothly in John's competent hands and Jane dismissed him to rack up for the night in Brighton and call for her in Hove the next morning.

Becky was delighted to see her but exclaimed at her look of exhaustion.

"Racketing about all hours of the night, I'll be bound! Come this instant minute and rest on your bed! Mary shall bring you a dish of tea and then you'll feel more the thing."

"Thank you, Becky, that will be delightful, but I will rest in my sitting room, I am expecting his lordship and will wait for tea until he comes. Perhaps you can spare some of his favourite macaroons?"

"To be sure I can, and he will soon put roses in your cheeks I don't doubt!" and she bustled off.

Jane had only time to take off her bonnet and pelisse and wash her face and tidy her hair before she heard Dominic's voice enquiring for her. He had stabled his curricle in Brighton and walked to Hove trying on the way to plan his meeting with Jane.

He left his coat and hat with Mary and was ushered into the sitting room before Jane had steadied herself to greet him in a cool, collected manner. It would have been wasted! Almost before the door was closed he was across the room, prepared speeches discarded, and had swept her into his arms.

"Darling, darling Elizabeth!" and any reply she might have made was stifled by his kisses. He lifted her off her feet and put her tenderly into the armchair by the fire and knelt beside her.

His head was in her lap and she could only just hear his low entreaties, "Forgive me, my dearest, forgive me!"

She was unable to reply for she heard steps on the stair and the rattle of crockery. Dominic heard it too and was on his feet looking out of the window when Becky and Mary came in bearing the tea tray and the newly baked macaroons.

"Put the tray there, Mary," said Becky with a sharp look at Jane. No need to complain of paleness now, a becoming blush coloured her cheeks.

With a satisfied nod to herself Becky said, "Mrs Brown must have know your lordship would be here today – something told her to make a batch of macaroons!"

This feeble attempt at humour had given Dominic time to master himself and he turned from the window and greeted Becky and sent his compliments to Mrs Brown, then Becky and Mary withdrew.

For a moment neither Jane nor Dominic broke the silence, then Jane, who had been bereft of speech by Dominic's breakdown, took refuge in commonplaces.

"Pray be seated, Dominic," and she began to pour out tea although her hands trembled.

Dominic dropped into a chair but made no move to take the cup she offered. The sight of his tormented face gave her courage to ask, "For what am I to forgive you, pray? That you would like to end our engagement ......"

"What!" He was on his feet again. "You cannot believe that!"

"What else am I to believe? You have shown unmistakably that you are deeply in love with Lisette!" she retorted bitterly, "The situation is intolerable and I agree that we should end it!"

"In love with Lisette? I?" he exploded.

"You give every appearance of being besotted, my lord!" By this time Jane too was on her feet.

"But I had to – don't you see? He expostulated. "Elizabeth, you have my whole heart!"

"Then all I can say is that you have a strange way of showing it!"

Dominic groaned. "I am going about this in the wrong way! I must explain – that is why I had to see you."

"It will take a great deal of explanation! There can be no excuse for your conduct over these last weeks!" all her hurt and humiliation informed her voice."

"I know it seems so, but I beg you to hear me!"

Remembering his embrace when he first arrived, Jane was puzzled – perhaps she should listen to him. It might be that his sudden infatuation had burnt itself out and he wished to return to his old allegiance. She had been so bitterly hurt that she could not forgive him, and yet her treacherous heart urged her to hear his plea.

"Very well," she said, seating herself again.

Dominic rook a restless turn round the room and began hesitantly, "First, you must believe me when I say that, all appearances to the contrary, I detest Lisette, she is but a means to an end. Elizabeth, you know that I am engaged in unmasking Napoleon's spies and she is involved with them."

Having broken the ice he sat down and gave Jane a detailed account of his activities. When he disclosed that he had undertaken to play the part of decoy Jane could no longer keep silent.

"But you will be in great danger! They will know through Lisette that you are the courier."

"There will be a little danger," he replied reassuringly, "It is to their interest to allow me to complete my journey, otherwise the Allies would change their plans and they would be ignorant of the new stratagem."

"I see," said Jane thoughtfully, "But why wait to tell me now? Surely you could have trusted me at the outset and saved me much pain."

"I beg you to forgive me," he repeated. "I had to make it convincing and, discreet as you are, I think you would have found it hard not to betray that fact that my penchant for Lisette was a sham. I am telling you now because – should anything go wrong – I am sure it will not – but just in case – I could not bear you to believe that you had been slighted, that my heart is not wholly yours."

Jane rose and went into his arms, "And mine is forever in your keeping, my darling."

As she came out of that embrace Jane caught sight of the tea tray. "Heavens, we must drink some tea and you must eat a macaroon or Becky will fuss and Mrs Brown will be mortally offended."

By this time the tea was cold but they both heroically swallowed a cup and Dominic ate two macaroons, "To take out the taste!" he said. Duty done, he rose.

"Must you go, my darling?" ask Jane.

"I must, I have to be back in Town by this evening, but I leave my heart with you!"

They exchanged a long kiss and as they drew apart Jane said desperately, "You <u>will</u> take care? You will come and see me as soon as you return?"

"Yes, to both those questions," replied. He smiled at her lovingly. "Now my mind is at rest I am almost looking forward to the adventure. I wonder how they will manage to steal and copy the plans," he added reflectively.

"I have no desire to know," snapped Jane tartly, "As long as you are unhurt, that is all that matters."

"Oh, I shall be safe," he said reassuringly and made for the door, then remembering, he turned. "For your comfort Mark Howard is in my confidence too, you can mingle your tears if I am late returning!" and with a laughing, mock salute he was gone.

Jane heard his voice bidding goodbye to Becky and the noise as the door closed behind him but she did not go to the window to watch him walk away down the street. She wanted to keep the picture of him laughing as he left her to take part in an adventure to which he said he was almost looking forward!

She could not rid her mind of the dread that he might not return to her. She had steeled herself during these last dismal weeks to believe that she had lost him to Lisette but it would be doubly cruel to lose him after their rapturous reunion. Sitting there alone she prayed passionately for his safe return and by the time Mary came to remove the tea things she had composed herself and was ready to join Becky and her sister in their sitting room and relate all her experiences at routs and balls and other gaieties.

When John called for her in the morning she paid a brief visit to Isabelle's and found it to be thriving. Mrs Gibbs had only one complaint, if such it could be called, they were overwhelmed with orders and she had had to take on two more seamstresses: she would like some more designs at Miss Darcy's convenience and Jane promised to send them. The twins had gained in poise and refinement and Maisie looked the picture of health.

Jane drove back to London reminding herself that she must not appear to be in good spirits in the face of Dominic's apparent dereliction but she told herself sadly that anxiety for his safety would keep her manner sufficiently subdued to satisfy the gossips.

CHAPTER 23

Dominic took a suitably regretful farewell of Lisette after driving with her in the Park and at dinner told his grandmother that he would be away for several days.

The Dowager, who was beginning to be aware of his neglect of Jane, replied brusquely, "We see so little of you these days Dominic, that you will scarcely be missed! When you return see that you pay more attention to your family and fiancée! I lose patience with these modern manners! I collect that we shall not have your company at Almack's tonight?"

Althea interposed, "You know he dislikes Almack's – thinks it dull – and any excuse not to attend will serve!" but, sure of Fitzallan's escort, she was not really put out.

Dominic ignored her and spoke to the Dowager. "Please excuse me, Grandmamma, I have business I must attend to as I am leaving at first light tomorrow. Jane will forgive me, I am sure," and he smiled at her.

"This once, Dominic," replied repressively, without returning his smile.

"Thank you, my love. Now pray excuse me," and he left the room.

Later that evening an officer and his orderly arrived at Delamere Manor. He carried a dispatch case secured by large brass locks which caught the light from the torches on each side of the door as he was admitted.

The two men watching in the shadows of the gardens opposite noted it and one went off to report. The orderly walked the horses until, after a while, the officer joined him and they rode off, without the dispatch case. Dominic finished his preparations for his journey and went off to bed to snatch a few hours sleep.

John had already played his part. In the mews, during the morning, he had grumbled loudly at his master's insistence on having four changes of horses for so short a journey to Dover. At Dartford, Rochester, Sittingbourne and Canterbury no less, and he, John, had to make a finicky ride to arrange it! Still grumbling, he set off, noting that a seedy-looking groom, a stranger to the mews, had made himself scarce just before he himself left, this to John's great satisfaction. "I wonder where them Frenchies will make their play? I only hope this lordship's right and they won't harm him. I've a good mind to follow him at a safe distance," thought John, but he knew better than to disobey his master and shrugged off his misgivings and settled down to his journey.

The next morning, while it was still dark, Dominic's horse was brought round and while the groom fastened on his lordship's overnight valise, Dominic himself secured the locked dispatch case in his saddle bag before mounting and riding off as the darkness lightened sufficiently for his mare to pick her way over the cobbles at a sober pace.

As he crossed the river the lightening sky was reflected in the water, turning it to a sheet of steel, cold and forbidding, but Dominic felt warmed by the brief note he carried in his inside pocket. It had been thrust under his door and said only, "My love and prayers go with you." It was not signed – cautious Elizabeth!

The light grew as he left the City behind. His mare broke into a canter and it was not long before the fringe of market gardens was passed and the wintry sun shone on open fields: the early lights of the scattered farmhouses looked warmer than the pale sun.

As he rode Dominic pondered on how the enemy would manage to take and copy the plans without making him aware of it. His consideration of the problem was quite detached as if it concerned someone else.

Dartford and Rochester were reached and passed without incident, although the mount provided at Rochester proved to be a sluggard. By the time he reached Sittingbourne Dominic had almost persuaded himself that his was a wasted journey, but there was nothing for it but to press on to the rendezvous with Jem at Dover.

No sign of pursuit between Sittingbourne and Canterbury, and to add to his misery a fine rain had begun to fall, the brightness of the early morning proving to be short-lived. The cathedral town looked as grey as his mood and Dominic was feeling sharp-set and out of temper. Could he and his superiors have miscalculated? Had their plan been too tortuous and, instead of pursuing him, were the enemy even now on the trail of the genuine courier on the road to Portsmouth?

He felt acutely depressed and called for hot coffee and a meal and was served promptly with ham and beef and appetising home-made bread and butter. The coffee was hot and strong and he began to feel more himself, but not for long!

As he left the Inn to mount his horse he broke into a cold sweat and the stable yard swung about him. His legs and arms felt powerless and refused to obey him. He made a desperate attempt to mount but had to lean helplessly again his horse. His last conscious thought was, strangely, one of triumph considering how dreadful he felt. "We have tricked them!" he thought and sank down in a lifeless huddle. Two travellers who had been staying overnight at the Inn emerged into the yard and, as Dominic collapsed, they ran towards him.

The first to reach him cried, "Jack, it is our friend, Delamere, in one of his fits! Poor fellow, let us get him inside."

The landlord hovered distractedly and talked about sending for an apothecary. The men reassured him.

"Milord is subject to these fits but they soon pass off and, after a rest, he is quite well again – it is but to take him within – he can repose himself on my bed and we will delay our departure until he is himself again," said 'Jack'.

The landlord was glad to have the matter taken out of his hands but it took the combined efforts of all three to carry the inert body to 'Jack's' bedroom, Dominic's six foot two was no light weight!

'Roland' waisted no time in searching Dominic's pockets for the key to the despatch case and had just held it up in triumph when there was a knock at the door and Dominic's baggage was handed in.

Jack seized the despatch case and, after several attempts, managed to open it. He settled down immediately to copy the papers while his companion considerately removed Dominic's boots, loosened his cravat, and cast a rug over the comatose figure.

146

For an hour there was silence, then Jack said, "Almost finished, it is a devilishly clever stratagem, our masters should reward us handsomely! How is milord?"

"Still fast asleep – his pulse is good, he should be recovering soon. When you have finished we ought to take our leave – regretfully of course! We will tell the landlord to be sure to give our regards to our friend – an urgent appointment forces us to go before he has completely recovered!"

Thus it was that when Dominic at last opened his eyes he was alone. The effort to do so brought the agonising pain in his head to a crescendo and with a groan he closed them again.

When the pain subsided a little he tried again and raised his head. The strange surroundings bewildered him and with a great effort he sat up and swung his legs to the ground and there he stayed, overcome by nausea. Through the mist which surrounded him he could just make out the basin on the wash-hand stand and lurched across to it in time to be devastatingly sick.

He was wiping his face with a towel dipped in the icy cold water in the ewer when the door opened. At sight of him the landlord's wife exclaimed, "My Lord, you should not be standing, come back to the bed," and she put her arm round him and helped him to lie down again.

By now Dominic's mind had cleared somewhat and the urgency of his mission returned to him. "I cannot lie here – I must get on!" and he sat up and held his head as the room swung round.

"Indeed, Sir, you should not attempt it," the landlady said worriedly. "You have been in a swound these two hours. Your friends said to tell you they were terrible sorry to have to leave you but they had urgent business and could not stay."

"I am sure they had," muttered Dominic, beginning to piece together the cause of his collapse. He looked round anxiously. "My baggage!"

"Be easy, sir, it's all here," and she indicated his saddle bags and despatch case on the floor under the window.

"Now," said the motherly soul, "If you take my advice you will take some nourishment and rest until tomorrow. You will be more able to travel then."

Dominic acknowledged her concern with a smile but answered, "I thank you, ma'am, but I am much restored and must continue my journey without further delay. Please to send someone to help with my boots and have my horse brought round, then I'll be on my way."

"But you must eat something, sir, you've nothing inside you!"

"Thankfully, no," replied Dominic. The thought of food made his stomach heave and the pounding in his head get worse. "Ma'am, I am in haste, pray do as I ask."

She acknowledged defeat and muttering, "Just like a man – no sense!" she got herself out of the room.

Dominic looked longingly at the bed but a look at his watch brought him to his feet. An examination of the contents of the despatch case showed him the slight disarrangement of the papers and he nodded in satisfaction, then wished he had not, for to move his head was agony.

The lad came and helped Dominic with his boots while he did his best with his crumpled cravat, then he made his way painfully downstairs. He paid his shot and refused offers of food and brandy but drank a glass of water gratefully. He was reduced to the ignominy of the mounting block before he was at last mounted and he looked so ill that the landlord expected him to fall off again before he reached the road.

However, Dominic stayed in the saddle and, once on his way, although even the sober pace of his horse jarred his head almost unbearably, the fresh air revived him and, after what seemed an unconscionable time, Dover was reached. The afternoon light was fading when, with the last of his strength, Dominic guided his mount to the down-at-heel tavern which was his rendezvous with Jem. The smuggler was waiting for him with mounting anxiety.

"You're late," he said sharply, "We shall miss the tide!" and he turned to his horse, already saddled. Receiving no reply he turned to look more closely in the half-light and was just in time to help Dominic as he reeled from the saddle.

"Eh – you're in no shape to sail," he ejaculated. "Shot the cat, have you?"

Dominic managed only, "Must sail, Jem. Get me there," before he was overtaken by retching which was the more painful since there was nothing left in his stomach.

Seriously alarmed, Jem shouted for help and Matthew, a lad of so few words that all but his intimates thought him to be dumb, came out of the Inn.

"He's ill, " said Jem, "I doubt we should sail."

"Get me to the boat, damn you!" uttered Dominic. The fury in his voice made up for its lack of command.

"Well, if you dies on us we'll have to tip you overboard, but you've asked for it," said Jem philosophically. "Matt, fetch the cart round, he can't ride."

Still without a word Matt went to where a ramshackle cart was ready, heaped with fish gear.

With the help of the two men Dominic was loaded into the cart and his baggage with him, then, with Jem on horseback and Matthew driving the cart, they set off for the jetty where their dinghy was moored.

Jem, Dominic and his baggage made the trip first and by the time Harry, the third member of the crew, rowed the dinghy back Matthew had unloaded the cart and sent it and Jem's horse back to the Inn in the care of the ostler who had followed them to the jetty.

The two men made short work of loading the nets and the pots and reached the single-masted lugger as Jem was beginning to haul up the anchor. With sail set they caught the last of the tide and were on their way.

Dominic was so nearly unconscious that the activity of securing the dinghy and hoisting the sail passed unnoticed by him and he sank into a deep sleep on a bedding of nets, covered by an old cloak, as the boat began its journey.

The long sleep somewhat restored Dominic although he was weak and his head still pained him. Jem was glad to get him to the safe house on the outskirts of Calais where the royalist hostess was shocked by his looks

While he changed into his shabby disguise she prepared a tisane and a bowl of gruel which was all he could manage and saw him go with deep misgiving. She had added her arguments to Jem's who had suggested that it was unnecessary for Dominic to struggle to the Allied Headquarters now he had outwitted the enemy, but Dominic had insisted that his journey must be completed.

"We are not sure how good their intelligence is. If they once suspect that these plans are a sham they will not act upon them and it is imperative that they do so. In any case they will not harm me: it is to their advantage that the plans be delivered; they will believe then that they can stage a counter-attack. "No," he said firmly, "I must complete my mission," and he set off on the tedious journey across France.

Each stage took much longer than usual. He still felt weak and could only manage meals of soup or gruel and even these occasionally made him sick. At last he reached Headquarters and found to his great relief that the genuine courier had arrived well ahead of him.

He was pressed to stay until he had made a complete recovery, but he longed to get back to Elizabeth. Thoughts of her had strengthened him at times when he had felt too ill to continue his journey. It had become a dreary pilgrimage, no need for heroics, no excitement – just an endless succession of plodding journeys interspersed with flea-ridden nights in filthy auberges and a persistent headache and sickness. He held the picture of Elizabeth and the sound of her voice in his mind as a man parched in the desert longs for cool water and his courage was renewed.

Now he was on his way home, more comfortably this time as a notary's clerk, able to travel in the slowest diligence's and lodge in poor but respectable Inns. It was only during the last stage of his journey to Calais that he became uneasy. The man in the opposite corner had surely been a passenger on the two previous stages. He was better dressed than his fellow travellers and could obviously have afforded a seat in one of the faster coaches used by people travelling long distances: yet he chose slow, local diligences that plied between closely situation towns. As they drew near Calais Dominic grew more and more suspicious and when they drew up at the end of the journey he delayed getting down from the coach until all the other passengers, including his suspect, had left.

His suspicions quieted, Dominic set out down the narrow back streets, his thoughts set on his meeting with Jem and on the next stage of his journey back to Elizabeth whose dear image filled his mind.

Again it was late afternoon – he seemed always to reach Calais at that time of day – and it might have been that because he was still very weary and far from well that in the gloom two attackers were suddenly upon him before he had gained the safe house and Jem. In the split second's warning that his tired senses had, Dominic put into practice a trick he had learned from a deserter from the 'Marseilles' waterfront: he dropped to one knee as the two men reached him from either side. The impetus of their rush was so great that they were unable to stop and collided with some force while Dominic rolled away from the and took to his heels, but he was slow and the swifter of his pursuers caught up with him and began a vicious thrust with a knife.

It was unfortunate that Dominic's right hand and arm were not at full strength and he only just managed to parry the blow and deflect it so that it inflicted a painful graze in his side instead of burying itself in his heart. By this time the other assailant was almost on him and Dominic gave himself up for lost. Although he was still prepared to give a good account of himself he sent a despairing cry of "Au secours," into the darkening alley and was then too busy defending himself to realise that the help for which he called was at hand.

Jem and Matthew were on their way to the safe house, where they had gone at intervals during the last few days, hoping to find that Dominic had arrived. All they could see was one man being set upon by two others and with no hesitation they flung themselves into the fray to even matters. The silent Matthew brought down the belaying pin, without which he never set foot on land, upon one villain's head while Jem used his fists on the other who took to his heels. Each time his fist landed Jem had cried, "Take that, you misbegotten Frog!" and in the midst of the battle Dominic recognised his voice.

"Jem! Thank God," he gasped.

"Well, by all that's holy, it's his lordship!" The silent Matthew was jolted into speech and bent to help Dominic to his feet. In an exchange of roles Jem had nothing to say, but, leaving the man Matthew had felled lying on the cobbles, took his lordship's other arm and the three made their way to the auberge.

By the time they reached it Dominic had almost collapsed and the landlady and Jem spent a busy time tending his hurts which included sundry bad bruises as well as the knife graze in his side.

Dominic hardly heard Jem say, "It's as well we have to wait for the morning tide – he's in no shape to leave tonight.

The landlady agreed, compelling her patient to swallow a draught which she had prepared, then they covered him warmly and left him to sink into a deep sleep from which he never stirred until, at first light, Jem shook him by the shoulder and said, "We should go now, if you are able – the sooner you're home the better."

The word 'home' brought Dominic into full awareness and, groaning at the pain of his stiffening bruises, he dressed as quickly as he could, helped by Jem.

Once more they jolted in the cart to the jetty and Dominic relapsed thankfully into the dinghy. On board Jem's boat, he settled down and, in spite of his many aches and pains, slept most of the way to Dover. By the time they arrived, however, he was feverish and in no state to ride so Jem settled him in the Inn, watched over by Matthew while he arranged for a coach to carry his charge to Ditchling.

He was seriously concerned about Dominic to whom he owed his life. When, on their first voyage together Jem had fallen overboard during a stormy crossing, Dominic had risked his life to save him. Like many another seafarer of his kind Jem could not swim and had given himself up for lost. Ever since his rescue, the smuggler had tried to pay his debt and now, many voyages later, an undemonstrative friendship had grown up between the two men and, although Jem would never voice it, he felt a deep affection for his rescuer.

He thought that Dominic should take to his bed for some days before continuing his journey and his grandmother should be informed but his lordship had been vehement in his command that his grandmother should not be told of his return and that he should be taken immediately to Ditchling.

Jem grumbled but obeyed, and soon he had installed Dominic in a fairly comfortable coach in which they made their way with the briefest of halts over the near hundred miles they had to cover.

Jem was more than glad to hand his lordship over to John who wasted no time in getting Dominic to bed and there he stayed for some days. Nurse was fobbed off with the tale that he old wound was troubling him and he only needed rest before joining the family in Town.

He was by no means fully recovered when he insisted on making the journey but agreed without fuss to be driven in the coach by John. He was anxious to make his report to the Horse Guards and to set in train the necessary steps to round up the gang of spies in England, led he was now sure by the two 'Counts', but as importantly, to be reunited with Elizabeth.

CHAPTER 24

While Dominic was making his painful odyssey across the Continent and back, Lisette was finding life tedious. Not only had Dominic disappeared but the two Frenchmen had left Town and she lacked an escort. She tried Mark Howard, confident that she had only to snap her fingers to summon him to her side. To her dismay, he failed to respond and she was forced to make do with a succession of callow youths who were flattered to squire an accredited beauty.

One comfort she had – Jane looked more and more forlorn, and Lisette rejoiced to think that, once more, she had triumphed over the cousin she envied with all her mean little soul.

Indeed Jane had no difficulty in looking worried. Try as she might to believe Dominic when he had assured her that there was little danger in his enterprise, she could not cease to feel apprehensive. Her anxiety increased as more than a sennight passed without his return and the fact that the true cause of her distress was not recognised and that there was no-one in whom she might confide made her pain almost unbearable. Mark Howard, with whom she might have shared her fears was now out of Town.

The whispers and scarcely veiled sneers of the ton passed her by, but both the Dowager and Althea were indignant on Jane's behalf as they became more aware of them.

At last the Dowager could bear it no longer when she saw Jane looking downright ill. As they returned from Almack's after a particularly unpleasant evening some twelve days after Dominic's abrupt departure, she swept them into drawing room and said commandingly as she sat down, "I will put up with innuendoes from that encroaching Lady Mordant no longer! She is the worst of them – ill-bred creature – but all the harridans in the card-room take every opportunity to sympathise with me for my grandson's outrageous behaviour, and I will suffer it no more! Elizabeth, tell me at once, what has gone wrong between you!"

Jane was so take aback by the suddenness of the attack that, luckily, before she could gather her wits together, Althea rushed into the breech.

"That scheming hussy, Lisette, has made mischief, Grandmamma. She has had my foolish brother on a string these many weeks. Were she not still in Town while he is away the world would believe they had gone off together!" and she broke into angry tears. Combined with her affection for Jane was the shock and grief that Dominic, her adored elder brother, should so fall from grace and behave like the general run of fallible males.

Jane could see no way out of her dilemma. She could not let Dominic be so misjudged by those dear to him and yet how could she reinstate him in their eyes without betraying his confidence? She must have time to think and for once in her forthright life she descended to subterfuge and burst into tears.

She said brokenly, "Aunt .... no more tonight – let us talk in the morning – my head aches so!"

The Dowager's anger was fast dissipating and, faced with two tearful girls, she abandoned her desire for a confrontation: emotional scenes were distasteful to her, although, most often, she herself provoked them.

She rose and said, "Very well, my dear, I agree. It will make more sense to discuss the matter calmly in the morning. Off to bed with both of you – we will see what the morning brings," and she preceded the tearful ladies up the stairs to their respective rooms.

The morrow brought Dominic!

The ladies rose late and gathered in the breakfast room for a nuncheon. Althea, dressed to go for a drive in the Park with William Fitzallan, had only time for a cup of coffee before she had to leave.

The bustle of her departure was scarcely over before Lister was welcoming Dominic. The Dowager had just said, "Now, Elizabeth ...." when the door opened and Dominic stood on the threshold. There were no words: Jane flew into his arms and they remained oblivious of the soft closing of the door and the Dowager's stupefied presence. Her indignation at such unceremonious behaviour soon gave way to satisfaction, however, and she waited with commendable patience for the lovers to become aware of the world about them.

Still in his arms, Jane spoke first. "Dominic, Dominic, you are safe – you are safe!"

"Foolish one, did you doubt it?" he replied and then became aware of his grandmother. Putting Jane gently aside he bent over the Dowager's hand and kissed her cheek.

"I am sorry, Grandmamma, to have been so long," he said, apologetically.

"As well you may be!" he responded acidly. She eyed him closely. "You are thinner and you have been ill. What have you been up to?"

By this time Jane had composed herself and joined them at the table. She poured a cup of coffee for Dominic and waited with relief for him to deal with the Dowager. She had spent a restless night trying to decide what she might with safety disclose and was more than glad that the matter was not out of her hands.

Dominic looked thoughtful. "It is a long story and not really mine to tell. I must ask your indulgence and your pledge of secrecy."

"Understood," replied the Dowager. "I knew you must be up to something, say on."

"Well, I have been on military business and it took longer than I thought. I am anxious that it should not be known – we might put it about that I have been at Ditchling because my wound has been troubling me."

"That does not account for your dalliance with that light-skirt, Lisette!" snapped his grandmother.

"She was part of the deception, Elizabeth knows," and he took Jane's hand in his. "But I must say no more. The matter is almost finished, it is but to tie off some loose ends. By the way, where is Althea? I would rather she knew nothing of this."

Fortunately she is out with Fitzallan – there is a match there unless I miss my guess," replied the Dowager, "And you need not trouble your head about her – you are in her black books and I believe she will scarcely speak to you."

"Good! I will make my peace with her later. And now, my love," he turned to Jane, "I must seek your nuisance of a cousin – a matter of some French perfume!" and his eyes laughed at her.

Jane smiled back. "It had better be a large flask, she has been deserted by her Frenchmen and Mark Howard will not come to heel."

"And he will never do so," said Dominic with satisfaction. "At least I nipped that little affair in the bud! As for her French friends,, they should be back shortly. But pray excuse me now. Continue to look forlorn, my darling we will talk at length later." And, regardless of his grandmother's presence, he kissed her passionately and went hastily from the room before she could protest at such rag manners.

The Dowager rose and, laying a gentle hand on Jane's shoulder said, "Now you may be happy, my dear, but remember not to look it!" Jane followed her to the drawing room composing her face to the required look of resignation while her heart sang a paean of joy.

Lisette, strolling in the Park with two of the young bloods who were competing for her favours, was bored and looked it, but when a curricle drew up beside them she saw the driver her face lit up.

"Dominic! Wicked one! You have been gone this age!"

Dominic acknowledged the two sprigs of fashion with an inclination of his head and replied, as he stretched down his hand to help her into the curricle, "I was delayed, but as you see, have come immediately to present my excuses."

He touched up his horses and they moved off, leaving the two young men affronted by such cavalier treatment, vying with each other in promises to make Delamere answer for such an affront, knowing full well how hollow were such protestations. They had not the hardihood or skill to make their pledges good.

Lisette was bubbling over with high spirits and gave voice to her most urgent question. "Did you bring my perfume?" and at his nod, asked perfunctorily, "And was your mission successful? You were an unconscionable time about it."

"Yes, to both questions. The perfume is in that box beside you and I was delayed by a trifling sickness."

She hardly heard him but fell upon the beribboned box with cries of delight.

"I shall not open it here, but I shall wear the perfume tonight at Almack's. I am quite out of my usual sort. I shall see you there, I trust?"

"Certainly, I look forward to it as ever ("Liar!", he thought to himself). But how is this? Do not your French friends escort you and keep you supplied with scent? Surely they still have contacts in France?"

She shrugged, "As to that, I have not seen them this age. They have affairs, you know, looking after such refugees as escape from Napoleon. They keep quite a register of the émigrés," she prattled on.

"The devil they do!" thought Dominic, "I should like to get my hands on it!" Aloud he said, "I had not realised that they occupied themselves with anything other than wining, dining, racing and card-playing. They have a lodging in Mount Street, have they not?"

"Yes, but their funds are limited," Lisette was repeating parrot fashion the tales she had been instructed to put about by the Frenchmen. She went on, "They were only able to bring part of their wealth when they fled here and now and again they go on a reparing lease to a less fashionable lodging in Blackfriars until their friends manage to transfer some more of their funds – how I have never understood." Except for her final remark this was the story the men wished to publish to account for their frequent absences.

"Wise of them, no doubt", Dominic commented and brought his curricle to a halt at Lady Hapgood's door. "Can you alight by yourself, my dear? As you see I did not bring my groom hoping to have you entirely to myself!"

Flattered, Lisette replied, "Yes, I can manage. Do hand my package to me when I am safety down. I would not drop it for the world!'" She climbed nimbly down from the high vehicle and, taking her present from Dominic, waved a farewell as she trod up the steps calling, "Until tonight, my lord."

Dominic bowed assent and drove off smartly. In two minutes he had put Lisette from his mind and was working on a plan to find and abstract the register kept by the Frenchmen. They would certainly have been furious to know that Lisette had let slip that they kept such a document.

For her part Lisette was feeling well pleased. What had started out as a light flirtation with Dominic to further the ends of the Frenchmen and with, as a reward, the return of her vowels and a glittering future at the Napoleonic Court, had worked in reverse. Seeking to ensnare him she had fallen in love, giving him as much of her heart as she was capable of sparing from herself.

She was convinced that he returned her regard and had begun to dream of a future as the Countess of Delamere, with the added spice that her triumph would be at the expense of the despised Jane. When, occasionally, a tiny doubt entered her mind that Dominic, bound by convention, might feel obliged to honour his commitment to Jane, she quickly changed the programme for her future to that she had formerly planned with Lucian. She was sure that Dominic, unlike Lucian, would be faithful to his mistress and, if their affair ended, would provide generously for her future. To be sure, to be his mistress was but a farthing dip to the candle of being his Countess, and she determined to make a strong bid for the greater prize. But first, the Frenchmen, she must have her vowels.

She had not long to wait, they returned at the end of the week and she made sure to meet them during the usual fashionable morning stroll in the Park. They looked pleased with themselves and she asked, "Did your plans succeed?"

"A merveille! We achieved all and more than we hoped for, soon the perfidious English will be where they belong, beneath our heel!"

Lisette looked round in alarm at this outburst of Gallic fervour, but it had not been remarked and she demanded, "So now I want my reward – my vowels, if you please!"

"All in good time," replied Jacques, "We do not carry them with us, you know. Besides, when you collect them we must arrange for our return to France. Napoleon is sure to be successful in this next campaign and we shall share in his triumph."

Lisette was about to announce that her plans had changed – she no longer wished to return to France – but a warning voice stopped her. First she must get back her vowels and, she hoped, some monetary reward. Self-interest and greed urged her to play for time.

"Very well," she pouted, "But I shall not wait long! Remember I can make things awkward for you if you try to go back on your promise!" and with that parting shot she walked on to join a group of friends.

The Frenchmen exchanged glances. "She is becoming dangerous, she will have to be dealt with. Nothing must interfere for the next week or so until we have safeguarded our agents and made sure of our own escape," said Raoul, as he exchanged polite greetings with acquaintances.

"Yes," agreed Jacques, "We must put off returning her vowels, they are the only hold we have over her here. But when all is ready she will accompany us will-nilly to France. There we can deal with her at our leisure and with no brou-ha-ha. It would be dangerous to leave her behind," and the two strolled on, the picture of men about town with nothing on their minds except, perhaps, the latest sartorial extravagance.

CHAPTER 25

Dominic had hurried off to put in hand enquiries into the Mount Street and Blackfriars' lodgings of the Frenchmen. Somehow the register they kept must be discovered – it was obviously the key to all the French agents in England. He was hopeful of gaining more precise information from Lisette and at Almack's attached himself to her as soon as she appeared.

Lisette looked breathtakingly lovely in blue gauze spangled with silver stars and with a silver ribbon threaded through her curls. She was wearing Dominic's perfume and was sure that tonight would see her triumphant. She meant to make Dominic declare himself and to that end enticed him into one of the many anti-rooms. The fact that he was a willing victim encouraged her in her fond belief, while his one aim was to extract the last iota of information she might possess.

The tête-à-tête began smoothly enough. Lisette held out her wrist and said, "Your perfume is delicious, do but breathe it, my lord."

She expected his caress to begin at her wrist and move up her arm to her breast – she was accustomed to allowing such liberties, and was dismayed when Dominic merely dropped a cursory kiss on her hand and said, "I am no connoisseur, I am afraid, all perfume smells alike to me. Perhaps your French friends have more expertise." He hope that she would follow his lead but, to his dismay, she abandoned her art of gently dalliance, cast herself on his chest and, putting her arms round his neck, whispered, "Do not seek to disguise your feelings, my love. Now that you have returned to me you may be sure that there is nothing to hinder you from making me yours! A runaway marriage would be but a nine days wonder and put an end to your foolish engagement to dreary Jane. I have never understood how she could have entrapped you – you must long to be free." She spoke confidently, his amorous attentions over the last weeks had ministered to her self-conceit as had his immediate return to her side after his recent absence.

Dominic had been so dumbfounded by this onslaught that he had made no attempt to stop her outburst, but now he tore her arms from his neck and thrust her roughly from him, exclaiming, "Are you mad?"

She could not believe that she was rejected and said, "No, my darling, only so in love that I cannot live without you!" She hesitated, trying to understand his withdrawal, then went on, "But, Dominic, if our marriage is not possible – if your marriage to Jane must stand – we can still continue our affair – such arrangements are quite accepted in the polite world."

The need to extract more information from Lisette vanished in the wave of repulsion that swept over him. He spoke between his teeth, "But not by me! What! To lie with you – you who are not fit to tie your cousin's shoe! The thought disgusts me! I can no longer breathe the same air!" and he left her standing aghast at the storm she had raised

Dominic had just sufficient self-control left to assume a composure he was far from feeling and managed to play his part for the rest of the evening without giving rise to comment. As soon as he reached home, however, he excused himself and went to his room.

"Tired out, I should think," said the Dowager. "Burning the candle at both ends and he is still not completely recovered from his indisposition."

Jane looked troubled, she was aware, in spite of his iron control, that Dominic was deeply disturbed, but she hoped that a good night's sleep would restore him.

Dominic, by this time feeling guilty when he thought over the means by which he had obtained information from Lisette, confounded John by demanding a bath immediately. He could not wait to wash away all traces of her and flung his clothes at his man and told him to burn them.

Only when he was in his night-shirt did he consider ruefully how intemperate had been his behaviour and made his peace with John by saying, "These women at Almack's drench themselves with scent – it make me sick!" He had only one more duty for John – to put a note under Miss Gascoigne's door, and then dismissing him, Dominic climbed thankfully into bed so emotionally exhausted that he fell asleep as soon as his head was on the pillow.

The note made an appointment with Jane for breakfast the next morning. The Dowager and Althea always breakfasted in bed and Jane and Dominic were alone saying that they would serve themselves.

Dominic took the opportunity to tell her more of his mission and ended with a bowdlerised version of the tête-à-tête with Lisette, stressing the information about the register and the Blackfriars' lodging already gained from his earlier meeting with her in the Park.

"Perhaps I was hasty in breaking off relations with her," (he did not reveal the provocation he had had), "But I think she knows very little more of importance and I was glad to end the connection. I must set Bow Street the task of discovering the Blackfriars' address and the Horse Guards to keep a close eye on the Frenchmen."

"How will you be able to secure the register, do you think and for what purpose?" enquired Jane. She felt thankful that the affair with Lisette was ended, but shuddered to realise in what danger Dominic had been on his recent journeys, although he had given a strictly edited account of his adventures.

"I am hoping to be able to search the rooms in Mount Street myself. It seems most likely that they keep the lists there, not in Blackfriars. Mark Howard will keep cave for me while the Frenchmen are at some Royalist function. Once we have a sight of the register we can prepare a substitute and exchange it for the genuine one – a tit-for-tat, you see – that's what they did with the plans I carried. We need to know who are the agents so that we may round them up.

"I can understand that, but why bother with a substitution?" she enquired.

A precaution in case they slip through our fingers – it will further confuse the French to have to work to a false list of agents in England."

"I see – will it be soon, your visit to Mount Street?" asked Jane, resigned to the fact that, until the 'loose ends' as Dominic had called them, were tied up she could not feel at ease about his safety.

"Tomorrow night. I have arranged for them to receive an invitation to a reception Castlereagh is giving for some distinguished Royalists – it is hoped that the Regent will be present, and two nights after that they will hardly dare to refuse to attend a soirée given by the Duc de Berri – they cannot afford not to be seen as fervent Royalists!"

"So that you will exchange the false register with the real one on that evening?"

"Yes – I have a feeling that time is of the essence. There are signs that they are making ready to leave the country, but of course, they will be arrested. And now, my love, I must tear myself away and send a note to Mark Howard. Be of good cheer, my darling, soon we will be able to put all this behind us." He gave her a quick embrace as he spoke and left her with a mock salute and Jane got ready for a morning walk in the Park with Althea which was to have unexpected consequences.

CHAPTER 26

Lisette's face was no longer beautiful when Dominic stormed out of her presence, it was convulsed with fury. For several moments she was consumed by hatred and despair and only the lack of an audience and her strong sense of self-preservation saved her from indulging in a bout of hysteria.

Fortunately no-one came into the ante-room and she was able to gain sufficient control of herself to play her part, like Dominic, for the rest of the evening.

In her room that night, she at last faced the collapse of her house of cards and was very glad that she had not told the Frenchmen that she no longer wished to go with them to France – it began to seem that that was to be the best future open to her – but was it? There festered at the back of her mind a soul-destroying sense of resentment against Jane, whom she saw as the author of all her troubles.

How to make her detestable cousin pay? She had failed in her bid to become Countess Delamere and triumph over Jane, and she now face the fact that there was little she could do further to harm her rival. But she could use her! She pondered – if she could persuade Jane that she, Lisette, was more sinned against than sinning, she thought, contemptuously, that her cousin would be fool enough to come to her aid and she would then attach herself to the future Countess and so cause the Earl as much embarrassment as possible. If she succeeded she could well abandon the Frenchmen and at last achieve a successful marriage in England. On this happy note she went to bed, unaware that Jane was doubly armed against her with the memory of the talk overheard in the pavilion at Cleeve to add to the misery of Dominic's apparent defection.

In the morning Lisette joined the promenade in the Park and soon sighted her quarry strolling with Lady Althea. She manoeuvred the group she was with until they came face to face with Jane and her companion. It was impossible, without rudeness, to avoid introductions and Jane soon found herself walking with Lisette behind Althea and their new acquaintances.

Listette said softly, "Jane, I must talk to you – can we fall behind a little?"

"I cannot imagine that you have anything of interest to say to me," replied Jane coldly.

"Only to apologise," said Lisette. "I have caused you some pain, I think, but, indeed, what was I to do when so handsome and charming a man as Dominic paid me such attention – I could not resist!"

Jane was about to make an angry retort when it struck her that Lisette had some justice on her side. Her cousin did not know Dominic's reason for courting her and who should know better than Jane how attractive and alluring he could be.

She answered discouragingly, "To be sure he is an attractive man, but he is pledged to me and that should have given you pause!"

"I know I was at fault and most sincerely beg your pardon," Listette answered placatingly. She wondered that the words did not stick in her throat – to humble herself to Jane – it was past bearing! However, she kept her goal in sight, "But Jane, I am so worried. Will you keep Cleeve when you are married?"

"I am not sure," replied Jane, "It does not, however, concern you.

"Oh, yes it does! It is my home, and if, when you are Lady Delamere your husband insists that you cease to pay my allowance, what will become of me?" She managed a tiny break in her voice.

Jane longed above everything to end the conversation. To be in close proximity with her cousin revolted her, but although she mistrusted Lisette, she acknowledged to herself that the future must look bleak to her.

"I can se that you have cause for concern, but I assure you that provision will be made, more I am not prepared to say now."

Lisette's rage nearly choked her – she wanted a definite promise and a named sum but realised that she had gone as far as she dared at a first approach, and replied with insincere gratitude, "Oh, thank you, Jane! I knew you would be generous and put my mind at rest." And while she indulged in a little artistic by-play with her handkerchief, Jane hurried to catch up with Althea and say, "I am sorry to take you away, but we shall be late for our appointment."

Unaware that they had an appointment, Althea was quite glad to leave the group which she found boring and, as the two girls made their way to the Park gates, Jane explained that she wanted to avoid continuing with Lisette.

"I understand," said Althea, "<u>Anyone</u> would make an excuse to leave Lisette!"

After the meeting in the Park Jane found, to her irritation, that she seemed constantly to find herself in Lisette's company but, short of giving her a public rebuff, she could do little about it.

Meanwhile Dominic had not been idle. He and Mark Howard made their way to the small house in Mount Street and, leaving Mark outside, Dominic opened the door with the key that John had abstracted from Henri the Frenchmen's valet whom he made his drinking partner at the near-by Inn frequented by the valet when his masters were out. Henri had not the head for English strong ale chased by Hollands gin and was soon absorbed in a fuddled way in shove ha'penny, a game which had caught his fancy and which he was determined to master.

A lamp had been left burning in the sitting room and Dominic went to the small desk, and, finding it unlocked, was not surprised when he failed to discover the register. The only other places in which it might be hidden were the bookshelves on each side for the fire-place. Failing them he must look in the bedrooms.

He made himself take his time. He found the work distasteful and would have liked to hurry to get it over. The task could have been given to a Bow Street man, but Dominic was not confident that a poorly educated constable would recognise a document written in French and he felt sure that there was no room for error so he had undertaken the matter himself.

Before he started on the bookshelves he went to the window and drew aside the curtain. All was quiet. Mark Howard was passing slowly along the street, turning after a few yards as if waiting for someone. Satisfied that he would get warning should the Frenchmen return unexpectedly, Dominic started on the bookshelves. He grew steadily more discouraged and, having dealt with one of them, began on the second with rapidly dwindling hopes.

It was not until he reached the lowest shelf on floor level that he found what he sought. The sheets of paper were secured at each end by strips of court plaster on the underside of the shelf immediately above the lowest one and he would have missed them had he not caught the edge of one as he withdrew a large volume of sermons.

For a moment or two he sat back on his heels while his heart and breathing steadied – he had not known how tense he had been. By lighting a taper from the lamp and lying down on the floor he managed to see how the papers were secured and then blew out the taper and sat up to consider how he might have a sight of them. He would need a careful look so that a replica could be prepared sufficiently close a copy to fool the Frenchmen should they take a look at the list before they began their final preparations to flee the country.

As far as he could see there were some five or six sheets and Dominic decided on a bold stroke. He would abstract one sheet from the middle which would serve as a model for the forgery and risk its absence being noticed before the substitution could be made.

He placed the lamp on the floor and with the utmost care, working while lying flat on his stomach, he eased the tape away from one end of the papers and with his finger nails managed to tease out one of them.

Very gradually he drew it out, careful not to disturb the rest. He replaced the plaster hoping that it would still adhere closely and reminded himself to bring fresh plaster when the false papers were substituted. He was almost sure there were five sheets to the register and thought, in any case, that five-forged papers would be enough.

He resisted the desire to examine the sheet he held and put it carefully in his inside pocket. Then he replaced the books he had taken out and, putting the lamp back on the table, looked round to see that there were no traces of his search.

He joined Mark in the street and gave him the key to pass on to John who could be relied upon to restore it to the befuddled Henri.

Dominic took his prize straight to the Horse Guards and told the expert forger who was waiting that five sheets would be enough for the substitution. Then, more weary than he would have thought possible, he made his way home. He was later joined by Mark and, over a restorative glass of wine they agreed that life of crime was not for them – it was too wearing to be attractive.

For a while the most noteworthy happening was the arrival in town of Sir Roderick Shadwell, Bart. He was young and rich and Lisette made a dead set at him, but so subtly that he was unaware of it and thought he was the pursuer not the pursued.

Jane was relieved. Lisette's preoccupation with the Baronet meant that she herself was less in her cousin's company.

Meanwhile, Dominic was elated – the papers had been successfully substituted and the matter of rounding up the agents listed in the genuine register was going on steadily but very quietly so that Messieurs Raoul and Jacques were not alerted. Dominic was not aware but would have been gratified to know that he had already given the Frenchmen a shock.

He had been dancing with Jane at Lady Hapgood's ball while Lisette was greeting the two Comtes at the ballroom door. She had not reported her break with Dominic so they had no reason to suspect his motives in conducting an affair with her. Tonight they, both at the same moment, caught sight of Dominic and spoke together.

"Sapristi!" – Raoul

"Mon Dieu! Il n'est pas mort!" – Jacques

Startled at their vehemence, Lisette asked ungrammatically, "Who is not dead?"

"Milord Delamere – we were told he had been dealt with in Calais!" replied Jacques angrily.

"Taisez-vous!" hissed Raoul. "It seems that rumour lied!" and he turned smiling to Lisette and swept her into the dance, leaving Jacques looking thunderous.

CHAPTER 27

Dominic gave Jane the latest news of the French affair. It seemed that one of the last of the agents arrested, when questioned and given a promise of leniency, revealed that he was due to take over the Blackfriars' house the next day while the two leaders made their escape by river to Greenwich where a boat awaited them. The watch on the jetty near the Frenchmen's house had been doubled as a precaution and the arrangements finalised to arrest the two men in Blackfriars before they had a chance to embark. "It will cause less stir than to apprehend them in Mount Street," he explained. Dominic proposed to spend the next day at the Horse Guards to hear of the arrest and to carry out his final duty.

"What is that?" asked Jane.

"To hand in my papers! I have had my fill of dirty work – besides I now have more important business to attend to!" and he took Jane in his arms. "Can you not guess, my love?"

She could, but wanted him to tell her. "How should I?" she replied teasingly.

"Because," he punctuated his remarks with kisses, "You are my future business,, you and our children, as you very well know!" With a final kiss he released her. "I shall not see you until tomorrow evening – to bring you the good news!"

"I shall wait at home for you, we have no evening engagement for once. Althea and I are in a party to Somerset House in the morning to see Sir Thomas Lawrence's latest portrait of the Regent – don't you wish you could escort us?" She laughed, knowing his opinion of the fashionable painter.

"No, I do not! I never thought to say it but I had rather face my Colonel than a likeness of His Royal Highness by that dauber!"

"Until tomorrow night then, my darling," said Jane. "I look forward to our meeting."

"So do I! So do I – passionately," replied Dominic blowing a kiss as he left.

Neither knew that their confidence was badly misplaced. True, they would meet the next day but in vastly different and dangerous circumstances from those they envisaged.

Jane spent the next morning, including the boring visit to Somerset House, in such a glow of happiness that it was a wonder that even her newly polished social sense carried her through without arousing comment.

In all her life she had never experienced such heart-warming joy – even more satisfying than the delirious ecstasy of Dominic's first avowal of love.

At the exhibition she saw Lisette studying the pictures – escorted by the Baronet and, in her present state of being in charity with all the world, wished her cousin every success in her pursuit of a wealthy husband.

Lisette and Shadwell were immediately in front of Jane when they were leaving and she saw the Baronet restore Lisette's reticule when she dropped it, but he failed to notice a paper, which had fallen from it. Jane picked it up and, with a feeling of deja-vu, saw that it was in French. As with Dominic's note in the garden she had read it almost before she realised. It said, 'Blackfriars – apres-midi-aujourd-hui, sans faute.'

Jane did not pause to consider the implications of the message but hurried forward to restore the note to Lisette. In the small crowd emerging from the exhibition she was sufficiently delayed so that she was only in time to see Shadwell's curricle with Lisette on board leaving at a sharp trot.

By the time she and Althea had reached Delamere House she had had time to take in the full import of the message to her cousin. Today the Frenchmen were to be arrested at Blackfriars! If Lisette were to call there she would inevitably be implicated in the Counts' treachery. It was now well past eleven o'clock – no time to send a message to Dominic – he might not yet be at the Horse Guards.

As the carriage drew up she made up her mind and turning to Althea said as convincingly as she could, "Oh, how vexing! I have forgotten to call for Aunt's ribbons – do you go in and I will get them immediately. I shall not be long."

Althea made no demur and alighted from the carriage. She did not hear Jane's direction to the coachman not to Carisonde's but to Hapgood House where, if she could not find Lisette, she could leave a message and hope that it would reach her in time.

She scribbled on a leaf from the tablet in her reticule, 'Imperative I see you before you leave for Blackfrairs, I will wait at Delamere House. Jane.' She could see from the carriage the shake of the butler's head as the groom handed over the note.

"The butler says Ma'am, that Miss Duclos is not at home, so I left the note."

"Thank you Brown," and to the coachman, "Home then, Jackson." Then, as the carriage began to move she called out sharply, "Stop!"

A guest of wind had blown back the hood of a modestly dressed woman who had mounted the steps from the area of Hapgood House and was walking quickly towards a hackney waiting some little way down the street. It was Lisette!

Lisette did not stop and reaching the hackney was almost inside when Jane came up and laid a firm hand on her arm, but her cousin pulled away and Jane, in her anxiety, followed her into the cab.

The coachman and groom were later to say to an angry Dominic, "But, your lordship, 'Ow was we to stop Miss Gascoigne? She was in and away before we rightly knew what was up. We followed as best we could but when we got to Fleet Street and the 'ackney turned off, the roads got narrower and narrower and we was forced to stop. I did send Brown to follow the 'ackney, but 'he lost it – 'he couldn't keep up, so we came 'ome." Jackson looked so distressed that Dominic curbed his anger and dismissed them saying, "I can see you did your best, Jackson. You lost them near Backfriars then?"

"Yes, your lordship," replied the groom, "Near the river."

When the two men had gone Dominic called for his horse with such a grim look on his face that even John forbore to speak but mounted and followed silently.

It was impossible to make good time through the crowded streets and they were barely half-way to their destination when they were hailed by a man travelling in the opposite direction.

"My lord – my lord, thank God I've met you," and he turned his mount to ride beside them.

"Well, man, what is it?" snapped Dominic. "We are in haste!"

The Bow Street man was too upset to be formal. "We've lost them – they've dodged us!"

Dominic, his mind on his beloved, seemed not to hear him. The man went on, "Sir, my lord, it's no use going to Blackfriars – the Frenchies have tricked us!"

This did penetrate and Dominic pulled up. The three horsemen formed an island round which people intent on their own concerns eddied and jostled.

Glad to have gained his lordship's attention the man went on, "I was riding back for further orders but your lordship will know what to do."

"I have other business," replied Dominic. "If they've escaped you, they'll make for Greenwich. Get the men at Blackfriars there to the Sea Hawk – Captain Willoughby is in charge and is waiting for the Frenchmen should they elude us at Blackfriars. You can explain your negligence later."

"Yes, my lord." The man gathered up his reins, "We don't know for sure but it may be that the two men who have taken a boat down river with their women are the two we're after."

Dominic, who had started off ahead of the man, pulled his horse up abruptly. "Their women! You had better explain yourself. Let us get out of this," and he turned into the courtyard of an Inn nearby. John and the man, Sergeant Bowles, followed him and they dismounted. Dominic's whole desire was to reach Blackfrairs but he had sufficient sanity left to realise that Bowles' information might be to do with Elizabeth and Lisette.

He led the way into the Inn and called for ale. The three sat down together and Dominic said, "Now tell me, with no excuses and no trimming, just what had happened.

Bowles obeyed. "It's like this, my lord, we was watching the house and our look-out reported that two men who matched the description of the Frenchies was coming. They was on foot and shabbily dressed – not like their usual, and they'd stopped to talk to two women," he paused and took a good gulp of ale.

"Yes, yes, go on," urged Dominic.

"One woman was shabby like them but the other was a fashion plate," continued Bowles.

"Oh, my God," exclaimed Dominic springing to his feet as if to hurry away.

John intervened, "My lord, wait, he says they lost them – we'd better hear everything."

Dominic looked at him as at a stranger. "My lord," said John urgently, "Please listen."

Dominic sank down again and John nodded to the sergeant who went on, "The four of them went into the house and we waited for the word to go in and take the Frenchies, but when we did, they wasn't there."

"What!" thundered Dominic, "They'd gone by the back door! You blundering fools! Was no watch kept there? And what of the ladies?"

"They wasn't there neither – and there's no back door – the whole street's back to back houses and we searched but there's no way through to the house in the rear. Then one of the lookouts came pelting in, the men and the women had taken a boat some way off down the street – there's passages through to the river and they were away down the river, rowing. We found a way through about six houses – a regular thieves run …. " Bowles was left in mid-sentences with his tankard half way to his mouth as Dominic and John ran to their horses and were off, clearing a way like madmen through the narrow crooked streets.

"Greenwich," gasped Dominic. "We'll be quicker riding," and saved his breath as they pounded on.

Dominic had good cause for anxiety. Having followed Lisette into the hackney Jane had stilled her cousin's protest.

"Listen, Lisette, you must not go to Blackfrairs! Tell the man to turn round!"

"I will do no such thing," snapped Lisette. "My visit is no concern of yours! I go to meet friends. In any case, how did you know …."

"I read this note," interrupted Jane, handing it over. "You dropped it from your reticule. I beg you, Lisette, to turn back!"

174

"Why should I? I know Blackfriars is not a fashionable quarter, that is why I have dressed like this. It is you who should turn back – your dress is most unsuitable for this place."

Jane looked about her, Lisette was right. Already they were in Fleet Street and could see the dome of St Paul's had either of them taken real note of their surroundings. However, both were pre-occupied, Lisette with the problem of how to get rid of her cousin and Jane with the dilemma of persuading Lisette to abandon her visit without betraying Dominic's confidence.

Before either had come to any conclusion the cab had turned right out of Fleet Street and was moving deeper into mean streets which grew more and more sordid and narrow. Then, without a command from his passengers the driver brought his cab to a halt and said, "This is as far as I goes – I can't turn me cab if I goes further."

"But I must get nearer the bridge," protested Lisette.

"Then you'll 'ave to walk! I ain't trusting meself down there!" and he pointed his whip at an even narrower street crowded with rough looking characters.

The men were ragged and brutish looking and the women slatternly with, in some cases, scraps of cheap finery to liven up their rags. The children who played in the gutter were most of them half-clad scarecrows with unchildlike eyes.

Jane shuddered at the sight and said to the driver, "But you will wait for us? Our business will not keep us long."

"Not me! I'll 'ave me money now and I'm off!" He snapped his whip at the crowd of children who were already surrounding his vehicle.

"Come back now, Lisette," begged Jane, "We must not be alone here.,"

"You go back. I never asked you to come! I must see my friends." On the only previous occasion that Lisette had been to Blackfriars she had had the escort of the Frenchmen. However, much as she was daunted by her surroundings desperation urged her to get back her vowels. She feared that, if her new-found Baronet should hear of her gambling she would lose him and she was determined to reach her goal.

175

Jane longed to retreat. Why should she undergo such a dreadful experience for Lisette, whom she disliked and who had always tried to harm her? Had not Dominic been involved she would probably have abandoned her cousin, but she could not forget that he had deliberately used Lisette for his own purposes and she felt in some measure responsible for she had condoned his action which she sorrowfully regarded as the one flaw in his otherwise sterling character. To her the end had never justified the means, while to him the safety of his country was paramount and sanctioned any action.

Still wrestling with her uncertainty Jane followed Lisette out of the hackney and, having been paid, the driver turned the vehicle with scant regard for the safety of the swarming children and made his rapid way back to the safety of the city. Too late, Jane thought that they should have refused to pay him until he had waited and driven them home.

Immediately their cab had disappeared the two girls were beset by the crowd of children and women begging and hurling insults and it might have gone badly with them had not Lisette suddenly called out, "Raoul, Jacques, a moi!"

Jane would not have recognised the dandified 'counts'. Their clothes were those of artisans and their faces and hands were grimy. This metamorphosis had taken place in Town. Two exquisites had called upon a compatriot and two workmen had left by the back door of the house and made their way on foot to Blackfrairs.

Lisette's call surprised them: they had thought to find her waiting at the house. They were late for their appointment with her having had to take evasive action in order to leave Mount Street unobserved. They had been aware for some time that the house was under surveillance, but did not know that their Blackfrairs bolt-hole was also watched, in such a district one or two more loiterers were unremarkable.

Without exchanging a word they made their way to Lisette, the last thing they wanted was attention to be drawn to them. To their amazement she was not alone and they recognised her companion. There was time for a quick, "We'll take them both," from Jacques, in French, before they reached Lisette and Jane.

They wasted no time in courtesies but each took the arm of one of the girls. "In here," and they urged them into the nearest hovel.

Jacques turned to Jane, "You cannot go about here dressed like this. Give me your hat!"

His peremptory tone offended Jane: in the brief time since she had recognised them she had realised that it was too late to save Lisette from embarrassment or worse so she replied stiffly, "I have no desire to remain here, M'sieur le Comte. If you will kindly escort me to where I may obtain a hackney …" she got no further.

With an oath, Jacques took the hat from her head and the reticule from her hand and called, "Ma!"

A slatternly old woman came out of the shadows and Jacques tossed the hat and bag to her.

"A cloak with a hood – quickly now!"

The old woman said nothing but snatched the things and went to rummage in a corner.

Lisette, still held by Raoul, was so annoyed and shocked that she never said a word.

Jane, outraged at such treatment, opened her mouth to scream and Jacques laid his grimy hand roughly over it.

"It would make nothing if you did scream, Miss Gascoigne, they would not need your cries here. However, we do not want a scene. Nod your head if you will keep quiet and I will take my hand away."

Jane felt sick – anything to remove his revolting hand. She nodded, and her lips were freed. Without her reticule she had no handkerchief to scrub them clean of his touch.

The old crone shuffled forward with a filthy cloak and Jacques flung it round Jane and pulled the hood well forward.

She took this to mean that they were to leave the hovel and she felt a gleam of hope knowing that Dominic's men must be all round. When they neared the Frenchmen's house she determined to call for help.

This hope was immediately dashed. Both the men drew knives whose thin blades glittered even in the dimness.

"In case you thought of making a fuss be sure we shall not hesitate to use these. To anyone watching you will appear drunk or ill and we shall support you." He and Raoul put an arm round each girl under their cloaks and Jane and Lisette felt the prick of the steel.

Lisette was almost fainting with terror. In spite of her knowledge of the ruthless character of the men, she had never thought that it would be turned against her and she stumbled out into the street fully needing Raoul's support.

Jane was rigid with disgust. She was frightened too but sustained by the knowledge that the men were to be apprehended and she put up no resistance when she was led out in the wake of Raoul and Lisette.

The short journey through the crowded, noisome streets was quite leisurely and seemed interminable to the two girls, but at last they reached the Frenchmen's house.

Here the tempo changed. Once inside the men acted swiftly. The girls were gagged, their hands tied and their cloaks and hoods drawn close.

As they worked Jacques said, "Did you think we would leave you behind? No, she," a nod of the head at Lisette, "Might talk, and you," as adjusted Jane's cloak, "May yet be useful as a hostage – in any case you will both provide a bit of sport!" and he laughed.

Then, to the girls' amazement, the men opened a cupboard to reveal a doorway. They urged the girls through and closed the cupboard and the door behind them. This manoeuvre was repeated several times, but by now both Jane and Lisette were too frightened and bewildered to count how many houses they passed through. No-one took the slightest notice of their passage and no-one spoke.

Jane's hopes of a speedy rescue died and she realised that she must rely on herself if she were to manage to escape; the chances seemed slight, the gag was stifling and her attempts to free her hands only made the tight cords cut deeper.

When they left the last house and emerged into the street, she had a wild idea of flinging herself to the ground and thus attracting attention whilst escaping Jacques' knife. She could not believe that no hand would be raised to help her, but, before she could carry out her plan, she was swept into Jacques' arms and carried across the street down a short evil smelling alley and on to a jetty where a boat waited with two men already at the oars.

"Got company, 'ave we?" laughed one.

Raoul, who had followed with Lisette, said, as the girls were passed down like so much cargo, "Can't leave the pretty birds to sing – beside they will pass the time!"

The Frenchmen jumped down into the boat and one of them said, "Almost wish we was going with you – we'd 'ave a bit of fun!"

Then they settled to their oars and began to hard pull against the tide slackening for the ebb.

There was no movement from Lisette, she seemed to have fainted, but Jane stared about her. Had her hands been free she would have pulled off her gag and appealed to the rowers, who, from their speech, were English and might have responded and helped them.

The afternoon wore on and the journey seemed endless. All the while Jane was thinking feverishly of how to take advantage of the moments when they would be transferred to a larger vessel – they could not row down the Thames forever - and it seemed unlikely that the Frenchmen would take to the land to travel to another port .... Then she remembered! Dominic had said that they had been informed that the Frenchmen had a ship awaiting them at Greenwich. Hope rose, she was sure that their captors would be prevented from sailing but her spirits sank again as she feared that she and Lisette would be used as hostages to bargain for the Frenchmen's liberty. Jane was balancing on this emotional seesaw as she and Lisette, who seemed to have recovered, huddled together in the chill wind which seemed always to blow over water.

Lisette, without Jane's knowledge of even a slight possibility of rescue, was sunk in hopeless misery. Her bitterness against her cousin increased. She attached no blame to herself for their predicament and was convinced that, without Jane, she would have been the cherished companion of the Frenchmen rather than their captive. She was sure that Jane's presence had caused them to believe that she, Lisette, had betrayed them and so they had taken reprisals. She was prepared, when once she was free of her gag, to convince them of her loyalty – let them do with Jane as they would, it would serve her meddlesome cousin right, but she, Lisette, was determined to save herself at any cost. The afternoon grew darker and colder as they made their slow but steady way to the Sea Hawk and the darkness was reflected in the spirits of the two girls.

CHAPTER 28

While Jane and Lisette were being carried down the Thames Dominic and John were galloping hard to be at Greenwich before them. Once over the bridge at Blackfrairs the sight of the Cathedral at Southwark struck a note of caution through the turmoil of anxiety that possessed Dominic and he steadied his horse and called to John.

"We must husband our mounts or they will founder before we reach Greenwich and we have no time to change horses."

From then on their pace became less headlong and Bermondsey and Deptford were traversed at the gallop, but at a pace the horses could maintain. With every beat of the hooves Dominic sent up a wordless prayer, "Oh, God – let us be in time – God guard my darling!" while the cooler part of his brain made and discarded plan after plan as to how to rescue his beloved.

They reached the Naval headquarters at Greenwich as the light was failing and Dominic enquired anxiously for Captain Willoughby. He was directed to the Custom's wharf and found, not Captain Willoughby, but a flustered Lieutenant who said, "I am sorry, Sir, but you have missed the Captain. He left for the Sea Hawk over an hour ago to be ready for the arrival of the enemy agents."

"Where is the Sea Hawk?" asked Dominic.

"This side of mid-stream – you can see her riding lights," and he pointed to where a three masted barque lay with her sails half-furled and riding lights lit.

"Then I must follow Captain Willoughby – pray order a boat," said Dominic.

The young Lieutenant reddened and hesitated. "I am sorry, Sir, but I have no orders …"

"You have mine!" snapped Dominic, "Major Templeton! And you will have the goodness to obey them!" He was beside himself with anxiety, every moment's delay fretted him almost beyond endurance, and this obstruction by a junior officer exasperated him.

The Lieutenant stiffened to attention, "Immediately, Sir," he replied, glad to delegate the responsibility for flouting Captain

Willoughby's order that there should be no communication with the enemy ship. He called an orderly and sent him to place a boat at the visitors' disposal.

Dominic thanked him and he and John were soon being rowed over the darkening water.

John ventured to speak reassuringly to his master. "The ladies are sure to be safe, Sir. After all our men hold the ship."

"That's as maybe," replied Dominic curtly, "But I cannot bear to entrust their safety to any other hands but my own. If anything went wrong ......" he could not go on. He could not dismiss from his mind the knowledge that in some measure his activities had placed Lisette and Elizabeth in danger.

As Dominic paused one of the men said under his breath, "Quiet, please Sir. Sound carries over water and we've orders to make no noise."

So it was in silence that they approached the Sea Hawk. Riding lights were now tossing gently on other vessels anchored in the river, but theirs seemed to be the only boat moving in the slight mist which was drifting over the water. In order not to raise the alarm the rowers, employed by Customs, wore no uniforms and looked liked ordinary longshore-men. When they reached the boarding ladder hanging from the rail of the Sea Hawk they did not hail her. Shipping their oars the men held the board steady as Dominic, followed by John, began to climb.

No sooner had he set foot on deck than he was roughly seized and, before he could protest, was hustled down to the saloon and thrust inside.

"The first of them, Sir," said one of his captors, "The other's being brought down now."

Dominic, held by a man on either side, found his voice. "Captain Willoughby, I presume?" addressing a portly, red-faced man in uniform. He tried to release himself without success as John was pushed into the saloon and held captive beside him.

"I am not aware that you have been given leave to address me." As Dominic made to speak he held up a minatory hand, "Nor how you know my name. I have to tell you that you are both under arrest and will remain in irons on board until you can be taken ashore in the morning and formally charged. Take them away!" he snapped and turned his back and sat down.

Dominic's wrath, the greater for having been suppressed, found voice as he violently resisted being dragged from the saloon.

"Sir," he ground out, "You are singularly uninformed! I am Delamere – Major Templeton of the Hussars – and I am here to .."

He got no further. "A likely tale," sneered Willoughby." You French plotters have a tale ready for any occasion! My orders were that no other boat except that carrying you Frenchmen, should approach this ship which is in our hands. Remove them!" he roared.

Dominic and John were putting up strong resistance but the odds were against them, when the door at the other end of the saloon opened and a tall young man in undressed Hussar uniform came in. He took one look at the struggling group and cried, "What the devil is gong on? Dominic! What on earth are you doing here?"

"Thank God said Dominic breathlessly. "Watty, tell these fools to stop man handling me!"

Lieutenant Jack Watkins grinned and said, "I don't know what you've been up to but," to the men, Let his lordship go, you numskulls – and his man!"

The men look uncertainly at Captain Willboughby, who had gone first red then white. He turned to the Lieutenant, "You know these men, Lieutenant Watkins?"

"I've served with the Earl of Delamere – Viscount Templeton he was then – for all of four years. Yes, Sir, I know him very well indeed."

The Captain said grudgingly to the men, "Then by all means, release them. Dismiss! Back on deck and be more careful whom you apprehend!"

"Yes, Sir," replied the sergeant in charge, resentfully, and got himself and his fellows quickly through the door.

Dominic, straightening his disordered clothing, turned to the Lieutenant. "Thanks Watty," and then at his stateliest, "And now, I will accept an apology from you, Captain Willoughby.!"

Willoughby swallowed, "Sir, you must see it from my point of view. You came unannounced – there were two of you, just as we had been led to expect – but yes, I apologise," he got out ungraciously.

"Good," replied Dominic, "Then we will consider the matter closed." Privately he agreed that there was something to be said for the Captain but he had taken a dislike to the pompous fool and was not going to admit it. "Am I to understand that you are not aware that the Frenchmen have kidnapped two ladies, my fiancée and her cousin, with some idea, I suppose, of holding them hostage in order to bargain for their freedom?" He was not about to betray Lisette's treachery. "Of course, they cannot know that their ship is in our hands and I am here to make sure that the ladies are rescued before the villains try to use them."

"The devils," exclaimed Watkins, "To think of Miss Gascoigne in their clutches!"

"I am trying to find it <u>un</u>thinkable Watty," said Dominic. "Had we not better go on deck to be ready for the rogues?"

The self-important Willoughby, having recovered from his moment of humiliation, rose, "Sir I have the matter in hand – my dispositions are made. I must ask you not to interfere!"

"Ask away," said Dominic going to the door. "<u>Your</u> interference so far has only served to hinder me – mine may be more effective!" and he left the saloon followed by John.

The Captain, enraged, would have followed but Watkins detained him.

"I'd let him have his head, Sir. He's a good man in a fix, I'd back him anywhere. If he's a bit sharp in his manner it's because he must be almost out of his mind with anxiety about his fiancée and her cousin."

As Willoughby made no response but continued to mount to the deck the Lieutenant ventured to put a restraining hand on his arm, "With respect, Sir, perhaps I should remind you that we should not show ourselves in uniform until we have the devils caught."

With a bad grace the Captain stayed deep in the shadow of the doorway. He did not, however, leave the matter without one graceless remark.

"Well, if this goes wrong, it will be your head on a charger!"

Watkins smiled, but forbore to point out that, military discipline being what it was, his Captain, as holding the higher rank, would have to shoulder the blame.

On deck Dominic and John joined the silent watchers in the shadows and waited. Thought was suspended and Dominic was aware only of his fears and his love as the sky grew darker and no boat came.

A short distance up river Jacques turned to Raoul, "We had better free their hands – they have to climb to board the vessel."

"And remove the gags if they will promise to keep silent – they will climb better so," replied Raoul.

"You heard?" Jacques asked the two girls – "Nod if you agree not to call out."

Even in her extremity Jane felt outraged that she and her cousin should be discussed as if they were so much cargo, but she would agree to anything to get rid of the stifling gag, so she nodded.

Lisette seemed to be only semi-conscious and did not respond. However, her assent was taken for granted and the men cut the cords round the girls' wrists and removed the suffocating gags.

The breath of fresh air gave new life to Jane and she began to rub her hands and flex her fingers and then, as Lisette made no move, began to do the same for her. Jane had no intention of keeping a promise given under duress and intended to cry out as soon as they had boarded the Sea Hawk. Of the four passengers in the boat she was the only one who knew that there would be friends on board the ship. She was afraid of Jacques' knife but hoped in the confusion of boarding to be able to elude it.

Under her ministrations Lisette began to recover and she said in a husky whisper, which was all either girl could manage after the brutal gags, "Are we not there yet? Raoul, I am on your side – my cousin is your enemy!"

"Tais-toi!" hissed Raoul. "Do you want the gag again?" and he brandished the cloth. It could not be seen in the gloom but his threatening gesture was unmistakable and Lisette subsided with a moan of fear.

One of the rowers spoke softly, "Sir, she is just ahead – shall I hail her."

"Be silent!" growled Jacques. "There is no need, we are expected – the boarding ladder will be in place – see?"

As they rowed along the side of the ship they came upon the ladder and the rowers shipped their oars and steadied the boat at it foot.

Lisette, urged on by Raoul, was the first to climb. Only the threat to drop her overboard, conveyed in a penetrating whisper, made her struggle up the ladder. Raoul was close behind her and as soon as she stepped on deck disaster struck.

Captain Willoughby, elated at the sight of victory within his grasp, stepped out of concealment and called, "Take him, men!"

Immediately dark lanterns were opened and what appeared, after the gloom, to be a blinding light was focussed on Lisette and Raoul and the men surged forward.

There were two quick-witted men on board. Even as John was ejaculating, "The damned fool!" Dominic snapped, "Off with my boots – quick!" and John, accustomed to swift, unquestioning obedience in response to that tone, tugged off his master's riding boots.

Raoul, the other man trained to quick reaction, immediately swung Lisette in front of him with his dagger at her throat and called loudly, "Jacques – va-t'en – depeche-toi!"

Dominic was already racing to the stern as Jane began to climb. She tried to go on but Jacques, close behind her, wrench her away from the rungs and both tumbled back into the boat. There was some confusion and by the time the men had got their oars into the rowlocks and were pulling away, the marksmen on deck were only just ready, under orders from the ass Willoughby, to fire at a disappearing target, and their shots fell harmlessly.

John, in his fury of anxiety so far forgot himself as to shout at the idiotic Captain, "You fool! Miss Gascoigne is in that boat!" Luckily so great was the noise, the egregious Willoughby did not hear him but continued to shout contradictory orders.

John turned to Watkins and said earnestly, "Sir, we must lower a boat and go after his lordship."

"A boat?" asked the Lieutenant in amazement.

"Yes, Sir – he's gone overboard after them – and I can't swim.

"Good God! You're sure?"

"Yes, that's why he took off his boots. He'll be in the water by now – they'll go back upstream and he won't want to lose them – please, Sir, we should hurry!"

His earnestness carried conviction and the Lieutenant took one look at the Captain, in the group surrounding Raoul and Lisette, giving hysterical, contradictory orders, and decided to act on his own initiative.

He called two of the Custom's men who manned the boats and he and John climbed into a boat and were lowered into the water. They set off up stream in the slack water before the tide turned.

Jacques' boat was also making way with an extra passenger of whose presence they were ignorant.

Dominic had shed his coat as he ran to the stern of the Sea Hawk and took a racing dive into the Thames. He trod water until he saw the enemy boat, almost invisible except from his low vantage point, and with a few strong strokes managed to grasp a trailing mooring line.

In the boat Jacques had struck Jane to prevent her from jumping over the side and she was huddled half-conscious at his feet. The Frenchman was concerned with his own safety not hers – and proposed to keep her as a bargaining counter just so long as she might serve his purpose.

Dominic's one idea when he took to the water was to keep in touch with Elizabeth and take the first opportunity to rescue her. His greatest fear, in the few electric seconds following Willoughby's ill-timed command, was that Jacques, with Elizabeth at his mercy, should succeed in reaching some unknown hide-away from which it would be difficult to flush him out – if, indeed, they could discover him in time to save his captive.

His could only pray, as he grew colder in the chill water, that the men in the boat would not discover him and that his numbed hands could retain their grasp. He knew that he could not swim fast enough to keep up with the boat now the rowers had found their rhythm and he took a turn of the line round his right wrist to make sure that he did not fall adrift.

Above the light mist which mantled the water early stars pricked the darkening sky. The half-moon would not rise for an hour or two and Dominic could hope to remain undetected until the boat grounded, then he might be glad of help from the moon. For now he concentrated on keeping afloat and fighting the drowsy numbness which threatened to overcome him.

Once the rowers in Watkins' boat had settled to their oars he turned to John.

"This is a mad idea – why are you so sure they will go upstream against an ebb tide? They would make better progress going downstream with the water."

"They've got half an hour of slack water before the tide turns to the ebb and downstream would take them into the country – these are town rats with their bolt-holes in the stews – that's where they'll be making for."

"Surely, Delamere cannot expect to tackle them one man, unarmed, against three?" exclaimed Watkins.

"No, but he'll know where they've gone. Don't you see, Sir, if once we lose track of them we shan't be able to help Miss Gascoigne – that's why his lordship took off. He's got a head on his shoulders has his lordship," and John concentrated on trying to pick up a sight of his master in the wide waters.

Suddenly he whispered, "There, Sir, see?" His straining eyes had caught one flash of white as Dominic took a stroke to ease the strain on his weak arm. Watkins had missed the momentary gleam, but urged his rowers to increase their stroke.

"No, Sir, begging your pardon," said John. "They mustn't suspect that they are followed. Let us keep our distance," and the Lieutenant agreed. Then John, who seemed to be assuming command said, "I've got it, Sir. See those two barges?" and he pointed ahead to where, on the right, two East coast barges were anchored stem to stern, just clear of the mud now being uncovered by the tide just on the ebb.

"If we went up behind them we could get ahead of the Frenchmen's boat unbeknownst. We could go on keeping an eye on them from in front. They'd not guess we were interested in them!"

One of the rowers protested, "We can't keep this up against an ebb tide!"

"And neither can they," replied John impatiently – they must stop soon."

Watkins agreed to the manoeuvre which, although they could not have foreseen it, proved to be a costly mistake. When they emerged beyond the barges, strain their eyes as they would against water which grew lighter as a pale glow in the sky heralded a rising moon, no other moving boat could be seen. Dismayed, John exclaimed, still remembering to keep his voice low, "They must have gone ashore! We'll have to cast back."

After one more searching look Watkins nodded, "Back men, slowly."

The tired rowers thankfully turned the boat and, with an occasional stroke allowed themselves to be carried slowly back while John and Watkins scanned the bank for signs of the Frenchmen.

After his one, cautious stroke, Dominic, against the noise of the water in his ears, tried in vain to hear a low-voiced colloquy between Jacques and the rowers. Could he have done so he would have heard one man say, "It's just along 'ere."

"No it ain't, Ben, we passed it minutes back!"

"I lives 'ere don't I," replied Ben belligerently, "Shut your trap, Alf!" and they settled to their oars going more slowly against the turning ride as they scanned the bank.

Jacques ignored the dispute. He was trying to make up his mind whether to get rid of Jane or whether she would still be more use to him alive. In the event he was forced to come to a decision as Ben's low voice said triumphantly, "There! Told you so, didn't I? Now, when we gets there it's only to knock three one long and two short and give the password, "The devil's to pay and no pitch hot," and we're in!"

The boat, almost aground, turned in a few feet of water to a broken-down jetty. Jacques though quickly – he could not safely drown Jane in such shallow water – her body would soon be discovered and even in this deserted stretch a hue and cry would follow, not only endangering him but the people on whom he depended for help. No, he decided, he must take his hostage with him and dispose of her in safer circumstances. Fortunately she never knew on how slender a thread her fate hung for those few minutes.

Dominic, too, had to make a quick decision. As he felt the boat make for the bank he realised that, in the shallow water, the men in the boat could not fail to discover him. Quickly, he released his wrist from the rope and let himself sink below the surface of the water.

The men tied up and helped Jacques to lift Jane on to the jetty. While they were busy, Dominic took a few gentle strokes and managed to conceal himself among the rotting piles supporting the jetty. By now he was so exhausted that, even had the opportunity offered, he would have been unable to help Jane.

She was just able to walk supported by Jacques. Her dazed mind was filled with despair and she made no resistance as the small cortege set off, the men in single file in front along the muddy path. They had not gone far from the river when Ben, who was in the lead, said softly, "There you are – see? What did I tell you?", and he pointed to the only gleam of light to be seen in the tumbledown hovels ahead.

Jane never understood what happened next. Jacques' arm was withdrawn, he stumbled against Alf and both of them fell. Had she been capable of movement she might have made a bid for freedom. As it was she witnessed the murders without mercifully realising it.

Jacques' knife had been ready and it sank into Alf's neck as they fell and was quickly withdrawn. Ben turned back in alarm at the short cry the doomed man gave and bent over the body on the ground. Like a snake striking, Jacques' knife struck up under the ribs to the heart and, without a sound, Ben collapsed over Alf's body.

Jacques got to his feet and came to Jane. She was too numb with cold and fatigue to feel fear of the menacing figure with the bloodstained knife who approach her. In the few steps he took Jacques again considered dispassionately whether to add her body to the pile, but decided against it. Bodies of wharf rats were not uncommon in such a neighbourhood and would give rise to little, if any, investigation, but the body of what was obviously that of a gentlewoman in such a situation would cause a stir and draw attention to his escape route, so, for the second time, Jane was spared. Instead he wiped his stained knife and hands callously on Jane's cloak and took her arm in a bruising grip.

"You will say nothing! You have seen nothing! Tu comprends?"

Jane's dry mouth could produce no sound but she nodded.

"Bien! Allons-nous," and he led her towards the gleam of light.

CHAPTER 29

As soon as he heard them leave, Dominic, by now almost too numb with cold to move, clawed his way up the mud to what passed for dry land – in this case slightly firmer mud.

He found the path but, in spite of the slowly increasing light from the half-moon, failed to see the two bodies in time and stumbled over them. He remained half-couched for an immeasurable time, convulsed with horror, and sure that Elizabeth's corpse lay there. He forced himself at last to inspect the heap and was so overcome with relief at finding only the bodies of the two men that tears streamed down his face he was so thoroughly unmanned, but for moments only. The two who were ahead of him had now reached the streak of light. He was too far away to hear the rhythmic, soft knock and the password, but saw the slit widen and the two figures pass inside.

He was galvanised into action – Elizabeth was alive and to be rescued! With a lack of feeling which would, in other circumstances, have horrified him, he robbed Ben's body of his heavy jersey, fortunately in so dark a colour that the blood-stains and the small rent made by Jacques' knife were hidden.

Dominic stripped off his torn and soaking shirt and had sufficient wit to bundle it up and throw it far into the undergrowth. Although torn and muddy its whiteness and quality would have marked him out as an interloper in these parts. He pulled on the jersey and began to feel warmer. He took the woollen cap, too, and pulled it well down. Finally, with no more compunction, he rifled the pockets of both corpses and took Ben's knife and the small store of money that each carried.

Thus equipped – his feet in muddy and torn stockings would past muster, he thought – he moved slowly towards the light. It proved to come from what turned out to be a dilapidated but sizeable Inn, identified by the old sign of a withered bush hanging over the lintel. The light escaped round an ill-fitting but stout door which he was sure was barred. He did not knock, which was as well as he could not give the password. He could hear a babble of rough voices and the occasional snatch of music from a penny whistle. He began to move carefully round the building looking for an insecure window or door by which he could make a covert entry

His hands, stretched before him, did not protect his feet and he stubbed his toe agonisingly on a ridge of stout wood in his path. He stood still, stifling the groan that the sharp pain brought to his lips, and then bent to explore the obstruction. As he did so he was startled to hear voices coming from beneath him and was only just in time to slip back into the shadows when the trap door over which he had stumbled, was thrown back with a thud and a gruff voice said, "They'll be along in the wane of the moon – not long now – but I'm not waiting 'ere in this perishing cellar – leave it, Bert, and let's get back to the fire."

There was a dim glow as from a lantern outlining the trap and a second voice replied, "We might as well, I suppose, nobody'll come tonight – they all knows the Wolf'll be by – 'e'll need the tide to get up to Rother'ithe. They'll be on their way to Rye with this lot of wool and leather as quick as they can. Boney's wild for new boots and uniforms and I'll bet there's a good load of laces and brandy waiting to be exchanged at Rye!"

The voice grew far away and the light grew dim and Dominic heard a door shut.

He waited a while and then reminded himself that 'the Wolf' was due and he had better take advantage of this unexpected piece of good fortune to enter the under-belly of the Inn.

He felt his way cautiously through the trapdoor and found a short, crude set of steps leading to the floor of the low cellar. Straight ahead a very thin shaft of light outlined a door – from its position at the top of more steps. Bending his head under the low ceiling, Dominic made his way with care along a narrow path between what he could feel and smell were roof high stacks of bales of wool and hides.

He mounted the steps and, with the utmost caution felt round the door. He found a wooden latch and, under cover of a burst of sound from the room beyond, gently lifted it. He was overjoyed to find that the door was not secured and he was able to ease it open an inch or two.

He found he could just see a small part of what was obviously a large white-washed room with a smoke-blackened ceiling.

After the cold outside, and the chill of the cellar, the heat smote him like a blow. The attention of the men he could see sitting or standing round a table was fixed on something out of Dominic's view, but from the sound of the penny whistle and the clapping of hands and stamping of feel in time to the music, some kind of entertainment was going on. Taking advantage of this distraction, Dominic eased himself through the door and closed it silently behind him. He found himself at the side of a huge chimney breast and moving quietly past it he could see the whole of the room.

The focal point was the great fireplace. A scree swung over the roaring fire carried a large soup-kettle from which came delicious smells. A fat man, streaming with sweat, was ladling stew into bowls for the men waiting at the long table which served as a counter. They were given pewter spoons and large chunks of bread, but each man had his own knife, and wicked blades they looked. At the other end of the table were mounted large casks from which another man, the landlord by his superior dress, dispensed wine or ale into the pewter pots proffered by eager customers. Dominic looked at the tapster's face in the light from the many lamps hanging from the rafters and shuddered. It was not unhandsome but the mouth was a slit and the eyes reptilian – they shone like pieces of jet and with as much feeling.

Scattered over the room were stools and benches and tables – a rather larger one in the centre and on this a coarsely handsome girl with a crimson skirt and low-cut black bodice was dancing with a great display of bare legs and much lissom swaying of her lush figure. The tempo of the music quickened almost to a frenzy and Dominic, while the heightened attention was focussed on the dancer, moved casually from the shelter of the chimney breast to the nearest table and picked up an empty ale pot. He made play with it as if it still contained liquor and surveyed the room.

At last he saw Elizabeth. She was a few tables away and sat on a stool propping up her head with one hand while with the other she held her hood close around her face – where was Jacques? As his gaze searched the crowd Dominic saw his enemy coming from the counter with two bowls of stew and a large piece of bread tucked under his arm. He reached the table and put a bowl in front of Elizabeth, then seated himself and broke off some bread for her. She turned away her head but he spoke sharply to her and she picked up the spoon and began listlessly to eat while Jacques began to gulp the stew ravenously – little of the Count in his table manner now! He had soon emptied his bowl and went off to the counter for wine where he engaged the man serving in earnest conversation.

After a few minutes, the landlord, if that was who he was, beckoned a man who was passing tankards and bowls through a tub of water to take his place and took Jacques round the end of the table and out of sight.

Jacques had sent a long look at Elizabeth before disappearing, but clearly felt that she was in no state to make a bid for freedom in such company and he made no bones about leaving with the landlord.

Dominic could scarcely believe his good fortune. Much as he wanted to call Jacques to account, he wanted more to rescue Elizabeth. He drifted casually until he could slip into the seat left vacant by Jacques.

"Elizabeth," he felt her start, "For God's sake, make no move but listen."

The horror of two murders, sensed rather than seen in the cold gloom, had so numbed Elizabeth's senses that she had responded to Jacques' commands like an automaton. The warmth and food in the Inn had begun to restore feeling to her body and mind and with it the desolation of utter despair – the nightmare seemed to be unending – and then to hear Dominic's voice! It was a dream – but it went on!

"Respond to everything I do. Are you able to walk? Nod if you are."

His voice brought a conviction – it <u>was</u> Dominic – he was here! She nodded and then felt his arms go round her and he drew her to her feet. For a moment or two they stood clasped together. The attention of the rest of the company was focussed on the centre table where a drama was developing. Another woman had joined the dancer and was endeavouring, in spite of red-skirt's protests – to display her own charms and the two were coming to blows egged on by their audience.

Dominic's eyes scanned the end of the bar where Jacques and the landlord had disappeared. Mercifully, they were still absent and Dominic began to move apparently aimlessly toward the chimney breast, drawing Elizabeth with him. Once they were hidden from the rest of the room he began to move purposefully to the cellar door and, whispering, "There are steps," drew her through the doorway. He held her close while, silently, he closed and re-latched the door.

A very faint light from the setting moon came through the open trap and Dominic almost carried his companion down the steps then began to lead her to the hatch and freedom. Elizabeth obeyed his every move as implicitly as she had obeyed Jacques – but with what a difference! Her spirits rose with every step, then, suddenly, Dominic checked.

Elizabeth began to say, "What ....?" but Dominic put his hand over her mouth and listened. Somewhere outside the cellar there was movement and Dominic almost groaned aloud. It would be folly to emerge from the cellar into the arms of men whom he guessed to be the Wolf's gang of smugglers. He dared not go back into the Inn. By now Jacques might have discovered that Elizabeth was missing, for now he urged her into a dark corner far from the trap door, and just in time! Two men came down the steps and, each having hoisted a bale of wool on his back, carried them out of the cellar.

In a few minutes the manoeuvre was repeated. Dominic reasoned that the first two men had not had time to deliver their loads and return so that four men were to be accounted for.

Only one man came next to visit the cellar, and, as he shouldered a bale, the glimmering of an idea came to Dominic. Had the smugglers always worked in pairs his idea would not have been practicable, but if there were single porters he believed it might work. He was desperate to find a way to get Elizabeth safely out of the cellar – their discovery would be inevitable as the last hides and bales were removed. Now Dominic thought that the sight of another man with a bale on his back would not arouse suspicion. The light, such as it was, was fitful and the identity of the carriers was impossible to establish.

Fired with his idea, he turned to Elizabeth and whispered, "I want you to be very brave. On your life do not speak or move!" and he seized the nearest bale and cut it open with Ben's knife. He took a large fold of cloth and wrapped it round Elizabeth from head to toe. "I will leave a small gap at the top for air he whispered as he worked and then used the cut rope to tie his bundle securely. The shape of his bale would not have survived close inspection but Dominic did not mean it to happen. He bent and lifted Elizabeth on to his back and began to move slowly forward to the steps giving time for the current visitors to heft their burdens and leave. Then he was on the steps. At the top he waited until they had disappeared and then made his way quickly into the undergrowth away from the Inn.

He laid his burden down and in the deep gloom, felt for the ropes. With great care he cut them and pulled back the cloth. Elizabeth made no movement and, for one horrified moment he thought she had died, suffocated by his rough and ready means of escape. He put a hand to her breast, so distressed that at first he could feel nothing, then the beat of her heart, faint but steady, filled him with joyful relief.

He held her in his arms until at last she stirred. The first thing she was aware of after the horror of the stifling journey was his gentle kiss, then his low voice, "Brave girl! Are you able to make one more effort? We must get as far away as we can while it is still dark."

She sat up and whispered, "I can do anything to be free."

He helped her to her feet and step by cautious step he felt his way towards safety.

All this while John and the Lieutenant were urging their sweating rowers to make their way back along the bank in the last of the slack water.

"They must have landed," muttered John. "We must get after them." He tried to see ahead but was baffled by branches of willow which dipped into the water.

Suddenly he said, "There – there's a jetty and a boat tied up!"

One of the rowers hissed, "Ssh ….. there's more than one boat about – coming towards us."

The other man said softly, "They'll be up to no good at this time of night – smugglers I wouldn't wonder."

"Wolf's lot," replied his fellow – "We've been after them for years!"

The Lieutenant exclaimed under his breath, "He's right – see – several boats coming with the tide!"

"We mustn't be seen," said John anxiously, and to the rowers, "Pull into the bank beneath this tree until we see what's going on."

They pulled in behind a large willow – the branches were almost bare but so full of twigs that they formed a perfect screen. There was no reaction from the oncoming boats so they were sure they had not been seen.

They counted three vessels, each towing an empty flat-bottomed boat: there were four men in each boat. As the first one drew near the jetty a man spoke in a low voice, perfectly audible to the listeners.

"There's a boat 'ere already, Wolf."

Another voice, authoritative and rather more cultivated, replied, "Then cut it loose – we don't need it. Then get to work."

The little flotilla had halted and the first boat was tied up to the jetty, the one that had been cut free to make room for it floated out on the incoming tide and drifted past the watchers. The two other boats were moored by tying them up to iron stakes driven into the mud.

Two men got out of the first boat and set off up, the path. One man stayed, sitting in the bow while the other climbed over the stern into the flat bottomed boat. In about ten minutes the first two men returned each carrying a bale on their backs. They unloaded them into the flat bottom while two men from the second boat squelched through the mud and up the path. As the man waiting helped to stow the bales one of the carriers said, "We came on two dead 'uns, Wolf, not far from the bush – right across the path they was – we slung 'em into the bushes."

"Were they ours?" enquired the man in the bows.

"Don't think so – we couldn't rightly see – but ours wouldn't be 'ere."

"True," replied Wolf, dispassionately. "Get on then. You go back on your own, Harry, Tom can stay to load – it's quicker with two."

The listeners were rigid with horror. Two bodies! Elizabeth and Dominic? John whispered, "He didn't say a woman – and he would have – but I'm going to see!"

"Don't be a fool, man," replied the Lieutenant. "They'll catch you."

"Not me, they won't. I've been on night patrol too often with the Major! Wait for me, Sir," and he stepped into the shallows and was gone.

The loading went on until the first tow was loaded and more hides packed into the boat. The leader, Wolf, stepped on to the jetty and called one of the men from the second boat to take his place.

"Away with you!" and the men untied and set off back up the river with the ride running strongly and the tow lying low in the water.

The second boat moved up to the jetty and the process of loading was repeated, and so to the third.

The last man to come from the cellar said, "That's the lot, Wolf – we've shut the cellar."

"You saw no-one?"

"No, and nobody saw us."

"Did Slitter come down?" asked Wolf, seating himself in the boat.

"No – it sounded as if he'd got a full house."

"Ah well, he'll let me know when the next load's due – pull away men!" and the rowers bent to their oars and, helped by the tide, passed the watchers in the willows at a good pace.

When they were safely past, one of the Custom's men said, "Well, that's a bit of luck – now we know where he loads. If we can find out when the next lot's due we'll have him!"

The Lieutenant was more concerned with John and the two they had come to rescue than with the problems of Customs and Excise and said, "If they've finished we can get up to the jetty –

it will be getting light soon and we should be able to set about finding his lordship and Miss Gascoigne." He was somewhat cheered that John had not returned to say that the bodies were those of Dominic and his fiancée.

As they were tying up, John joined them. He gave the Lieutenant a hand up and said, "They were two longshoremen at a guess. One was half-stripped and I found this," and he waved the white bundle he had carried under his arm. "It's his lordship's shirt!"

"Surely they've not murdered him or carried him off!" exclaimed Watkins.

"No, Sir. Don't you see – he's taken the man's jersey and thrown away his shirt – it's still sopping wet."

"That means his lordship's not far away," said the Lieutenant jubilantly. "Did he kill the two men I wonder?"

"No I did not!" replied a voice from the shadows, and John turned crying, "It's my lord! Oh, Sir, thank God!"

Dominic stepped on to the jetty with his arm round Elizabeth. For the next few minutes everyone was concerned with getting her to safely into the boat.

Dominic's quick, "Thanks, Watty, more later. We must get Elizabeth home first," were the only words spoken.

They were all so pre-occupied that they had no eyes for the menacing figure who had just emerged from the path followed by the landlord, Slitter, and two of his men.

"Seize him," commanded Jacques.

"Just a minute," interposed Slitter.

Dominic said urgently, "Go, you two – get Elizabeth home!"

Watkins turned to the rowers, "Off with you! Take the lady to a safe shelter." Then he cried to Dominic, "We're with you Major – it will be like old times!"

Elizabeth, settled in the boat, was too bemused and exhausted to protest and the boat shot off.

Jacques, infuriated at the sight of Elizabeth being snatched from him, said angrily, "Take him, men!"

"Just a minute," repeated Slitter quietly. "I give the orders! These are my men!" His expressionless eyes rested on Jacques and Dominic in turn and gave nothing away. His word was law here and his men did not stir. The two groups faced each other in the growing light.

Dominic, quick to hear the antagonism in the landlord's voice said, "It seems to me, M'sieur le Comte that your quarrel is with me! Settle it yourself, unless you have no stomach for fighting your own battles!"

Jacques looked murderous, but made no move. He was good at planning the removal of all who got in his way but he saw to it that others did the killing. His was the knife that struck the unguarded victim when there was little chance of reprisals.

As he hesitated, Slitter spoke again, "That seems fair – I have no quarrel with this man – besides, I knew nothing of the woman – I never allow a skirt to interfere in my business." To Dominic he said, "I take it you have no dispute with me and will leave me to mind my own affairs – you and your friends.?"

Dominic was quite happy to give this assurance. He was not speaking for the Custom's men in the boat – besides they were no longer present! His overwhelming need was to settle his account with Jacques man to man, and here, unless he missed his guess, was his opportunity.

"So be it," said Slitter. "It's between the two of you. We'll stay to see fair play!" and with that he and his men stood back.

John and Watkins were aghast. Dominic, to their minds, was in no fit state to tackle Jacques after the exhausting trip through the river, apart from any calls that had been made upon him while rescuing Elizabeth – besides, there was his weak right arm.

John, "Sir, you can't!"

Watkins, "You must be mad!"

Dominic became suddenly the fighting major they both knew. "Keep out of this! That is an order!" and he turned to face Jacques.

The Frenchman gave a hunted look round. Blocking the path were Slitter and his men and behind Dominic were Watkins and John. Like a single rat Jacques would rather run but, like a rat, when cornered, was prepared to fight. He cast off his tight fitting coat and tore off his cravat. As Dominic advanced upon him his knife was in his hand.

"Like that is it?" said Dominic quite pleasantly, and Ben's knife flashed in reply.

The match looked uneven. Dominic was the taller but looked almost slight against the stocky Frenchman. As well, Dominic's feet were bare with only the rags of his stockings to protect them while Jacques' hessians were thick-soled and stout. A lot can be done with a boot in a fight in which no holds are barred.

Jacques' knife hand came up to be met by Dominic's and sparks flew while he planted a punishing left into the Frenchman's body. Jacques relied almost solely on his weapon while Dominic's bouts in Jackson's Parlour stood him in good stead.

The Frenchman fell back gasping and Dominic moved in to follow up his attack. This time the Frenchman used his foot and stamped down heavily on Dominic's unprotected instep, at the same time striking upwards with his knife. Despite the pain in his bruised foot Dominic had the quick reflexes of the practised fencer and swayed aside to avoid the full thrust of the knife which inflicted a deep scratch in his side and another rent in Ben's much abused jersey.

Slitter was viewing the fight impassively, his men with professional interest, but John and Watkins watched with mounting anxiety.

Jacques was triumphant, he thought his knife had inflicted real damage and he rushed in for the kill.

To his friends' horror Dominic threw his knife away and dropped to one knee – they thought he was at the Frenchman's mercy. Then, like the hired bullied in Calais, Jacques was unable to halt his rush and, as he plunged forward he was given a heave by his adversary which catapulted him over Dominic's head and, as he landed his knife was knocked out of his hand and it was a wonder that his slide did not take him over the edge of the jetty. Before he could recover Dominic was upon him, his hands, despite the weakness in his right, round Jacques' throat. The pent up fury which drove Dominic when he thought of Elizabeth's sufferings at this man's hands would have resulted in murder had not John's urgent, "My lord, my lord – you'll kill him!" brought a return of sanity to his master. He slackened his grip, but there was no more fight in the Frenchman and he got up.

"Tie him up," he said wearily, "We will take him back to pay in full for his crimes."

Then he thought of Slitter, wondering whether the man would interfere, and turned ready to confront him, but Slitter and his men had vanished. The landlord had no desire to embroil himself in a conflict which did not concern him. Besides in his twisted and devious mind he despised Jacques and felt some admiration for a man who, against the odds, had defeated his enemy.

CHAPTER 30

For three of the four left on the jetty, the situation had turned from drama to farce. They had no boat – there was no hope that a boat could make its way to them against a tide now almost at the flood and little hope as yet of a boat going upstream. The three sat on the edge of the jetty in the growing light ignoring the curses and obscenities of the trussed up Jacques until John could bear it no longer.

"Shall I gag him, Sir," he asked.

Dominic looked at his beaten opponent and said quietly, "Hold your tongue – my man will gag you else!" Jacques looked in the pitiless eyes and fell abruptly silent, while Dominic, dismissing him, said to Watkins, "I have no notion how you managed to get here, but thank you."

"Fat lot of use we were," replied his friend. "We didn't even find you or Miss Gascoigne, and if you want to thank anyone, thank your man – he organised the whole thing."

"But without the Lieutenant's authority I couldn't have managed, my lord. He ordered the boat and made the men follow you."

"I see honours are even," commented Dominic with a smile. "Thanks to you both at least we have Miss Gascoigne safely away and must possess our souls in patience until the river traffic begins to stir."

In spite of his cheerful words and Ben's jersey the early morning cold was making him shiver and his foot was swollen black and blue and giving him great pain

Watkins was cudgelling his brains to devise a way to get Dominic to shelter when John exclaimed, "A boat!" and he pointed to where, on the flood tide, a boat seemed almost to fly towards them.

John and Watkins stood up and shouted and the boat pulled in to the jetty. It was manned by Customs men and one of them addressed the Lieutenant, "Captain Willoughby has sent us to find you, Sir. He orders you to return to the Sea Hawk immediately."

Watkins was so relieved at the timely arrival of the boat that he replied frivolously, "I suppose I am to fly – or are you prepared to row me back?"

"Against this tide? No, Sir, it can't be done."

"Then let us waste no more time. We had better make for the Strand," and he and John helped a very lame Dominic into the boat and wrapped him in a spare boat cloak.

"What about him?" asked one of the crew, pointing to Jacques. They were consumed with curiosity but reckoned they would get the story from their fellows who had manned the original boat.

"Put him in the bottom," ordered Dominic, "He must be handed over to the authorities," and the luckless Jacques was dumped like so much ballast.

The journey to the Strand was swift. Watkins tried to get an account of what had happened after he and John had left the Sea Hawk but the rowers had been ashore at the time and had been despatched up-river at first light by signals from the ship.

Dominic was past caring. He was so tired and battered that his only sentient thought was of Elizabeth and these men would, of course, have no news of her. He had no energy to spare to wonder about the fate of Lisette. Later he was to blame himself for this dereliction, although his concern would have been too late.

At last they drew in to the steps and, leaving the hapless Jacques in the puddle of water in the bottom of the boat, the men concentrated on getting Dominic safely ashore. It was no light task. He could not put his foot to the ground so, as soon as he was lifted out of the boat, the Customs men made a chair with their linked hands and carried him to where John, who had gone ahead, had a hackney waiting. Dominic would not drive away until he had thanked the men, then he turned to Watkins.

"Watty, will you take our prisoner to Bow Street? He can be kept there until Horse Guards are informed – they will deal with him. Do not forget that he is a very dangerous man. On your lives do not let him escape." He smiled at the Lieutenant, "Then perhaps you'll join us at Delamere House – we can at least feed you and give you a bed!"

His responsibilities discharged with the last of his strength, Dominic lay back in the cab and let John convey him home.

At sight of him the Dowager, with tears of relief streaming down her cheeks, which she ignored, exclaimed, "Thank God!" She answered the question before he had time to ask it. "Yes, Elizabeth is here – she is sleeping. The doctor has given her a draught and said that there is nothing wrong with her that rest will not cure. I wish we could say the same for you!"

Her tears dried, she gave her orders briskly: the doctor was summoned. Dominic was carried to his room and the sweat and grime of his adventure removed in a long, hot bath, by which time the doctor had arrived.

He dressed the deep scratch but was more concerned over Dominic's foot. "Some broken bones, I am sure, but, until there is less swelling it is difficult to know the extent of the damage. Meanwhile you must not put it to the ground – you do not wish to be permanently lame, I am sure, my lord." By this time Dominic was falling into an exhausted sleep and the doctor expected and received no answer. He left a draught for when his patient woke. "He will be in considerable pain and must rest. I can assure you that there is no permanent damage, your ladyship, but do not let him stand on that foot."

"He will not," replied the Dowager firmly, "Even if we have to tie him to the bed! My grandson is an obstinate creature."

"But I am sure you are a match for him, ma'am" said the doctor with a twinkle. "I will call again tomorrow to look at that foot. Good day, your ladyship," and he took himself off, satisfied that his patient was in good hands.

After a few hours Dominic stirred, but he was only half awake and not sufficiently compos-mentis to protest when he was given the doctor's potion and after, sank into a long-lasting, deep sleep.

The next morning the doctor declared himself satisfied with his patient's progress. "A few more days in bed, your lordship, and I will find out the extent of the injury."

Dominic did not waste time informing the doctor that he did not propose to stay in bed, but asked, "You are quite sure that Miss Gascoigne has suffered no serious hurt?"

"Quite sure, my lord. She is a remarkable young lady – does not indulge in the vapours which might be expected of a delicate female. In fact, she declares her intention of leaving her bed today. I have no objection as long as she does not over exert herself. I will leave a draught for your lordship should the pain become severe," and he bowed himself out.

"Pompous ass!" ejaculated Dominic impatiently. "Now John, I will get out of this confounded bed!" As John protested, "Calm yourself – I will not dress – breeches would not go over this thrice-cursed foot. A dressing gown and slippers will serve, but I must be shaved and then I will see Lieutenant Watkins." With that he threw back the bedclothes.

John was in a quandary. The Dowager and Althea had paid Dominic an early visit and then left to make a round of morning calls so there was no one in authority to forbid this reckless behaviour. He did his best, but his master's mind was made up and by hopping on his sound foot Dominic was soon installed in an easy chair, shaved, and with his injured foot supported on a stool. It was found to be still so swollen that it was impossible to get a slipper over it.

Dominic would not admit it, but he found himself to be so tired after his efforts that he was glad to sit back and drink the glass of wine brought by John.

There was a knock on the door. It was Elizabeth's maid – her mistress would like to know if his lordship was able to receive a visitor.

Dominic heard the message and called, "Please tell Miss Gascoigne that I should be delighted to see her if she is sure that she is well enough."

The maid curtsied and left and Dominic, in a state of confusion quite unlike him, said, "Am I tidy enough, John? We don't need this stool – I must get a slipper on!"

John was soothing. "Now, Sir, you are quite tidy and you must keep the stool. Your lordship knows full well that we cannot get a slipper on that foot, but we'll put a rug over your knees and cover it." He brought a light rug and arranged it so that the bruised foot was covered and then set a comfortable chair ready for the visitor.

When Elizabeth scratched at the door he opened it and said, "If you'll excuse me, Miss Gascoigne, I'll go and arrange for a tray to be brought for his lordship's nuncheon, and may I say that I am very glad to see you so much recovered."

Elizabeth smiled at him, "And no little thanks to you and the help you gave to his lordship. Do you think, John, that I might share his lordship's nuncheon.!"

"Indeed, yes, Miss Gascoigne, I'll go now and arrange it – I'm afraid it will take a little while, though," and with a bow Cupid's surrogate made himself scarce.

During this interchange Dominic's mind was filled with the thought that he might never have seen her again and the joy and delight he felt at sight of her almost suffocated him and he could not utter.

Elizabeth's heart was so filled with thanksgiving that she too was speechless and she went, without a word, to take him in an embrace so passionate that it spoke for her. She ignored the chair placed for her and knelt beside him.

"You must think me shameless to thrust myself upon you so," she said demurely.

"In my bedroom too!" he responded teasingly. Then, gathering her to him he could only say, "My darling, my darling – I thought I had lost you."

"I had nearly give up hope," she confessed. "But Dominic, you are hurt – what is this?" and she twitched the rug from his foot. "Good God! How did you come by this? Oh, it is all my fault!" and she buried her face in her hands.

He took them away. "Blame it rather on Jacques' boots! My, dear, do not distress yourself, he got far more than he gave and is in safe custody."

"We have so much to tell each other, darling," she stood up, "But now we should be more decorous! What will John think?" and she touched the swollen foot with the lightest of caresses and retreated to her chair.

"John thinks, as I do, that you are the greatest piece of good fortune that has befallen me," said Dominic tenderly.

"Very well said, Sir!"

"I could say more! But to serious matters. I must find out about what happened after I left the Sea Hawk. We will have Watkins up – or perhaps John can tell us. There are still Lisette and Raoul to be accounted for."

As he spoke the door opened and John entered followed by a footman bearing a loaded tray which he set down on a table John placed between Elizabeth and his master.

The man said, "Excuse the liberty my lord but belowstairs are glad that you and Miss Gascoigne are back safe and sound.

"Thank you William, though not as glad as I am!" Dominic smiled at the man who bowed and withdrew.

John served Elizabeth and his master. As he poured wine for him Dominic asked, "John, what happened to Miss Duclos and the other Frenchman after I left the Sea Hawk?"

"I couldn't say, sir," John replied. "There was a struggle and some shooting but me and the Lieutenant were too busy getting a boat ready to follow you to notice what was going on. Captain Willoughby was doing a lot of shouting. I don't know if Lieutenant Watkins could tell you more, Sir, but he isn't here," he added.

"Do you mean that he had gone out?"

"No, sir, he's never been here."

"But he was supposed to stay the night."

"Well, sir, he never did. I 've not seen him since he went off with the prisoner."

"This must be looked into," exclaimed Dominic. "You have never explained how you turned up so providentially."

"Well, sir, I knew you'd follow Miss Gascoigne and I thought you'd need help – you were one against three, so I got Lieutenant Watkins to commandeer a boat and we set off after you but we nearly lost you when they tied up. We had to wait while that Wolf and his men loaded his boats before we could get to the jetty."

"The Wolf, eh," said Dominic thoughtfully – "you must tell me more later, but now we must find out about Lieutenant Watkins and Miss Duclos and Raoul." He looked at Elizabeth, "My dear, you are eating nothing.

"I am not hungry, Dominic. I am getting very worried about Lisette."

"Well, drink your wine and John can take the tray." He had eaten very little himself, pain from his foot and anxiety about lack of news had taken away what little appetite he had.

As John took the tray he thought, "Curse this foot – I should be at the Horse Guards!" Aloud he said, "John, when you come back bring me pen and paper, I must send a note."

"Yes, sir," replied John and left the room.

Elizabeth could not bear to see Dominic looking so pale and drawn and said comfortingly, I am sure everything is being taken care of, my darling, after all there has been very little time ….."

She was interrupted by John's return. He carried a small travelling writing desk but said, as he gave it to his master, "Sir, a Major Brown has just arrived and asks if he may see you."

"Brown? Harry Brown? He will have news – by all means send him up."

When John had left Elizabeth rose and said, "I will leave you. If he has news of Lisette, you will let me know?" she asked.

"Be sure I shall. If he has no news he can set about finding some. You will return after he has gone?" he asked anxiously.

"Yes, if only to make sure that you are in your bed where you should be, my love," and she kissed him and left him.

Major Brown was ushered in a few minutes later.

"Harry – I hoped it was you!" exclaimed Dominic. "What are you doing here – in England, I mean?"

"Brought despatches," replied the Major seating himself. "I am due back in a few days, but as I knew you they asked me to see you. Sorry you've been damaged," nodding at Dominic's foot.

"That's nothing," Dominic said impatiently. "What's your news? What has happened to Watkins?"

"Oh, he is under arrest"

"What! Why?"

"For abandoning his post without leave, I understand. There's a fine hornets' nest at Horse Guards."

"That fool Willoughby, I suppose," said Dominic disgustedly. "Watkins did noting of the sort – he came after me! Oh, we will sort it out. But Harry, have you news of what has happened on the Sea Hawk? My financée's cousin was kidnapped and the last I saw of her she was being held at knife point by a French spy."

"That is what I have come about. I don't know all the details but I have brought a Customs man who was present. Shall we have him up?"

"Quickly!" agree Dominic. "John," he called and John came from the dressing room to which he had retired.

"Bring up the man who came with Major Brown and, before you go, give the Major a glass of wine." John did so and went out. He returned with the Customs man.

"Preventative Officer Johnson," said Brown. "This is Lord Delamere."

"I am glad to see you," said Dominic. "Bring up a chair." The man did so and seated himself.

Dominic asked, "Now what have you got tell me?"

Johnson looked ill-at-ease. "Nothing good, I'm afraid, my lord. After you left the Sea Hawk – I was there you see," in response to Dominic's enquiring look. "There was confusion – some of Captain Willoughby's men were ordered to shoot at the escaping boat and others were confronting the Frenchman. I don't know whether you saw, sir that he had his knife at the lady's throat and no-one quite knew what to do. Then Major Willoughby ordered them to seize him – he said the Frenchie would never dare to hurt the lady ..." He paused.

"Go on, man," urged Dominic.

"He was wrong," said Johnson bluntly. "The lady was screaming to our men to save her, she was on our side – well, we knew that – but the Frenchie called her a name – it sound horrible – and slashed her cheek with his knife."

"Oh, God," said Dominic, sickened.

"Then our men rushed forward and I couldn't see but one of them told me afterwards that she struggled like and the Frenchie stabbed her. One of our men used his gun-butt and when the skirmishing was over the lady and the Frenchman were both dead." He mopped his brow and at the sight of Dominic's ashen face said miserably, "I'm sorry, sir, very sorry."

Dominic mastered himself sufficiently to say, "It is not your blame. Thank you for carrying out a most unpleasant duty. John, take Officer Johnson down and offer him refreshment while he waits for Major Brown." He fell back in his chair as the men left the room and Brown was on his feet holding his glass of wine to Dominic's lips.

"You really need brandy," he said. "What a horrible story."

"And all my fault," groaned Dominic. "I brought her to this – I used her and I left her."

"Nonsense, Dominic," said Brown bracingly. "That other spy has talked. He did not know his partner was dead and he is busy spreading the blame and implicating Miss Duclos. She was in it from the beginning he says."

"The rat!" snarled Dominic. "I should have killed him!" He sat up and spoke earnestly. "Harry, this must go no further. Miss Duclos is a cousin of my fiancée but they have not been close – indeed Lisette – the cousin – has been Elizabeth's enemy from the time they were children. I cannot have her embroiled in this scandal broth!"

"Do not distress yourself, my good fellow." said Brown reassuringly. "We know how to be discreet. The spy will be dealt with in camera. I was sent to ask what is to be done with Miss Duclos' body."

"She must be brought here and Elizabeth must decide about what she would like to be done. Oh God, Harry, I have to break it to her!"

The Major was in a quandary, it was obvious that his friend was in no fit state to deal with anything. Fortunately for him help was at hand. The door opened with a snap and the Dowager sailed in.

"What is the meaning of this, Sir? My grandson should be in bed and is forbidden all visitors!"

Dominic intervened. "This is my very good friend, Major Harry Brown, Grandmamma, and he has done me a great service. Harry – the Dowager Lady Delamere."

The Major bowed and looked to make his escape but the Dowager was not done with him, "Kindly wait for me downstairs, Major Brown, I should like to speak with you before you leave."

"Ma'am," bowed the Major and escaped the storm centre, metaphorically mopping his brow. He would rather have faced an enemy charge than this diminutive virago.

The Dowager turned her attention to her grandson. His appearance alarmed her but, as usual, she translated concern into an expression of annoyance.

"You were told to stay in bed and have no visitors – you are behaving like a child, Dominic!"

"Don't Grandmother," he pleaded. "Lisette is dead and I have to tell Elizabeth".

"Great Heavens!" she exclaimed, and then, "Well, I cannot say I am sorry – she was an unpleasant young woman and obviously still causing trouble now she is dead!"

"But she was killed – horribly!"

"In that case you are not to tell Elizabeth. I will inform her of her cousin's death. I suppose Lady Hapgood has been told. Where did Lisette die?"

"On the Sea Hawk – she was kidnapped with Elizabeth and I … I left her …." He could not go on.

"Now that's quite enough of that! John!" she called. He came from the dressing room.

"Get his lordship back to bed. Did the doctor leave a draught?"

"Yes, your ladyship."

"Then he is to take it. Now what?" as Dominic began to speak.

"I have to make arrangements …. Lisette's body …"

"I collect Major Brown knows all the details?" He nodded. "Very well, you may leave the matter to me. I shall inform Elizabeth's man, Mr Whitney, he will deal with the formalities."

Having disposed of the matter she turned to the door. "When I have seen the Major and broken the news to Elizabeth, I shall come back to make sure you have carried out my orders!" and she swept out of the room.

John said gently to his master, "Come now, sir, let me help you. It's as much as my place is worth to disobey her ladyship."

Dominic was so worn out by the traumas of the morning and the pain in his foot was sickening him, that he made no demur and was soon in bed and taking the doctor's draught.

Downstairs the Dowager heard the shocking details from the Major and thanked him for undertaking such an unpleasant duty. She said that she would inform Miss Gascoigne's man of business immediately and he would attend to matters.

Major Brown took his leave and left with an awed Preventative Officer who had never, in all his experience, encountered the likes of the Dowager.

The Dowager ordered her carriage to be at the door in half-an-hour and despatched a note to Mr Whitney asking him to call on her on a matter of great urgency. Then she went to Elizabeth's room.

She made no attempt to soften the news, but neither did she pass on the horrific details of Lisette's death. Elizabeth was saddened but not grief-stricken. She exclaimed, "Oh why would she not listen – I might have saved her!"

"My dear," said the Dowager, "She brought about her own ruin – you have nothing with which to reproach yourself. I have sent for Mr Whitney. He will wish to see you to take your instructions, I feel we cannot leave the funeral and such matters to Lady Hapgood – after all she is not a relative."

"Oh, no!" said Elizabeth, "I must be responsible – but Lady Hapgood should be informed – she has been very kind to Lisette."

"Indeed she has – do not worry my dear, I will see her. I shall just look in on Dominic – I have sent him to bed, the foolish boy is blaming himself for your cousin's death.

Elizabeth knew why Dominic should feel conscience-stricken and she grieved for him. "I should go to him," she said.

"Not at present, my dear. The doctor left a draught and I hope to find him asleep. As well, you should be preparing to receive Mr Whitney if you feel well enough."

"Of course, aunt – oh, you are so good to me – taking my burdens on your shoulders – you are so wise."

"I have lived longer," the Dowager replied drily. "You call me Aunt, but I regard you as the daughter I never had, but let us get through the next few weeks and we shall be able to think only of happiness. Now I must go," and she kissed Elizabeth and went to her carriage, pausing on the way to make sure her recalcitrant grandson had obeyed her and, to her great satisfaction, found him sound asleep.

CHAPTER 31

When Mr Whitney was announced Elizabeth went to meet him, her mind full of all the difficulties before her. As usual, a few minutes with her life-long friend calmed her and she found her problems dealt with most efficiently. He expressed no grief at hearing of Lisette's death and said that he would take care of official details.

"Where would you like her to be buried?" he enquired matter-of-factly."

"At Cleeve," Elizabeth replied without hesitation. "Her mother and my parents are there and they loved her."

"Very well. I gather it will be a very private ceremony?"

"Yes," she said and then paused. It came to here with something of a shock that she herself was Lisette's only relative. Lady Hapgood had been her cousin's friend and benefactress, but there was no tie of blood. The tragedy of Lisette's aloneness brought the tears she had not shed at the news of her cousin's death.

"There, there, my dear," soothed Mr Whitney. "Lisette is now at rest. Had she lived she would have gone from disaster to disaster – there was nothing in her nature to make for true happiness."

"How wise you are," said Elizabeth drying her eyes. She went on, "I shall attend the funeral of course. When can it take place?"

"In about five or six days, I should judge," he replied. "I will write to the Rector at Cleeve and it should be possible for Lisette's body to begin the journey tomorrow – I doubt, in the circumstances, that there will be an inquest. I myself shall start out for Cleeve in the morning. The notice of your cousin's death can be sent to the appropriate journals here and in Gloucestershire today. If you approve, it should just read, 'Suddenly', with no details.

"I am sure that will be best. Will you tell them at Cleeve to get the house ready for me, Mr Whitney?" Elizabeth asked.

"Who will come with you, Jane?" he smiled at her as he exercised his prerogative to use her childhood name.

"I shall bring my maid – I cannot think of anyone who would care sufficiently for Lisette to undertake the journey."

"They may not care for your cousin, but they do for you – too much to let you face such an ordeal alone," he protested.

He had almost immediate support for this argument. Before Elizabeth could reply, the Dowager, returned from Lady Hapgood's, came in and greeted Mr Whitney and asked, "You have settled the details concerning Miss Duclos' affairs, I collect?"

Mr Whitney gave an account of the steps agreed upon and when he mentioned Elizabeth's intention of travelling alone to Cleeve, the Dowager spoke her mind.

"Of course, I shall accompany you, child, so will Dominic. He can travel with us in the coach – then he will have to rest his foot. We will not trouble Amelia Hapgood – her age will excuse her the journey." Considering that the Dowager could give her ladyship some ten years in seniority this trenchant speech earned a concealed smile from her auditors.

Her ladyship waited for no agreement from either of them but went on, "Althea shall stay in Town. Fitzallan's people have invited her to visit them and it will be convenient for her to accept for while we are in Gloucestershire." She turned to the lawyer, "Thank you, Mr Whitney, you are, as ever, a tower of strength. I will bid you good day – we shall start for Cleeve the day after tomorrow," and she went briskly from the room almost before Mr Whitney had had time to rise to his feet.

For the first time for many days Elizabeth laughed. "She is wonderful, is she not? So kind and so good."

"Indeed, yes," he agreed. "Her encomium almost brought me to the blush." He bowed, "I leave you in good hands, my dear Jane. Be assured that everything will be arranged to your satisfaction – I will see you at Cleeve."

Alone for a moment before she went to her room, Elizabeth stayed to utter a prayer of gratitude for the love and care which had lifted her heavy burdens.

The following day was a busy one. Dominic, much recovered, arranged, through John, the preparation of the travelling coach and a second coach to carry the two maids and the luggage.

The dowager saw Althea safely installed in the Fitzallan's Town house and returned to supervise her packing quite sure that, without her oversight, something vital would be omitted. Elizabeth had only her own packing to organise and then, while the Dowager was resting, she joined Dominic whose spirits, in spite of the melancholy reason for their journey, had considerably improved. He had felt less than adequate since returning home and welcomed the prospect of action even if only at second hand.

But his mood was sombre as he tried to express his regret at Lisette's death, "It was my fault .... That fool Willoughby ..."

"You had to choose – my safety or Lisette's – we should not be here now if you had chosen differently."

Dominic was startled. He was learning a bitter lesson: he had believed that he was adequate to all situations, that he controlled all eventualities, a mental and physical arrogance that had been fostered by his natural abilities and his rank.

He felt humbled and guilty, "Had I not used her she would not have come to such a pass!"

"You may have hastened the end, but both Aunt Helena and Mr Whitney have pointed out that Lisette's ruin was inevitable – brought about by her own nature, and I am bound to agree with them."

"I find little comfort in that," replied Dominic. He was dismayed that she offered so little sympathy and had not attempted to mitigate his part in the tragedy.

"Then find some comfort, my dear, in the fact that she is now safe from further harm." He looked downcast and she took him in her arms. She knew he had expected her to say that she found no fault in him.

"My dear, we are none of us faultless – we all make mistakes. I could not love you half as much if you were a pattern of perfection – with all my errors and weaknesses how should I match you?"

He held her close. "To me, you are the sum of all virtues. You have given me a standard against which to measure my life. You have taught me that a spy needs to have not only courage, but the ability to touch pitch and not be defiled. It takes a greater man than I for this. You were right, my darling, the end does not justify the means, and I will have no more of it."

His confession healed the small wound she had suffered when he had persisted in using Lisette, however honourable he believed his motive to be, and she stayed quietly in his arms, utterly at peace.

They were disturbed by John, who tapped on the dressing room door and, bidden to enter, after Elizabeth had seated herself decorously in the 'visitor's' chair, said, "Her ladyship sent to remind you that dinner will be early tonight. She says you should not be late in bed in view of the early morning start for Gloucestershire."

The message delivered, John became more himself and warned, "Her ladyship's sent for the doctor, sir. He is to strap up your foot."

"I don't want him! My foot is very much better – send the fellow away!"

"It would be much better to do as your grandmother wishes, my love," said Elizabeth persuasively, "It will be as well to avoid further damage.

As she spoke there was a knock at the door and John admitted the doctor.

Elizabeth rose, "Your patient is much improved, doctor. I am sure he will be grateful for your help," and with a minatory look at Dominic she went out.

Dominic's foot was much less swollen and the doctor had brought a small, padded splint to which he bound the foot. "This is to prevent your flexing it – the broken bones should be kept immobile. Your lordship should now use crutches."

"I will do no such thing!" declared Dominic. This strapping will do all that is necessary, although I shall not get a boot on, that is certain."

"No indeed – a lambs wool stocking will be best," replied the doctor. "If you will not use crutches at least use two sticks and keep your weight off the foot. If you are careful your journey should give you the rest you need. I will look in again when you return to Town, my lord," and he turned to go.

Dominic's good manners asserted themselves and he said, "Thank you for your help and advice, doctor. I own I am an ill-tempered patient!"

"Not at all, my dear sir. Compared with many whom I treat you have been a model of forbearance. You have not sworn at me or hurled missiles! Indeed, you have been most patient!" and with this feeble witticism he left.

The journey to Cleeve with John as courier went smoothly and the enforced rest did all of the travellers good. They journeyed in an enclosed world and Dominic and Elizabeth grew ever closer during the two evenings they spent in the cosy Inn parlours when the Dowager had retired early to bed.

It was a strangely non-passionate interlude. Emotion seemed to be suspended – perhaps the ghost of Lisette hovered. Whatever the cause they spent the hours in exploring each other's minds – they knew each other's hearts.

Dominic found Elizabeth to be well informed, thoughtful and decisive but not dogmatic, so different from women he had previously encountered and as they talked she charmed him more and more.

For her part, she was surprised to discover the depth and range of his thinking. So far his virility and physical courage had been more evident than his mental prowess, which she now found to be impressive.

On the second night she asked him, "Now you are selling out and no long intend to engage in espionage, shall you occupy yourself in managing your estates."

"No, I have a very good agent who keeps me well-informed – I am no absentee landlord. Elizabeth, I have a mind to enter politics – I have long thought our tax system was iniquitous – association with the smuggling fraternity has taught me that! It is an evil trade and should be rendered unnecessary and I should like to have a hand in such measures. Should you dislike being a political hostess, my darling?"

"I should enjoy it. It is strange, Dominic, but at Cleeve I so hated meeting strangers and only felt safe following a well-trodden path and even in that I felt so inadequate. Now I take pleasure in meeting people and in new experiences – with the exception of being kidnapped of course! – and I find I have quite a talent for organisation."

"The ideal wife for a rising member of His Majesty's Government in short!" laughed Dominic and brought the meeting to a close with a kiss.

The last day of their travels brought them to Cotswold country and Elizabeth delighted in pointing out loved landmarks to her companions. It was a halcyon day in early Spring, wild daffodils and primroses were pale reflections of the sun but the varnished petals of the celandines competed bravely with the heavenly gold. The country was looking its best and, in spite of the sober nature of their journey, her spirits rose with each mile nearer to Cleeve.

When they reached Elizabeth's home the Dowager looked with approval at the rambling manor house. In the afternoon sun the grey Cotswold stone was warmed to a pale honey and the shining casements twinkled a welcome.

The staff were drawn up to greet the travellers and Mrs Reynolds was presented to the Dowager.

She curtsied and said, "I have had the Stuart room prepared for her ladyship, Miss Gascoigne, and the Tudor room for his lordship."

"Excellent," replied Elizabeth. "Aunt Helena, may I take you to your room? Ellen and your boxes should be there by now." To Mrs Reynolds, "Perhaps you will show his lordship the way – his man will help him up the stairs," then she and the Dowager mounted the oak staircase, which rose from the hall to a landing which branched right and left.

As they went Elizabeth said, "The Stuart room was my parent's room. The legend has it that Prince Charles once spent the night there on his travels after the disaster at Worcester, but my father thought it very doubtful."

As they entered the spacious room where her maid awaited her, the Dowager replied in the same vein, "I collect that Bluff

King Hal honoured the Tudor room with one of his many wives?"

"As to that it was thought that Henry VII, journeying to or from Wales, rested there. Again, my father thought it all a hum but for convenience the labels are still attached to the rooms. Dinner will be at six o'clock, Aunt Helena – if you are too tired, would you prefer a tray in your room?"

" No, child, I shall rest for a while and then change and I will join you at dinner." Ellen came to help her mistress and Elizabeth made her way to her own familiar room.

At dinner, with Mr Whitney present, the talk was all of Cleeve but when the tea tray was brought and the servants had withdrawn, he told them of the arrangements for the funeral which was to take place the next day.

The Dowager would remain at the Grange and he and Dominic would accompany Elizabeth to the service.

"Miss Duclos' body will rest in the church overnight – the Rector and I did not think it was necessary for a vigil to be kept and I can assure you that all is in order as you would wish. The carriages will be ready at ten o'clock: the senior staff have expressed a wish to attend but there will be no other mourners." They thanked him and then went to their rooms.

Elizabeth was haunted by the phrase ' no other mourners'. Did no one grieve for her cousin? Before she went to bed she sent to the stables for a carriage to be ready in the stable yard at seven o'clock the next day and sank to sleep with the comforting thought that this time tomorrow the distressing experience would be behind her.

At seven the next morning after a hasty cup of chocolate she went to the carriage. Standing beside it, leaning on his two sticks, was Dominic.

"Dominic," she cried in astonishment. How did you ….?"

"John was in the stable last night," he explained. "He is to drive us. I collect that we are going to the church?" and he handed her into the carriage.

As he climbed in somewhat awkwardly she said simply, "Yes, I wanted to say farewell to Lisette. I cannot bear to think how lonely she must feel."

He took her hand, "My love, remember she is where loneliness cannot trouble her. If we believe anything we must believe that she is now comforted."

"I know, I think I am seeking comfort for myself and forgiveness for never having loved her."

He pressed her hand and they sat in silence for the rest of the short journey.

"Go in, my dear, I will follow," he said, as John helped her from the carriage, and she went alone into the little church where the first rays of the sun through the coloured windows painted the cold stone with gold and rose and blue.

The coffin stood on trestles in the nave covered with a pall of white lilies. There were lilies too in large vases by the steps leading to the chancel.

Elizabeth stood for a while and then knelt and let the stillness and beauty calm her spirit. All bitterness and resentment fell away and she could mourn Lisette's untimely death sincerely – sad that her cousin had not been granted the capacity to give as well as to receive love.

She rose from her knees to see Dominic waiting quietly by the door and went to him with the healing tears still wet on her cheeks.

Without speaking he took her in his arms and held her for a moment, then collected his sticks and they went out into the sunshine.

On the way back to the Grange she said, "I am so glad I went and your being there made it doubly heartening," she added, "We will not mention our journey to Aunt Helena and Mr Whitney, shall we, Dominic?"

"No," he agreed, "It was a very private experience."

The funeral service was simple. Men from the estate carried the coffin to the Gascoigne vault where Lisette was put to rest with her mother and aunt and uncle.

As they left the church Elizabeth noticed a tall man near one of the rear pews and when they had left the vault to return to the carriage he came forward.

"Miss Gascoigne – Jane – I will not detain you, only to offer my sympathy. I came to pay my respects to your cousin because Lucian loved her."

Elizabeth was moved by his sincerity although she knew it to be based on a false premise – Lucian loved no one but himself.

"It was kind of you to come, Sir Lennox. May I present my fiancé, Lord Delamere? Dominic this is Lucian's father, Sir Lennox Chancellor."

"I am honoured to meet you, Sir," said Dominic. He saw in Sir Lennox a man who had suffered and whose kindness and honesty was written plain on his careworn face. He had not deserved to have such a scoundrel for a son.

Elizabeth said, "Will you not return with us to the Grange? It is so long since we have met. Lucian is abroad, is he not?"

"Yes, in Barbados – the estate there needs his attention." He did not elaborate but went on to decline the invitation to the Grange but hoped to see more of Jane on a less melancholy occasion.

They parted and, once in the carriage, Elizabeth said indignantly, "Lucian deserves to be whipped – to cause such grief to his father who is one of the kindest and most upright men I know."

"Sadly, it is often the case that the kindest of fathers are cursed with dissolute sons. Perhaps they are too kind to their children in their youth." Commented Mr Whitney.

"It does not necessarily follow," declared Dominic. "My father was very kind, though strict, and I believe I am not dissolute!" He hoped to bring a smile to Elizabeth's face and succeeded.

"Perhaps you are the exception that proves the rule," she said, and, as the carriage drew up, she went to change from her deep mourning to something less funereal.

After the details of the funeral and the meeting with Sir Lennox had been reported to the Dowager she said, "Well, now we can put this tragic business behind us. I think we should rest tomorrow and set out the day after. It is time to look after Althea, without her Grandmother to hold the reins she will be in all kinds of mischief I'll be bound!" She rose without waiting for agreement from her companions and, escorted to the door by Mr Whitney, left the lovers to plan for the next day.

Elizabeth was glad of the opportunity to spend some time with Mrs Reynolds who had looked after the house so well in her mistress' absence, and Dominic wished to visit an outlying farm with Roberts, the agent.

"He, Roberts, has persuaded the tenant to try a new improved seed drill which he believes is working well on sloping land, and will take me to see it at work. You have a good man there, Elizabeth, willing to make sensible experiments."

Satisfied with the thought of the tranquil day before them they said goodnight.

CHAPTER 32

The Dowager spent the next morning in the succession houses and was given a basket of early fruit by the gratified head gardener.

Elizabeth inspected the house and visited the kitchen. She expressed her gratitude for the way in which the domestic staff had so loyally served her.

"Shall we be seeing more of you now, ma'am?" asked Mrs Reynolds. "For the wedding perhaps?"

"The wedding?" repeated a startled Elizabeth. "I ... I .. had not considered ..." She grasped at a plausible excuse. "So soon after Miss Lisette ..."

"Quite understandable, ma'am," said cook darting an admonitory glance at Mrs Reynolds. "Time enough when Miss Gascoigne has got over her cousin's death."

"Thank you," replied a relieved Elizabeth. "You can be sure that you will receive early notice of any arrangement necessary. Thank you again for all your good work," and she escaped to her room thoroughly shaken by the conversation.

She felt the need for a time of quiet, solitary reflection and, putting on her bonnet and pelisse, went for a last walk to her favourite haunts.

She had come to no solution of her problem by the time she came to the edge of the wood and saw the fallen tree to which she had retreated on the momentous day that had seen the start of her adventures.

She sat down and gazed without seeing at a river of daffodils swaying in the light breeze. At her feet the scent from clumps of primroses rose like faint incense but the perfume went unbreathed.

The housekeeper's question had confronted her so abruptly that she realised with a shock that she had not, as yet, even thought of her wedding.

The answer was not far to seek. So many things had happened since last she had sat on this log dazed and wretched with shock.

First, there was her flight from Cleeve and setting up her business in Brighton: then the meeting with Dominic: then her kidnapping by Lucian: then the discovery of Dominic's spying activities: then – and here she became lost in a delightful reverie – Dominic's declaration of love!

From that moment life should have been a flower-strewn march to the altar, but once more the shadow of Lisette had fallen on her path and the misery and doubts which followed had only been ended by the abduction of herself and Lisette and her rescue and Lisette's death.

Small wonder that plans for a wedding had not engaged her thoughts, but now, surely, there could be no just cause or impediment. It was usual, she knew, for the ceremony to take place from the bride's home, but Elizabeth shrank from the thought of being married in the church where so lately Lisette's body had rested. Besides here there was no family and few intimate friends to support her.

It was a teasing question and one she felt that should be settled with advice from Dominic and the Dowager. She hoped that they would not suggest an elaborate ceremony in Town. And what of the period of mourning for Lisette? She could not bear the thought of a delay of twelve months before she and Dominic could be united. Fretted by these bothersome thoughts she rose and began to return to the house, her steps leading her as before across the lawn to pass the rear of the pavilion.

She was almost at the very spot where the adventure had begun when she was halted by the sound of a crash and a full-blooded oath followed by a string of curses. Dominic had not wasted his time in the army and had a fund of expletives to suit every occasion.

Elizabeth ran to the front of the pavilion and found him sprawled on the steps with his sticks fallen just out of his reach. In her haste Elizabeth tripped over one of them and came down heavily on top of Dominic.

In a moment it seemed they were on the grass clasped in each other's arms: lips to lips, breast to breast. Dominic's kisses covered her throat and his seeking hands pulled her dress from her shoulders. Elizabeth almost drowned in an ecstasy of passion, and strained ever closer to him, her body clamouring for fulfilment.

There could have been only one end to their fierce coupling but a gasp of pain and a sharp recoil from Dominic broke the spell. A few seconds later and no pain, however agonising, could have recalled him to his senses but his damaged foot, flailing as the lovers embraced ever more ardently, caught his stick wedged against the steps with a force that turned him sick. In the momentary break they disengaged and gazed at each other in wonder and some consternation.

Holding his throbbing foot to still the pain Dominic groaned, "Forgive me …."

"For what? Showing me that love is not only comfortable coses and chaste kisses? Forgive you? I thank you!"

She began to straighten her disordered clothing and rose. "My darling, is your foot too painful to stand?" She smiled mischievously, "I am persuaded that we should sit for a while and compose ourselves before returning to the house."

Dominic could find no words. What other gently nurtured woman would have responded so to his onslaught? He marvelled at the unique quality of his beloved – refusing scornfully to deny her own passionate reaction to his fervour.

With her help he managed to stand and, with the aid of his sticks, to negotiate the steps which beforehand had proved his undoing.

Decorously they sat somewhat apart in the pavilion and could not at first find anything to say. Then both broke the silence.

Dominic, "Elizabeth …." both stopped and began to laugh., Elizabeth, "Dominic ….."

Dominic was the first to recover. "Since you will not accept my apology I too will offer thanks and congratulate myself on loving a woman too honest to affect false modesty." He paused and then broke out, "Oh, my love, how long must we wait?"

"Strangely enough," she replied, "I have been thinking about our wedding. Perhaps your grandmother will insist on black gloves for a twelvemonth!" she said despondently.

"She will not!" a crisp voice replied, and the Dowager appeared at the foot of the steps. The two in the pavilion had not taken their eyes from one another and had not observed her approach.

"No, do not get up, I will join you, this is a pretty place in which to discuss our plans," and she seated herself between them.

"We have to decide the time and place – we have the loved ones!" and she put out a hand to each.

"We cannot wait for a year," declared Dominic.

"No," agreed his grandmother: she had drawn her own conclusions from the slight dishevelment of their appearance. "That is out of the question, for one thing we shall find ourselves caught up in preparing for Althea's nuptials before long unless I am much mistaken and you should be settled first."

"But, Lisette?" said Elizabeth doubtfully.

"You owe her nothing," replied the Dowager. "However, convention must be served. Three months' mourning may not be long enough to satisfy some sticklers, but we shall not care for them! So, in three months – that will bring us to the beginning of June – May is unlucky. Now where? Strictly speaking, Elizabeth, you should be married from Cleeve – is that what you would like?"

"Oh, no. I have no family and very few friends here and, besides, the church is haunted by Lisette," replied Elizabeth.

Dominic, knowing it was a foolish desire was ready to press for a marriage next week! He was thankful, however, for his grandmother's concession, generous from one of her traditionally minded generation, and held his peace.

"I collect you would prefer a quiet wedding – indeed our haste is bound to set tongues wagging and the less noise we make about the marriage the better – a nine days wonder is soon over," said the Dowager.

"We will hope so," agreed Elizabeth. "Aunt Helena, would it be possible for the wedding to take place at Ditchling? I have found such happiness there."

"An excellent choice," replied the Dowager approvingly. "You can be married from the Dower House."

At Dominic's start of surprise she went on, "It should be in order by the end of the Season: I put the matter in hand before we left for Town. Elizabeth and Althea and I can stay there while we prepare for the wedding."

Dominic gazed at the Dowager in awe. "Grandmamma, you are a wonderful woman – who but you would have been so forehanded!"

"Somebody must – you children need a wise head to think for you and I doubt if wisdom is your prime attribute to this moment!" and she directed a look of shrewd amusement at each of them in turn.

Elizabeth blushed but Dominic acknowledged the wit with a glance of appreciation and said briskly, "Well, now our affairs are settled we can get back to Town and deal with Althea," and they made their way slowly back to the house.

The return journey was smooth and comfortable under John's capable aegis. The evenings spent in the cosy Inn parlours were as tranquil as before. Passionate demonstrations of affection had reached their climax at Cleeve and by unspoken mutual consent were now in abeyance. Elizabeth wanted to hear more about the Dower House.

"It is about a quarter of a mile from the Manor. It was built in the time of Queen Anne and is, I think, quite perfect," said Dominic. "An old aunt of my father's lived in it in his time and she used to give us children gingerbread men and we thought somehow that she was the witch in Hansel and Gretal. It has been cared for by a housekeeper since she died and once a year servants from the Manor give it a thorough Spring clean, so it can be made habitable quite quickly."

"Dominic, I am sure we do not wish to dispossess your Grandmother – surely she would prefer to stay at the Manor?"

"There you are wrong. She came to look after us from a sense of duty and disposed of her house in Bath at the time, but she has never liked the Manor; her own marriage was spent there and was unhappy. She had told me often that when I married she would like to go to the Dower House – she has grown fond of Althea and me, you see, and would like to remain near us."

This reply stilled Elizabeth's doubts. "If Althea marries Fitzallan she will live in Norfolk when she is not in Town, will she not? Would Aunt Helena not prefer to live nearer to her?"

"Are you suggesting that she cares more for Althea than for me?" he asked in mock indignation. "No, you are the attraction. She had told me often that you are the daughter she longed for but never had – besides she looks forward to her great-grandchildren!"

This retort had the effect of causing a laughing, blushing Elizabeth to retire hastily to bed.

On the second and last evening of their journey Elizabeth said, "We have spoken of the Manor House and the Dower House, but what of Cleeve, Dominic?"

"That is for you to say, my love. For my part I liked it exceedingly. It is in hilly country, like my native Downs but sterner and more dramatic, and I found it a very refreshing contrast. Unless it has too many unhappy memories for you we could keep it and visit it as often as we wished – for the hunting, perhaps?"

"I am so glad – in spite of some miserable times I have happy memories of the Grange and should enjoy visiting it with you – it was just that I did not wish Lisette to be associated with our wedding ..." she looked at him for understanding.

"I too shall be glad to have no shadow of past mistakes falling over that day," he replied. "Then we keep Cleeve – good!"

"There is something more I must say, Dominic. On hearing it you may wish to break off our engagement." He looked thunderstruck, but before he could speak she went on, "I must confess that I am no lover of the hunt – I have been out with my father but I always come home before the kill – I am too sorry for the fox!" and she looked ruefully at him.

He looked stern. "That is, of course, a serious defect – certainly a just impediment to our marriage!" He could keep his countenance no longer, and roared with laughter. "You little wretch! My love, you should see your face! Now it is time for my confession. Since I have in my turn been the hunted not the hunter, my sympathies have been with the quarry. That is settled then – we will ride but neither of us will hunt. A good ride will be sufficient justification to keep Cleeve."

"There is one other use I have in mind for the Grange, if you approve," she said shyly. "I have always felt sorry for the younger son in a family. Often he has only an inferior property or none and is expected either to live in idleness on an allowance, sometimes inadequate, or follow some profession for which he has no taste or aptitude. I though our second son, if, that is, we have one, could have Cleeve," she ended with a rush.

Dominic smiled at her tenderly. "I see now why you appeal so strongly to my Grandmamma – you feel and think so clearly for others. Bless you, my darling, our second son shall have the Grange and we will acquire sufficient properties with which to endow the rest of our progeny!" and he swept her lovingly into his arms.

Althea was restored to her family the day after they arrived in Town and after the flurry of greetings she said, "Grandmamma, William would like to wait on you and Dominic this afternoon, if you are both at liberty."

The Dowager and her grandson exchanged looks.

"We shall be pleased to receive him, my dear, I will send a note."

"Thank you, Grandmamma," replied Althea demurely, "There is no need. Unless I write to say that it is not convenient he will call at three o'clock."

"And we know for what purpose, do we not?" asked Dominic, drily.

"I am sure you do," said Althea composedly, in spite of a faint blush, and then, eagerly, "It will be all right, won't it?"

"From our point of view, yes," answered her grandmother, "But what of Lady Fitzallan?"

"She has approved of her son's choice." Althea's tone was an imitation of that of her future mother-in-law's. "She is sure his father would have given his consent! But only if you and Dominic agree." She went on despondently, "She said, as well, that we must have a long engagement, because I am so young! It won't have to be too long, will it?" she looked anxious.

"Not too long, puss," her brother reassured her.. "Of course Elizabeth's and my marriage must come first."

"What!" exclaimed Althea, "A whole twelve month?" Her voice rose.

"A little less in alt, my dear, there is no need to be so shrill!" said the Dowager. "Dominic's wedding is to take place three months from now. A year's mourning for Lisette is not called for – the sooner she and her dreadful end is forgotten the better!"

Althea turned impulsively to Elizabeth, "I am so glad – and so sorry ...." She stammered incoherently, "I mean ..."

"I know what you mean, dear," replied Elizabeth. "Lisette is in the past and Dominic and I are as eager to be united as you and William. Come and talk while Lucy unpacks for me. I have brought you a length of French silk I found in my Aunt's chest at Cleeve," and she and Althea left Dominic and his grandmother to discuss the coming interview with her grandchild's suitor.

Good news had greeted them at Ditchling. Napoleon had been deposed on March 31st and on April 11th, not long after their return, he abdicated and Louis XVIII was proclaimed King of France in Paris.

There was general rejoicing but everyone was so busy that beyond a collective sigh of relief only the Dowager commented. She dismissed the event with, "Good! Now we can leave the French to sort out their own muddles," and she returned with renewed zest to harrying the staff at the Manor to put the finishing touches to the Dower House and the end of April saw the three ladies installed in their new abode. Her ladyship little knew what a false prophet she was to prove to be.

Elizabeth echoed the Dowager's sentiment. At last Napoleon would cease to interfere in her life and so, with the thought, joined the older lady in the ranks of false prophets.

Elizabeth took little part in the move: she was engrossed in designing and putting in hand her wedding dress and trousseau, Isabelle's workrooms had never been so busy.

Althea was to attend the bride and waited with unaccustomed patience for the wedding garments to be finished before a whole new wardrobe for herself could be begun. No modest country wedding for her! Her nuptials, to take place a the height of the Season, were to be the most magnificent for a decade.

Dominic, excluded as a mere male from this feminine brou-ha-ha, spent much time overseeing estate matters which had, of necessity, had little of his attention of late, and in supervising alterations at the Manor required for the comfort of his bride.

The news that peace was to be signed in Paris on 30th May was timed, according to some villages sages, so that the Beacon could be lighted as part of the wedding festivities on 1st June.

CHAPTER 33

It was a perfect day, the sun soon dissipated the slight mist and a little breeze sprang up to temper the heat. It seemed as if half the inhabitants of Sussex were lining the route from the Manor to the Church. Small children with baskets of rose petals were ready to strew the path of the bride from the lychgate to the porch.

Inside the Church a most unusual congregation was gathered. Dominic, viewing the assembly from the vestry, was struck by the contrast with that of Society weddings he had attended. Guests on such occasions were less interested in observing the service than in being seen and envied for their rank and, in the case of the women, admired for their looks and the toilettes in which they hoped to outdo each other. Gossip, mostly malicious and by no means sotto-voce, was exchanged until the entrance of the bride demanded a perfunctory silence for the service. Of reverence there was none.

Here, to be sure, there was murmuring in the church, but it was clear that all were present to participate in the service and the warmth of good feeling for the bride and groom was almost tangible.

On one side the nave was filled with upper servants from Cleeve, led by Mrs Reynolds, squired by Roberts, the agent. They sat beside Becky and her sister and behind them most of the workers from Isabelle's agog to see Elizabeth in the gown they had stitched with such love and care.

Across the aisle, the Dowager, accompanied by Sir Maurice and Lady Cholmondely-Brown, Adrian's mother and father, sat in regal splendour. Adrian had, at first, protested bitterly at the idea of being a page at a wedding. Only the reminder of Elizabeth's prowess at cricket and the promise of a knock-up with the two groomsmen in the afternoon, not to mention a description of the feast to come, persuaded him to don the uniform, in which, be it said, he looked very point-device.

Behind the Dowager's pew were ranked men and women from the Manor and the estate led by Nurse, Mrs Knowles the housekeeper and Lister, the butler from the Manor who were later to entertain their opposite numbers from Cleeve. Domestic protocol would be strictly observed and the ranking guests from Brighton and Cleeve, Becky and her sister, Mrs Reynolds and Roberts would be entertained in the housekeeper's room at the Manor, while the Manor servants and the workers from Isalbelle's made merry in the Servant's Hall.

Dominic's musings were cut short by a reminder from William Fitzallan that he and his groomsmen should now take their place by the altar rail to await the bride. Subdued murmurs of admiration greeted the appearance of the three personable young men and rendered Fitzallan and Mark Howard somewhat self-conscious. With the first step towards the fulfilment of his impatiently awaited desires, Dominic became oblivious of his surroundings, from which detachment only Elizabeth could release him, and he sank to his knees to thank God for the gift of his beloved.

The cheers outside the church rose to a crescendo and all heads turned to look towards the back of the church.

This was to be the proudest moment of Mr Whitney's life. He had been chosen, by the Dowager of all people, in the absence of a male relative, to give the bride away and, as he walked up the aisle with Elizabeth on his arm, his love and pride was unbounded.

He was unremarked. All eyes were upon the bride. Her gown of supple ivory satin enhanced her lovely figure and the wonderful embroidery of single roses in a faint flush of shell pink with seed pearls of stamens and a diamond dewdrop at each heart drew gasp of admiration. An Angouleme bonnet framed Elizabeth's face with a spray of rose buds under the brim. Embroidered roses were strewn over the short train born with anxious care by a subdued Adrian and Althea completed the picture in a gown of silk gauze of a slightly deeper shade of pink with silver ribbons.

As Elizabeth approached the chancel steps Dominic rose and the two exchanged looks unconscious of all else. In that moment Elizabeth achieved beauty – her love transfigured her and was matched by the glowing look of devotion which lit his countenance.

236

By some miracle they played their parts in the ceremony without faltering and responded adequately to the good wishes showered upon them as they left the church.

Back at the Manor, they behaved correctly as host and hostess to the small party of guests. Adrian, shorn of his finery and stuffed full of delicacies, was early removed by William and Mark for the promised cricket practice and was sufficiently weary to make no demur at the early departure decreed by his father. William and Mark took their leave, escorting the Dowager and Althea to the Dower House and, at last, the lovers were alone. Lister and his minions had gone to join the parties in the Servants' Hall and the housekeeper's room.

There had been only one odd incident during the party. Just after the toasts to the bride and groom had been drunk, Lister had approached his master and Dominic with a word of excuse, had followed the butler to the library where he had received a note brought by special messenger from Brighton. He wrote a brief reply and returned without comment to the wedding guests.

After waving off his grandmother and her party Dominic turned to Elizabeth and said, "And that is the last of this topsy-turvy wedding – the guests all leaving instead of the bride and groom – now at last able to begin their honeymoon in peace!"

As they turned to go in, Elizabeth said, "Would you rather have gone on a wedding journey?"

"And waste more hours!" he replied indignantly. "Hurry, my love, and dismiss your maid – that gown is very fetching, but I have a mind to see you in something less formal."

She paused on the stairs and looked back at him, "I have a white negligee, suitable for a virgin – I might as well wear it for the short time it will be appropriate!" and with this bold, provocative remark, she kissed her fingers to him and fled up the stairs, just too quickly for him, bounding after her two at a time, to catch her before she reached her room, once his, and the chaperonage of her maid.

Baffled, he went to his dressing room, and told John as he helped him to prepare for the night, "Have the carriage ready for eleven tomorrow morning, I have to go to Brighton"

"Tomorrow, sir?" ejaculated a startled John, "But …"

"I know, but it is a summons I cannot ignore. Be off with you now."

His curiosity unsatisfied, John bade his master goodnight and went to join his fellows whose merry-making and that of the villagers crowding round the flaming Beacon bade fair to last till morning.

Dominic knocked gently on the door to his bedroom and was bidden to enter but no more words were needed. The tenure of the virgin negligee was short and the passionate consummation denied them at Cleeve more than made up for the months of delay.

Later, when their first hunger had been assuaged, Dominic looked at his beloved. The bed and window curtains were open and a moon, low in the sky, sent its rays across her sleeping face. A smile curved her lips, slightly bruised by his kisses, and even in the calm of sleep, there was an air of vitality and happiness that had long been absent from her waking face. Even as he looked she stirred and, murmuring his name, turned into his arms, and, gathering her closely to him he, too, slept.

CHAPTER 34

Dominic woke early and went to his dressing room without disturbing Elizabeth. He rang for John and took more than his usual care in his choice of dress, murmuring at one point to a mystified John, "Not silk stockings and knee breeches," and finally choosing impeccable morning wear of buff pantaloons, a quiet waistcoat and black, perfectly fitting coat. He was ready to leave his room when a letter was delivered.

"Special messenger, your lordship. No answer, he said."

The note was impressively sealed and Dominic frowned as he opened it. He looked thunderstruck as he read it and said to John in an exasperated tone, "Enquire of her ladyship's maid if her mistress is awake."

She was and eagerly awaiting him, sitting up in bed and drinking her chocolate. Her maid curtsied and retired and Dominic removed the cup and gave her a most satisfying good morning kiss. Emerging from his embrace she looked at him in some surprise.

"You look ready to pay morning calls – I thought … "

He interrupted, "You have hit the nail on the head, my dear. I or rather we have to make a special call. I have to tell you that we are summoned by His Highness to be in Brighton at noon."

Elizabeth was bereft of speech and gazed at him in astonishment.

"I meant to tell you," he said, "Prinny sent a note yesterday afternoon commanding my presence immediately. I replied in suitably respectful phrases that I was in the process of marrying a wife and therefore could not come, but said that I would wait upon him this morning."

"But he is not your commanding officer any more! You have sold out!" cried Elizabeth indignantly,

"He is still for all practical purposes, my sovereign, my love. What is more, I have just received a further note asking me – no – commanding me to bring my wife!"

"But he has never met me!" exclaiming Elizabeth.

"It seems he wishes to do so now," replied her husband. "I am sorry, my dear, I have no notion what is in his mind, but I am afraid we must go – can you be ready. I have ordered the carriage for eleven o'clock.

Reminded of the time Elizabeth sprang out of bed, and putting aside all the questions she was bursting to ask and to which, clearly, he had no answers, said drily, "How fortunate that I am provided with an eye-catching trousseau! I will join you at eleven, my lord!" and she pointed commandingly to the door.

He caught her fingers and kissed them. "Admirable woman! Does nothing daunt you?" and left as Elizabeth's maid came back hurriedly in response to her ring.

The vision that descended the stairs at the appointed time was one to make any husband proud. From burnt straw bonnet and apricot gown with a slightly darker pelisse, to bronze slippers, she was elegance personified.

Once in the carriage Dominic turned ruefully to his wife. "This is not how I planned to spend today. I almost wish that we had gone on our travels to be out of reach of the Regent's whims – I wonder what he is up to now!"

"Something trivial, I have no doubt. His starts seems to be more outrageous when he is bored – perhaps he is finding life a trifle dull now his affair with Mrs Fitzherbert is coming to an end," she replied. "But here we are and our curiosity will no doubt soon be satisfied."

However, the Regent did not immediately come to the point. His manners, when he chose, were impeccable and he exerted his considerable charm upon Elizabeth. She was too slender for his taste – he preferred the objects of his gallantry to be opulent and colourful – but he complimented Dominic on capturing such an exquisite lady for his bride.

The courtesies over, he came to the reason for summoning them. They were to go to Paris, leaving in four days from Portsmouth. A frigate would carry them to Le Havre from where they could post to the capital.

It was as well that Elizabeth was sitting down – she felt that she would have collapsed with shock.

Dominic was equally stunned but angry. With difficulty he pulled himself together to say, 'Your Highness' wish is our command, but may I ask why we should travel to France when our honeymoon has scarcely begun?"

The Regent answered Dominic's tone which bordered on the peremptory. "To serve your country." He replied coldly, then softening a little, "Let me explain, Lord Delamere. The situation in Paris is uncertain to say the least. The Bourbon's have no head for Government." He stopped abruptly, realising that the last monarch in France had literally lost his head on the guillotine! " I mean," he went on hastily, "That they are swayed by every wind that blows and have little notion of what the people and the country really needs. At the moment Russia, Prussia, Austria and a host of other interests are pushing their claims. We need someone from Britain to steady Louis, and Cathcart, the man who should do it, has gone down with mumps!"

Dominic spared a sympathetic thought for the embarrassment of a grown man stricken by such a childish ailment, but offered the Regent another argument.

"But surely, your highness, the Ambassador ......?"

"Too official – he will do his possible but he needs help, someone who can speak the language, knows the country and has his head screwed on."

Dominic despairingly tried another caveat, "But, sir, there must be many men more qualified than I!"

"No doubt, but they are out of reach – either with Wellington who has his hands full or shooting in Scotland or some such. It would take too long to get hold of them. You are accessible and I must add, available." His tone left no doubt as to his mood of growing annoyance.

Elizabeth felt it time to intervene. "Your highness, I hope, will pardon our hesitancy. We have been taken by surprise, but I would like to thank you, sir for bestowing upon us such a wonderful wedding gift," and she smiled gratefully at him.

He looked flustered and confused and Dominic looked searchingly at her, wondering what new facet this surprising wife of his was now to display.

She went on, "A honeymoon in Paris! I collect that it is rapidly being refurbished and will soon be the centre of the polite world as it used to be, and thanks to you, sir, we shall be among the first to be part of it!" she said enthusiastically. She turned to Dominic, "My trousseau will not be wasted on rural Sussex after all," and her look warned him to support her.

Dominic bowed his agreement.

The Regent looked pleased and became affable. "Yes, Lady Delamere, just so. For you to accompany your husband will remove any idea of official representation, what could be more natural than a wedding journey now that the Continent is one more open to us, and where better than Paris to display your trousseau," he added archly. He became business-like and turned to Dominic, "Then you will join the frigate in four days' time – all the necessary papers and instructions will be awaiting you."

The Prince rose and held out his hand in dismissal, but when Elizabeth, curtseying, made to kiss it he turned it and kissed hers and said playfully, "We shall expect to see more of you when you return from ...exile, my lady."

"We shall look forward to attending on your Highness, when we are again in Sussex," and she swept a second magnificent courtesy as her husband bowed and the Regent left them.

Dominic managed to hold his tongue until they were safely in the carriage on the way back to Ditchling, then he said, "You wretch! Wedding gift! Honeymoon in Paris indeed!"

"Well, I could see you were getting more and more angry ..."

"And so you proceeded to twist him round your little finger. You are a dangerous woman, but since we seem to be embarked on a quasi-diplomatic mission you are proving to be amply equipped for the work! How many more surprises have you in store for me?" and he began to laugh.

" I still do not see what you are supposed to do," complained Elizabeth.

"Oh, I have seen it done before – drop a word here and there, bring the right people together and so on, but I expect we shall have clear instructions at Portsmouth. Prinny will get the Foreign Office to brief us."

"Then we can forget about it all for four days." exclaimed Elizabeth happily.

"I am more concerned with the nights!" he said wickedly as they drew up at the Manor.

They mounted the steps and Elizabeth asked thoughtfully, "Which of us said that Napoleon would no longer interfere in our lives?"

"Both of us, I think," replied Dominic, "But you are wrong – not Bonaparte but Bourbon!" and, laughing hilariously, they embarked on four days of married bliss.